The Chase

Written by: Danie Jaye

In dedication to my high school English teacher who advised, I would never make it in writing. And to my uncle who taught me that creativity begins with an Elephant having eight legs.

Part One

"If growing up means it would be beneath my dignity to climb a tree, I'll never grow up, never grow up, never grow up! Not me!"

-J.M Barrie

Chapter One

The smell hits my nose and sinks into the pit of my stomach. It's there that it churns around and around until my mouth pools with salvia. I can't decide if whether I want to throw up or spit up, so I choose to go with the latter, because it seems to be more of a discreet option. Some tension frees from my body, as I sink into the stiff pink tufted sofa. A cloud of dust releases from deep within its fibers, which my nose simply cannot ignore. I choose, however, not to stifle my sneeze as I reach into my pocket to pull out my sorry-excuse for a tissue. And as I do this, curious eyes peer in through the glass-inlaid door, which I pretend as though not to see. There they are engaging in their little side conversations; most likely discussing my place in all of this mess—like it is any of their business.

I owe no one an assessment of my current emotional state. I mean, isn't it obvious that I am damaged beyond repair and completely disconnected from this world? Nothing about anything makes sense anymore, and I have no desire to try to make sense of any of it either. If I had it my way, I would choose to remain coddled by fear and denial. I would refuse to accept the reality of the situation, believing that there is still time to go back and change things, and time to make everything all better now. How stupid of me, I know.

You see; I was not prepared to count down days, hours, or even minutes. I was not prepared to listen for a ticking clock or to watch the sand pour silently into a figurative hourglass that I never could quite see. I honestly thought that everyone that I loved including myself, were these infinite creatures. I believed we were timeless, each with our internal clocks ticking away in harmony with one another's. These, however, were terrible misconceptions of mine. Yet, why am I still holding on tightly to these delusions?

I feel like this is all a dream. A part of me wanders through a dreamlike world ignoring the reality and tangibility of whatever is happening all around. I can feel the hard surfaces of the furniture. I can smell the air that circulates the room. And most of all, I can feel every single emotion strike at my heart like arrows to a target. Still, none of it feels real, so I choose not to believe in this world's existence. And the only thing that does make sense is to walk away and pretend like everything is as it always was before, and that this is all just some crazy dream that I am waiting to wake up from. The sad part of it all is, is that I never will wake up, but I refuse to believe that too.

I lean hard against the backing of the couch. I have somehow turned this rather large coat closet into a place of refuge. It conceals me from the aftermath, which outside of these confines, forces me to face. From the small glass inlay, I can see that the entire place is now swarming in black. It reminds me of a herd of black cattle, slow moving and unaware. Thankfully, the color is rather concealing. I not only blend in with the herd, but my noticeable difference, doesn't quite stand out as much. I look the same as I always have before. Minus my red swollen eyes and my tear stained cheeks.

My trembling hand glides across the arm of the sofa as I feel the start of more tears begin to develop. I stare down at the coats, wondering if everyone realizes just how unseasonably warm it is outside. Nevertheless, it is here that I count the number of buttons, keys left in pockets, as well as the wallets left by many trusting individuals. Soon, though, my mindless preoccupations turn stagnant as I cradle my head in my hands.

"Emma?" An unfamiliar voice pulls me away from my thoughts. I look up and see a tall guy with familiar blue eyes—not as vibrant, but still recognizable. And from under the dim lighting of the room, his hair glistens softly, which not even his high and tight haircut could take away from him. "Your mom said that she saw you come in here," he continues to speak to me, shutting the door softly behind him.

My eyes burn towards his direction, but I can't seem to focus on him or anything else. The few droplets that have formed out of the corner of them provide momentary relief, before drying up once more. A damp and shredded tissue hangs loosely in my hand, and I am finding it hard to replace it with a new one, in fear that it would subconsciously give my eyes permission to endure yet another round of crying. I have barely said two words to anyone all day, and as of right now, I am having trouble formulating a comprehensible response.

"You don't recognize me, do you?" He brushes his hand through the top of his dirty blonde hair. I watch as it sends a chill down my spine.

I look into his eyes. I do know him. Well, I know *of* him, for that matter. He, the elusive big brother who took off years ago and never returned. I carry a lot of resentment inside of me for what he did. And even though he did it to Logan and his dad, it makes no difference; because I consider them extensions of myself and took it very personally nonetheless.

The words struggle upon my lips, "I know you," I say, "Of course, I know who you are."

"I bet you do."

"So, you come back now, huh? What you couldn't have visited during happier times?" I wipe my nose with the back of my hand

"It's not like that."

"Then, what's it like George? Please tell me."

"Listen, Logan and I made amends, all right?" His hands go up defensively.

"He didn't tell me that," I look at him rather surprised. Logan tells me everything, which makes it hard for me to believe what he is saying.

"I am sorry if he didn't tell you, but we did." He looks at me with the same red in his eyes that I have in mine. I know that he must be hurting, but I can't believe for two seconds that he is hurting more than I am. What does he know about the life and family that he abandoned? They are more my family than his. A struggling comparison on who owns the right to express the most grief. In my heart, I feel like I would win.

"Well, I don't believe you."

"Listen, I just came over to introduce myself and to see if you were okay, that is all. I didn't intend to start an argument with you," he says, looking down at his feet.

Every fiber of my being ignites. I glare up at him wanting nothing more than the chance to tell him exactly how I feel; but how can I? How can I, in a place like this? Logan would never approve of me creating a scene here out of all places, and the last thing that I want to do is upset him. Therefore, I take a deep breath in and release it calmly into air that surrounds us. I hope that he knows just how hard this is for me.

George continues to stand uneasily beside me. His eyes gaze out of the glass inlay while his feet remain planted in the floor below. I try to ignore his presence and my fury within, but when I hear him suppress a sniffle, my heart changes its mind. He too is in pain. How selfish of me to deny that.

I allow an apology to slip through my tightened lips, which he accepts without any question. Timidly, I watch as he moves in closer and sits down beside me. The current smell dangling in front of my nose like the unwelcoming wreath upon the front door, quickly replaces by nothing more than the scent of his musky cologne. For a swift second, I inhale, but I don't smell the wind in his hair, the fields of grass, or what my dad would call the mixture of 'hard work and fun' emit from him. He possesses none of these smells, but I know exactly who does.

"Have you seen Logan?" He whispers, staring down into the coats.

"Not yet," I say.

"Neither have I. I just don't know what to say to him; you know?"

"You could start with an apology," I say, immediately regretting my words. "I am sorry," I apologize again. "I am really not trying to be this rude to you." I pull his gaze back up with mine.

"Well, no, you're right. I could begin with an apology," he says, before reaching his hand into his pocket, and pulling out a tissue. The tissue, like mine, is barely usable. The only difference is that mine contains smudges of makeup, whereas his doesn't. He uses it to blot underneath both of his eyes, before sticking it back into the confines of his pocket. But for some reason, neither one of us can look at each other. I think it's because we fear that our tissues may not support the consequence if we did.

"Do you want to go outside and talk? There are a lot of people out there, and I don't know about you, but I could use some fresh air." He peers out through the glass inlay.

"Yea, I could too; but shouldn't we go see Logan first?"

"We probably should wait anyways. There were a few people already talking to him before I came in here."

I leave behind me the pile of coats and follow George outside. The back of the funeral parlor sits on the same bed of land that our family farm does, but the ambience is not quite the same. It feels rather cold, sterile, and strangely foreign to me. For all I know, I could be in a different country right about now. I can almost hear the coat closet calling out for my immediate return.

Behind George, I continue to follow his lead. My awkward gait exhibits the repercussions of my immobilization for the past few days. He slows down when we reach the edge of the parking lot, where a small memorial garden sits a few feet beyond. My gaze extends out to the brush. It's the same brush outlining the farm just down the road. It brings a wistful smile to my face as a flood of memories burst into my mind. But I try not to think about them all right now. It is much too painful to think of such happy things.

George weaves through several rose bushes to get to a couple of wooden benches built in the memory of families' loved ones who had passed away several years ago. My hand traces along the plaque engravings before I sit down. The metal is oddly cold against my flesh for such a warm day. And as we both take a seat, we instinctively look back towards the parlor longing for answers to questions that we know we will never receive. I don't know about him, but at this moment, I am grateful for the distance we have placed in between.

"I know you didn't ask, but I have a feeling that you want to know why I left?" he asks breaking through our temporary silence.

An expected breeze blows on by me, and I smell a hint of the farm beyond the fields. It pulls me in for a second, allowing me to escape as I run through the fields of a faded memory.

Then, when the breeze releases me, I am left facing only George's gaze. Its penetrating effect burns a thousand fires within my already damaged soul. *Such similarities they possess, but I much prefer the original. He appears as nothing more than a remake to me.*

I am perfectly aware that his question warrants a response from me, but I already know the answer that will follow. I am aware of why he had left; Logan told me all about it. But something tells me that he wants to give me his side of the story and the least that I can do after being so rude to him, is to let him tell it.

"I couldn't handle it, you know?" He begins without my solicitation. "She and I were close—much closer than I was with my dad. When she got sick, I lost it. And when she passed away, I lost it even more. Everything about this place—the farm—the house—the land—Logan—and dad reminded me of her. I just couldn't take it anymore. I had to get away—I had to give myself time to heal," his words stutter upon reveal. "And then this happened…"

"They were hurting too, you know, but they didn't just pack up and leave."

"I was ten years old for heaven's sake!" He throws his hands into the air.

"I know," I nod.

"You see; dad had the farm, and Logan had my dad. And in a sense, I felt like I had no one after my mom died." His voice suddenly goes silent now as the sun momentarily hides behind a cloud above. "After a while," he continues, "I *did* start calling home a lot. Did Logan tell you that?"

I nod again. I know that he called home. In fact, I accidentally overheard some conversations Logan had with him in the past, but I don't tell him that.

"But every time I would call, my dad never wanted to speak to me. He would either hang up or give the phone to Logan. I mean, there were many times that I wanted to come back home, but I thought he would end up turning me away; therefore, I just stayed where I was. I did try though…"

I would be a fool not to hear the desperation in his voice as he yearns for some level of forgiveness from me, but why from me? Who cares what I think. I mean nothing more to him than any other person back inside of the parlor.

"And then when Grandpa Charlie—"

"I know," I meet his gaze again, "but can you at least understand to some degree how your father must have felt? He lost his wife and then technically his son. But only one of those two people actually chose to leave." The words shoot out as fast as a lizard's tongue, sharp and fierce.

"You really don't hold back on saying what it is that you are thinking, huh?" He chuckles. "Logan told me that you were a bit of a spit fire." The tension in his face seems to ease.

"Yea, well did he tell you that he can be a real horse's ass sometimes?" I smile; however, the words do not sit well with me.

He releases another chuckle into the air, which is then, carried off by the wind. It echoes back to me, and through that echo, I can almost hear Logan's voice emit from his. And in one swift movement, I watch as he slides his hand across his lap and into his pocket again. However, this time, when his hand resurfaces, he doesn't bring back what I presume to be his tissue; he brings back an envelope with him instead. "Logan gave me this, it's all about you," he says, holding the envelope out in front of him. "Says it's everything I need to know."

The white envelope waves gently between his fingers and catches hold of a few of the sun's rays. I stare at it as though trying to pierce through the paper to reveal the contents inside. I am baffled by this and completely taken off guard.

"I don't understand. What would he think that you would need to know about me?" I sit back firmly against the bench. I stare at the man sitting beside me and marvel at the similarities between the man that I love and this man that I hardly know. He is as unknown to me as ninety percent of the people back inside of the parlor; yet, he seems to know a lot about me, at the hands of Logan, that is. The thought almost sickens me to the point that I want to throw up again. *Could it be?*

I stare out into the brush and contemplate Logan's motive. I so desperately want to be chased right now. Clear into the brush to escape where the land meets the flowing river. I so badly want to feel the wind against my face and the way that the sun burns against my skin. I want to plummet to the earth side by side to the one person in the entire world that I love more than I love myself. But as I turn my head back towards the parlor, I don't see him. He doesn't come outside. He doesn't make his way down here and sit beside me. It's as if he doesn't even know where I am. I should be sitting here with him instead of George.

"Well, I have been given strict instructions on revealing this to you," he smiles.

"What kind of instructions?" I lean back further into the bench, feeling the wooden planks dig into my shoulder blades.

"Well, let's just say that I am to expect the same introduction," he pauses. "And he said that I am not to take any crap from you."

"Oh, did he now?" I can actually picture Logan saying, that, which makes me smile.

He smiles too, "Sure did. So, about this introduction…" His voice trails off, as his foot inches closer to mine. Although, it takes me a good second or two to realize what it is that he is doing.

"Go ahead, these shoes aren't new," he almost wiggles his foot out to taunt me.

A tear rolls down my cheek, which I quickly brush away. "I can't," I say to him.

"Well, he said that you would say that, so now I am left with no choice but to give you a running head start," he says getting to his feet. "You have until the count of ten. One, two—"

I look down at his feet and shake my head, "You know I can't."

"I know," his eyes acknowledge his awareness of my situation, "but I will go easy on you...Three."

I try to block his voice out, but I am unsuccessful. I watch as he now tucks the envelope back inside of his pocket, "Five—six," his lips move, but I hear nothing but the sound of my own beating heart.

"Seven." His voice comes alive once more.

Suddenly a burst of familiar excitement hits me. I am hesitant to embrace it, but it overflows in my veins, forcing my heart into action as I hear him call out, "Eight." My eyes then fall to his black leather shoes; just as I hear the number, *nine* reach my ears. I pry my eyes upward and face the giant blue sky. It sparkles and shines down as though wrapping around me like a hug. And without a second's hesitation, my foot lifts into the air and then stomps down hard against his shoes. I take off running, just as I hear him yell, "Ten!"

And with the wind against my face, and the grass beneath my shoes, I take off between where the here and now merges with the there and then…

Five Years Ago...

Chapter Two

"Chase me!" I yell at him, as I dart across the pasture and into the open fields. The grass whips across my ankles, but I continue charging right through it. The smell of the farm wafts through the air and hits my nose in a strangely pleasant manner. It used to be that I couldn't stand the smell, but now it just screams home to me. From a short distance away, I can hear the sounds of the grass crunching beneath his shoes. He really is picking up speed now, which only pumps up my adrenaline even more. "You will never catch me!" I continue to yell back at him. I don't know why I even provoke him, especially when I know that he always catches me in the end.

"I will get you Emma Rae!" He calls out to me, but I keep running. A quick turn of my head, I see him rapidly approach. "You know I always do!" He continues to call.

Faster and faster, we run against the fields as the sun beats down upon our faces. My destination is approaching. I never go past the river. I always stop just as the rolling water tickles the tops of my shoes. It is the same place where he always catches me and wrestles me to the ground. Perhaps in the future I should just declare it a safe zone.

For a girl though, I always put up a good fight. He always wins, because in my mind, I think it's because I let him. But of course, if you were to ask him about it, he would tell you that that isn't the case. It must be a boy thing, or better yet, it must be a Logan thing. He is the most stubborn person I know.

Within a moment's time, I reach the river and just as I turn around, he jumps out from behind the brush and tackles me to the ground. "You're a real horse's ass Logan Solway!" I yell from beneath his flailing arms as he continues to try to pin me to the ground. Left with only one defense, I pretend to start crying, which subsequently makes him loosen his grip on me. And just as soon as he does, I turn him onto his own back and pin him to the ground instead.

"Works every time," I say with a devious grin.

"You know, one of these days you are going to cry for real, and I am just going to think that you are joking."

"Yea, well when there are real tears, then you will know."

When I release him from under me, we roll over onto our backs and begin to bask in the sunlight. It permeates our skin until it produces a somewhat calming effect, as it steadies our breathing and siphons the remaining energy we had left in us. I feel the heat from the summer sun as it warms against my flesh, but I don't heed the warning. I have been burnt all summer long and I really couldn't care less if I get in one final burn before it is over. Therefore, I just lie back and close my eyes, while listening to the birds chirping in the trees above.

So much about this day has been perfect. Logan and I helped around the farm; my mom made us a great lunch, and we even had time to explore like we always do. I remember this one time, a few years back, we convinced ourselves that pirates buried treasure in our land, and we spent a good week digging random holes throughout the pasture and fields to try to find it. Our parents were not pleased at all, especially since the cows were not too bright and kept falling into the holes. We really meant no harm and even told them that we would share the treasure, but that didn't seem to diffuse their anger in the slightest.

Another time, we believed that there were uncharted territories beyond the river and woods that no man had ever set foot on. We each had packed our own backpack with exploring gear and a few snacks, and set off on what we thought to be an adventure of a lifetime. When we finally made it over the river and through the small wooded area, we discovered that our suspicions were completely inaccurate. The land we believed to be uncharted was full of newly built homes and a small convenience store. And the only things that we got out of the exploration were a couple of sodas, which Logan spent some of his allowance money on for us.

Today, like those days, I can feel the excitement of adventure in the air. It is laced with the urge to explore and to discover. I want to get lost in some fairytale or story where we escape the world we are in and venture into the world of make believe. I want to sword fight with evil pirates. I want to pretend to fly as Logan pushes me on the tire swing. I want to hunt for dinosaurs in the woods. And most of all, I want to play those games like we used to, but, sadly, we are much older now and our reasons for explorations and adventures are diminishing. Our imaginations just don't work like they used to. Then again, to be quite honest, they work just fine, it's just that we feel kind of foolish for even using them now.

I have come to learn that growing up on a farm does seclude you a bit, but for Logan and me, it never bothered us at all. When my parents bought the neighboring house to the Solway farm about ten years ago, Logan's dad quickly gave my dad a job and the two have been working together ever since. You see, when Logan's mom died when he was about three years old, it became just him and his dad, especially after some other things happened as well (but more on that later). So I guess in a way; our moving next door made him feel like he finally had a family again. I mean; we do kind of act like brother and sister.

I gently caress the top of the grass with my eyes still closed. My mind wanders back to the first day that I met Logan. I must have been about five years old at the time. I don't remember much, but the one thing that I do remember was that after our parents introduced us to one another, I stomped down hard upon his foot and told him to chase me. He chased me then just as he chased me today. The only difference now is that I know this land like the back of my hand. Unfortunately that day, I ran straight into the river where I thought I was going to drown. I was never a strong swimmer, not even now for that matter, which is the main reason why I never run past the river, not unless Logan holds my hand across.

"Did I tell you," Logan speaks up, "My dad said that I am finally old enough for more responsibilities around the farm, instead of just taking care of the animals."

I turn on my side and face him. His dirty blonde hair glistens in the sunlight, but his eyes remain closed. If they were open, the blue coloring from them would blend in perfectly with the sky above. I always told him that he had skies for eyes.

"Like what?" I finally ask. Farm responsibilities have always been divvied up equally between us, so I am surprised that he has been given an increase in duties, whereas, I haven't been.

"I don't know, he didn't say. Perhaps it means that I can start riding the tractor now," he says with a hint of excitement in his voice. I sit back and watch a smile creep across his face, and his dimple begin to form.

"Logan, your dad would not let you ride that thing until you are much older. You are only thirteen," I say.

"Yea, but I will be fourteen come December. Besides, he let me ride it once, you know."

"No, he didn't."

"Yes, he did," he argues back.

"Oh, yeah— and where was I?"

"I don't know, cooking? Isn't that what you women do when you're in the house?"

"That's not nice Logan," I shoot back. "We can ride tractors too if we wanted."

He turns to his side, opening his eyes to me. "I suppose you could," he smiles. By the tone in his voice, I know that he is trying to apologize to me for what he said without *actually* having to apologize. And as usual, I accept it just the same. I find myself such a pushover with him sometimes.

"But he at least agreed to let you come with me, right?"

"Nope;" his smile flat lines.

"But it's high school! Aren't you the least bit curious what it would be like not to be homeschooled for once?" The excitement in my voice doesn't match what I really feel inside. In fact, I am against the whole idea. All I have ever known is being homeschooled alongside Logan. My mom would spend a good six hours with us a day, giving us breaks to rest, eat, and of course, to help around the farm. What will become of my duties without being able to help Logan? Who will keep him company? Better yet, who will keep me?

"Maybe, but my dad needs me around the farm. He always tells me that I am the extra set of hands that he doesn't have to pay for. Well, besides what he gives me for my allowance. I just think it's best if I stay back and help him; you know?"

"What am I chopped liver? I help too! Doesn't he need me?"

"Face it Emma, you know I do a little bit more than you do around here. And I am only going to continue doing more."

"Whatever," I sulk. "So, does that mean that my mom is still going to home school you?"

"I guess it does."

We continue to lie with our backs pressed firmly against the grass without a care in the world. As I have noticed with all previous summers, there is a moment where you can actually smell the scent of it passing. And for some reason as we lie here, I can smell it now. My arm extends as my hand reaches out into the air. In my grasp, I try to hold onto whatever is left of summer, but with time running out, there really isn't much left to hold on to.

I look to the right of me at the old sycamore tree where our fathers built us a shared tree house when we were both about seven. So much time has passed since then, but all throughout those years, I have never once been without my best friend. And to think that, now I will be, makes me want to climb up there and hide until graduation.

A breeze hits us, and I can see the effects it has on the trees above. The vibrant green leaves sway, and I can't help but returning my attention back to our tree house again. We barely go up there now. *We are too old*, Logan always says to me when I ask. But something about being up there always felt magical to me. It was like being in our own little world.

I remember this one night when we tried to have a sleepover up there; a bat ended up flying inside, which made Logan panic. He literally fell out of the tree house trying frantically to climb out, breaking his arm upon impact. And when I climbed down to meet him, I just couldn't stop laughing. It was similar to the time that I fell off my bike and dislocated my shoulder. He laughed at me for weeks about it! I only laughed at him for a few minutes though, before I ended up decorating his cast with drawings of bats when we left the hospital that night.

The river flows ahead of me, and I can hear the occasional splash from a few birds dipping themselves in for a little bath. I try focusing my attention on that, because I am having a hard time wrapping my head around the idea that in one week's time, I will have to leave him. I understand that it's just during the day, but we have never been apart. I can't imagine facing the horrors of starting a new school, especially high school, on my own. He is my partner in crime, my co-pilot, and first mate. There is no one else I would want by my side, and it saddens me to know that he can't be there.

You see, other than Logan; I have no friends, and I never really needed anymore anyways. Logan is all that I need and even though new people will soon surround me, I promised myself that I would never make friends with any of them. The last thing I would ever do is be disloyal to him and by making new friends; it would feel like I would be.

I do wonder if he feels sad about me leaving though. He really hasn't said much about it, and I was kind of hoping that he was still trying to get his dad to let him go. But it's apparent now, that I am in this all alone. I wonder if there is any way for me to get out of it too. It is worth a try, I suppose.

But for some reason, my parents seem overly excited about my change in education. Last week, in preparation for school, mom took me out shopping and bought me a bunch of clothes outside of the standard jeans, t-shirts, and the occasional Sunday dress that I would have to wear to church around the holidays. She had me trying on all kinds of skirts, blouses, and everything girly that she could lay her hands on. When we got home that day, I showed Logan all the clothes that she had picked out for me. His nose scrunched up in distaste. It wasn't very reassuring. He told me that I should just wear what I usually wear. And when I asked him why, he told me that school shouldn't change the way a person looks. I couldn't argue with him there.

Soon, the clouds roll in and block out the sun's penetrating rays. I sit up, brush the grass and dirt off my clothes, and jump to my feet. "My mom is going to call me soon for dinner. We should probably head back," I say.

"Ok," Logan says, getting to his feet, as well.

We set off on foot through the brush and into the field. Once our feet hit the pasture, we sprint across, waving towards Logan's dad as he rides along in his tractor. Reaching the front of the farm between our two homes, Logan and I go our separate ways.

"See you soon ya big buffoon," he calls out to me.

"In a flash you horse's ass."

I head up the front porch steps where I tear off my shoes and place them down upon the boot mat. Mom hates it when dad and I track mud into the house, so we have been told to leave our shoes outside. I open up the front door, greeted by the smells of roasted chicken and mashed potatoes. When I head towards the kitchen, I spot my mom tending to something in the oven. Her hair is tied up in a ponytail, and her apron is a mess as usual. She sees me just as I am about to sit down at the table.

"Now, Emma, why don't you go clean up before dinner? You know the rules," she says to me, without taking her eyes off the stove.

"Looks like you may need to clean up before dinner too," I chuckle, pointing to her messy apron.

"Don't you laugh at your mother," she giggles back. "This dinner better be delicious. I am pretty much wearing half of it."

I clamber up the stairs and down the hallway towards the bathroom. Grabbing the bar of soap from the shower, I quickly scrub my face and hands until I know that I have reached my mother's standards for cleanliness. The last thing I want to do is come all the way up here to start over, which has happened a time or two.

After a good rinse, I stare into the bathroom mirror to examine my work. During the summer, my red hair gets these tiny strands of caramel throughout it. At first, I thought it was permanent until I noticed that by the fall, it all fades away. And as of right now, though, I can spot a few in the mirror. Not to mention the few freckles that have carefully decorated my face, courtesy of the sun; thank goodness that they will fade too.

As I exit the bathroom and wipe the remaining water residue off onto my shoulder, I accidentally bump into the console table, which displays one of mom's many crystal vases. I steady the table with one hand, while I hold the vase with the other. The last thing I need is for her to yell at me about breaking something else of hers, which I have a tendency of doing from time to time.

Our house is what most people would look at as being a typical farmhouse. The wooden floorboards creak underneath your feet. It has a rustic and homey charm to it that I love. And not to mention, the smells that float in from the farm whenever you leave a window or door open. However, there are various pieces of modern furniture, and décor scattered throughout it, which have a tendency to stick out like sore thumbs, thus, changing the overall character of the house. However, mom refuses to merge everything into one style, so she just considers herself eclectic.

I always laugh to myself when I think that my parents used to live in a big city. Neither one of them knew a thing about farming, but after living what dad called "the fast life" for years, they decided to start a new chapter in their lives somewhere else. My mother, however, had no clue that the new chapter would lead them to a farm. But they got used to the work and lifestyle pretty quickly. Although, sometimes I see this twinkle in her eyes, and I wonder if it's because she is dreaming of the big city. The twinkle I assume is the residue from all of the lights.

Just as I head back downstairs, dad enters the kitchen and gives mom a kiss on the cheek. He is dressed in a flannel shirt and Carhartt overalls that have more stains on it that anyone of us could begin to identify. But even with his messy appearance, he always keeps himself clean-shaven and well groomed. A deal that he made with mom after she told him that she would never kiss him with a beard.

"Now Ted, you go on upstairs and get yourself cleaned for dinner. I just sent your daughter up there. She smells just like you," she smiles, as he kisses her again on the cheek.

"Well," dad sees me as I enter the room, "that's the smell of hard work and fun," he says releasing mom and swooping me up into his arms instead. "Isn't that right Emma?"

"Right—Hey," I say, once my feet touch back down on the surface of the linoleum. "Is Mr. Solway going to let Logan ride the tractor?"

"What?"

"Logan said that he is getting more jobs around the farm, and he thinks that he will be able to ride the tractor now, is that true?" I find myself almost whining. I would be lying if I said that I wasn't a bit jealous when he told me that a little while ago.

"I don't think so," he scratches the top of his head.

"Good, because that horse's ass can barely wheel a wheelbarrow straight," I gruff, sitting down at the table.

"Young lady, you had better watch your language," mom yells at me. She wipes at her face, causing some residual eye makeup to make its way on the side of her hand. She really has no need to wear it. But she says it's the only thing that makes her feel like normal again—whatever that means.

During dinner, all I can think about is leaving Logan. I find it unfair that he has to stay back, and something tells me that he really wants to go with me—contrary to what he says, that is. I bring this up to mom and dad who only tell me to mind my own business. But what they don't understand, is that Logan *is* my business.

"Well, I don't want to go then," I say, setting my fork down. "If Logan can't go, then neither should I."

"You are going with, or without him, Emma," mom looks at me sternly from across the table. "You will go to school, get good grades, and then, maybe, college."

"College?" I almost spit out my food. "I am not going to college," I push my plate away.

"Finish your dinner," she stops my plate dead in its tracks. "And yes, you will go to college. Your father and I both have our college degrees—"

"Yea, but you don't use them, do you?" When the words slip out, I am afraid to face either one of them. I cower into whatever is left of my mashed potatoes, praying that the moment will pass.

Thankfully, when dinner ends, I run upstairs to my room and dive head first into my bed. I don't even care that my clothes are filthy as they smudge against my white blanket. The only thing I can think about right now is that I hope this last week of summer goes by slowly. I just want to be able to savor what time I have left before things begin to change for me. Doesn't anyone else see the problem with separating Logan and

I? It's as though I am the only one cognizant of the potential repercussions.

Of course, I can't help but to think of Logan returning to the lonely little boy that he once was before I came into the picture. Then, I wonder about his elusive older brother, the older brother who took off after their mom died to go live with Logan's grandparents in Denver. He doesn't talk about him much and neither do I. And I doubt that he will be visiting anytime soon to make up for my absence. In the end, I agree that this is all too much to think about right now. And as my face kisses the cottony threads of my pillowcase, I allow myself to drift off into sleep, only to be woken up six hours later to Logan's voice.

"Come in Echo Romeo, this is Lima Mike," Logan's voice emits from the walkie-talkie that I have sitting on my nightstand. Last summer, we saved up all of our allowances to buy them. To us, it is imperative that we have access to communication at all times.

"Come in Echo Romeo, this is Lima Mike," Logan repeats himself. Logan learned the military phonetic alphabet when he found out that his dad was once a Marine. The "Mike" is appropriately coded for Michael, which is his middle name.

"This is Echo Romeo," I yawn into the walkie-talkie, "over."

"You up for a little stargazing?" he asks.

The question immediately dissipates any more of my remaining yawns, as I quickly jump out of bed to go meet him outside.

Chapter Three

The moonlight catches me and shines upon me like a spotlight. I am as conspicuous as a neon sign. A few feet away, I spot Logan making his way down his front porch steps, carrying his outdoor blanket underneath his arm. And when the moonlight releases me and embraces Logan instead, his blue eyes twinkle against the light, bringing a piece of the day into the night.

As he approaches me, I notice that he is wearing his pajamas. Flannel bottoms with a dark colored t-shirt. *At least he changed;* I think to myself. As for me, I'm still wearing what I had on earlier that day, but only one of us looks as though we actually got any sleep.

The grass begins to move softly under our feet now, as we make our way across the street. Stupidly, I wore my house slippers outside instead of proper outdoor shoes, but I did so because I didn't want to create any extra noise upon my escape. Mom and dad would never approve of me leaving the house at night. Regardless if it is, just to stargaze.

Once we cross the street, we enter into the front yard of an old abandoned house. The house always looks rather creepy to me at night. And on several occasions I have asked Logan if he thought it was haunted. He never took me seriously and just assumed that I was only trying to get him scared. Needless to say, it has become our usual stargazing spot, so I have no choice, but to put on a brave face as best as I can.

Shuddering at the image of the dark grey house, Logan pulls the blanket out from underneath his arm and gestures for me to come lay down beside him. And for the next hour or so, we stare up at the night sky side by side, just long enough for time to escape us and for me to forget just how terrifying the house is beside me.

"And that one looks like a donkey. Well, you see the donkey used to be a horse until a wicked witch cast a spell on him, which then turned him into a donkey," I say, pointing to a small cluster of stars that I swear up and down resemble a donkey.

"Well, why did the witch do that?" Logan asks earnestly.

"Well," I peer over at him, "legend has it that he was being a real horse's ass," I say laughing aloud into the night.

"Ha, ha," he says back. "Wait—so wouldn't that mean that she just turned him into a jackass instead?"

I sit up slightly, "Hmm, I guess it does," just before we find ourselves bursting into another fit of laughter.

Our laughter carries us into many more made up stories with birds, monkeys, and even a princess who instead of a prince, was once a frog. Nights like these, I absolutely love. And even though we are occupied with our storytelling, a part of me wants to ask Logan how he feels about me heading off to high school without him. But for some reason, I can never find the right time to bring it up.

"Can I tell you something?" Logan breathes up towards the stars.

"Sure," I say, while bracing myself for what I assume to be his moment to tell me how he feels.

"I come out here without you sometimes."

I turn and face him. "What do you mean?"

"I mean, I come out here at night without you sometimes."

Startled by this unexpected confession, I pull myself out of my lying position. My eyes penetrate through the darkness at him, "Well, why do you do that?"

"If I tell you, will you promise not to laugh?"

I nod, "Promise."

"Well, I come out here and talk with my—" he hesitates with a gulp, "my mom."

I lean heavy against my arms unsure of what to say. A part of me wants to remind him that his mother is no longer with us and for him to double-check exactly who it's been that he has been talking to, but those words reek of pain. The other part of me is saddened by this confession. Not because he chose not share these conversations with me or even invite me along for that matter, but because I never knew her death still lingers painfully in his heart. I assumed he was always bothered and hurt by it, but not in a consuming way. I look up at him, noticing the wet glare forming in his eyes, but I pretend as though not to see it. "Well, what do you talk about?" I finally ask. It seems like the safest question to present him with at this point.

"My life, the farm, and things like that. I tell her that I miss her and that dad misses her. I even tell her that George misses her as well, because I am sure, wherever he is, that he misses her too. And I also talk about you," his voice trails off and gets lost in the darkness.

"You talk about me?"

"Yeah, I talk about how much fun we have and things like that."

"Oh." I desperately want to ask him where he directs his conversations to, and if he feels like she responds back, but I am afraid. Many nights I have been asleep in my bed completely unaware of what intimate conversations transpired in the darkness beyond. I would have never suspected that he would venture out without me; but then again, I would never have suspected that he would be venturing out to speak with his mother either. I must remember to choose delicate words; the last thing that I want to do is offend him.

"I know what you want to ask me," he leans up from the blanket until we are shoulder to shoulder. "You want to ask me if she talks back to me, right?" A half-smile appears on his face. I can tell because I only see half of his white teeth gleam against the glare of the moon.

"Yes, I suppose," I reply nonchalantly. *He knows me so well.*

"I don't know if she responds, but I do feel like she is listening when I talk to her though."

"And how do you know that?" I ask delicately.

"By the way that the trees sway and the earth around me behaves after I say something to her. It's like she is sending down signs to me; you know?"

I nod and before I realize it, the question burning in my mind, slips through my lips faster than I can stop it. Instinctively, my hand shoots up to cup my mouth in embarrassment, but it stops midcourse when I see him begin pointing up at the sky for me. My eyes turn upward as my hand falls loosely to my side. I am now gazing at the spot where he is pointing, while grateful by the smile on his face that he is not upset with me for asking.

"There," he points, "that is my mom."

The constellation of stars that his finger is circling doesn't look like much of anything. But out of the corner of my eye, I can see that to him, it does. He continues pointing and telling me that she watches down from the sky at him every day. "She is not all those stars," he explains, "She is just the one that I am pointing to, the one in the middle."

I locate the star and smile, "She is beautiful, Logan," I say to him.

"Thanks," he says, bringing his eyes down level with the grass. Some of the wetness makes it way out from his eyes and rolls down his cheeks. Casually, he brushes it aside, and I pretend as though that I still don't notice.

I have only seen a few pictures of his mother. There are a few hanging up around his house and the one that Logan keeps in his bedside drawer; but other than that, nothing. Logan says that his dad finds them too painful to look at, but Logan on the other hand, wants to keep them up to remember her by. To me, she looks just like Logan and George. She has bright blue eyes and the same color hair. Logan's dad is the complete opposite, however, having dark brown hair and brown eyes. The only similarity that I ever picked up on between Logan and his dad was the small dimple that would appear on both of their left cheeks whenever they would smile, chew, or even laugh. Logan calls it his cheek crater; I call it the Solway trademark, which Mr. Solway is presently hiding beneath his beard.

After several yawns that lead to unexpected dosing, we drag our bodies up from the ground, fold up the blanket, and head back across the street. Logan must have been really brave tonight to share that secret with me, and I think on some level, it would be nice of me to repay that gesture. Therefore, I muster up the courage as soon as we reach the middle of our front lawns, to tell him how I feel about leaving. I want him to know that I am not excited about it. And maybe then, he will feel better knowing that it hurts me too.

"You know Logan, I don't want to go," I say, just as I am about to head up the front porch steps of my house.

He looks at me through the darkness. "You should though."

His reply confuses and surprises me at the same time. "Why?" I ask.

"Because, you are really not much of a farm girl," he laughs, before taking off towards his house and shutting the door behind him.

The next day, I wake up with the rising sun. I change into a new set of work clothes and head outside to begin feeding the animals. As I make my way towards the barn, the moist grass from the morning dew suctions to the soles of my shoes, which release as soon as I approach the doorway where I spot Logan. From only a short distance away, I can tell that he didn't get much sleep last night, which means that there is a good chance that he may be grumpy today, *hooray for me.*

The half-moon circles hanging like deflated balloons underneath both of his eyes tighten with the release of a yawn every few minutes. I watch until it becomes contagious, as an unexpected yawn releases from my lips and enters into the barn ahead of me.

"I already picked up most of their messes," he says, pointing to the shovel and the bucket now swarming with flies.

"Ok," I plug my nose at the smell. "I will get the rest."

The smell is putrid, burning the hairs within my nose. Sometimes, Logan and I tie handkerchiefs around our faces to block out some of the smell, but mine is currently in the wash. "Do you have an extra handkerchief?" I yell across one of the horse's stalls to Logan. But in response, all I hear is the sound of his boots, shuffling their way out of the barn.

For the rest of the day, however, no matter what I say or do, Logan doesn't say much in return. He listlessly gets through his chores and heads back home without so much as a goodbye or even a wave. Dumbfounded, I hang out in the middle of our two front lawns, believing that his attitude is nothing more than a rouse and that in a few moments, he will be coming out of his house to yell, *gotcha!* But he doesn't. And sadly, this supposed jokes goes on for days.

* * * *

Hard-pressed and unsure of what to do about Logan, I drag myself into the kitchen for dinner with a defeated slump. Almost a week of trying to deal with his unnecessary behavior leaves me frustrated beyond words. But he doesn't seem to care. Does he not realize how much time he has wasted? But it's too late now, because it's the night before school starts and life as I know it, is about to change.

Mom serves up our plates while dad makes his way inside, smelling like a hard day of labor. As soon as he sits down, he begins rattling on about his days in high school, all of which go in through one ear and out the other for me.

"You will be attending the same high school that I went to," he says, taking a bite of his meatloaf. Mom nods her head as though to affirm the information to me. Then, before I know it, he takes me down memory lane where he talks about his football years and the winning touchdown he made against the school rival team. He actually gets up from the table to demonstrate the miracle play for me; which looks like nothing more than of him trying to dance around the kitchen with a loaf of bread.

"You're going to be a freshman", he says to me as though as I had no idea. He sits back down at the table somewhat winded with a huge grin upon his face. "One of the best years of my life…" His eyes begin to glaze over.

"And you will do great," mom chimes in. "Thankfully your dad was able to pull some strings with the principal and get you accepted. Your dad went to school with Mr. Harper; they are old friends." She sips at her drink.

"That's right," dad comes to, "Mr. Harper is friends with the superintendent, so that is how all that worked out. You could have gone to your mom's high school in Syracuse, but we really had no connections there."

I quickly finish my plate just when I hear dad begin to talk about another one of his miracle plays. I scramble up the stairs and climb into bed, because I can barely stand anymore of dad's football talk and mom's need to reassure me every five minutes that 'I will do great.'

The stress of this whole situation wears on me considerably. Am I the only one who sees this? Am I the only one who cares? I close my eyes, hoping for some kind of relief, but all that greets me is the haunting images of a place I have never seen before. The winding hallways, the unfamiliar faces, and the fears of never seeing Logan again, all of which begin to terrify me behind closed eyes. No one seems to understand what this change means to me. Better yet, what it is doing to me, as well.

My eyes suddenly burst open. I turn over and look at my alarm clock, which is a rooster that stopped crowing about two years after my mom bought it. Now it just faintly whirs whenever the alarm clock goes off. I notice that the time reads a little after eight o'clock pm. Have I really only been in bed for an hour?

Reaching up, I turn my bedside lamp on and gradually pull myself out of bed. After dinner, I never bothered to change out of my work clothes, so I think it's best to change quickly before mom finds out that I tried to sleep in them. Stiff from dried mud and the residue from sweat, they drop to the floor with an imaginary clunk. And after I change into my pajamas and kick the dirty clothes off to the side, I climb back in bed, just when I hear the sound of a knock upon my bedroom door.

"Hey sweetie, it's dad. Can I come in?"

"Sure," I say, hoping that his unexpected visit is not to reenact any more of his football memories. Thankfully, I don't have anything in my room that resembles a football.

The door creaks open revealing my dad sans the recollecting smile he had on his face throughout dinner. He worked a little later than usual tonight, because he and Mr. Solway have been spending their evenings fixing the barn roof after it suffered a partial collapse a few weeks ago. And as he makes his way further into my room, I can smell the farm as it violently radiates off of his clothes and into the surrounding air. My mind immediately goes to Logan.

"I know you must be nervous about tomorrow, but don't be. Auburn High School is a great school. You will fit in and do just fine." He tousles my hair between his dirty fingers. "Mom is going to drive you to school each morning. The busses don't come this far out; I'm afraid. However, I am surprised you are still up kiddo. Shouldn't you be sleeping?"

"I was, but then I got up just a few minutes ago."

"Well, you should really get some rest for tomorrow, okay?" He gently taps me on my knee.

I watch his face radiate with pride as though I have done something remarkable. But all I want to do is to tell him that I don't want to go—not without Logan, at least. But I waver on the idea, because I don't want to disappoint him. I hate disappointing him. And right now I feel like I would be by telling him.

The soft anchor that was once his body at the edge of my bed lifts as he makes his way back over to the door. But just as his hand graces the handle, I find myself at a moment of panic and stop him. "Dad?" I say, watching him turn back around. "I want you to know that I am kind of sad about tomorrow. It's just that I wish that Logan could come too; you know?"

His shoulders slouch, as he releases a deep breath through his unaffected smile. "I know; but who knows, maybe in a year or so, Logan could join you. Just because he isn't going with you now, doesn't mean that he can't come another year."

"I never thought of that." My eyes twinkle with delight.

"Just remember, you are defined by you. Not by whom you are with another. You are perfectly capable of doing things on your own," he says, just as he shuts the door behind him.

I am not quite sure what he meant by that. But what I do know, is that I can't describe myself without including Logan in the description. I wait barely a half-second, before I rush towards my nightstand and grab hold of my walkie-talkie. Logan needs to know that there is still hope and that he still has a chance to come with me after all. Maybe this will get him to loosen up and knock off his attitude.

"Come in Lima Mike, this is Echo Romeo. Do you copy?" My breaths release jaggedly through the mouthpiece. I am as winded as though I just ran across the pasture to convey this message.

Waiting for him to respond, though, I take a deep breath in, releasing it as I check the volume on the walkie-talkie. I repeat myself for a second time into the mouthpiece, but he doesn't respond. The power button is on, so I know that the batteries are not dead. I wait a few more seconds and repeat myself again, "Come in Lima Mike, this is Echo Romeo. Do you copy?" But strangely, there is no answer. I continue holding the walkie-talkie firmly in my grasp as I feel my lips press into the holes of the mouthpiece.

I decide to bring it over to my bed with me as I try to reach him several more times. Some attempts sound rather desperate, but I am just anxious for him to say something—but of course, he doesn't. I ponder over the idea that maybe *his* walkie-talkie is the one that needs new batteries. I would hate to think that he is purposely ignoring me. *I mean, what did I do?*

"Logan, are you ignoring me?" I yell with a sense of agitation in my voice. I don't even care that I have just broken our privacy code about revealing our real names—something that Logan said we could never do. Apparently, it doesn't matter though, because he still says nothing in response. My reply is nothing more than the faint sound of static mixed with my own staggered breaths.

Frustrated, I throw the walkie-talkie off to the side. I don't have time for this. I climb into bed without another peep. I have to get some sleep, and I refuse to waste the night trying to get him to talk to me, when it is obvious he doesn't want to. I shut my bedside lamp off and pull the covers up to my chin. The emotions swirling around inside of me make my stomach churn; thus, making it hard for me to fall asleep. I flip from my right side to my left like a fish. But no matter how I try to position my body, I cannot get comfortable. Of course, I blame Logan for this.

Morning is here before I know it and even though I technically am able to sleep in an extra forty-five minutes that I normally do; I end up lying awake in bed for most of it. I stare up at the ceiling, trying hard to listen for any sounds coming from the barn, but through my double-pane window, I hear not a thing. Then, out of nowhere, my mom bursts through my bedroom door, opens up my blinds, and begins to sing some good morning tune to get me out of bed. She is overly excited about today and immediately I find that familiar twinkle in her eye. The only thing is, is that I am not going to the big city; but I think in her mind; it's close enough.

"Now," she says, opening up my closet door. "I have already picked out your outfit for today," she says, bringing me back a khaki skirt and a multi-colored patterned blouse from my closet. "You will look absolutely pretty for your first day!" She exclaims, clasping her hands together. She is never this excited, even on Christmas.

"Can't I just wear jeans?" I groan, recalling what Logan said about how school shouldn't change the way a person dresses.

"You can, but not on your first day. You want to make a good first impression, right?"

Not in the mood to argue, I head to the bathroom for a quick shower. I slip out of my pajamas and stand under the faucet for as long as I can before my mom yells through the door for me to hurry up. I'm barely able to properly dry myself off before she charges into the room with my clothes in her hands. What makes things even more difficult for me, though, is that she keeps trying to dress me as I am trying to dress myself. Her limbs begin to tangle with my own and I am beginning to think that she and I are going to wind up wearing this outfit together.

Fully clothed, she twirls me over to the mirror so that I can see how I look. "Don't you look beautiful?" She beams at my reflection. "The colors in this blouse bring out those emerald green eyes of yours. Don't you think?" She asks as though I care.

And without waiting for my response she continues, "Now you go on downstairs for some breakfast and I will meet you there to do your hair."

For being a freshman in high school, I feel more like a kid going off to Kindergarten with my mom dressing me and doing my hair again. She doesn't even do this on Sunday mornings or even holidays for that matter. Her behavior is rather bizarre, but I can understand why she is doing it. She never gets to dress me up and make me into the little girl that she always pictured me as; I just hope she takes a picture of how I look, because this is the last time that I will ever let her dress me up without a fight. I feel absolutely ridiculous in this outfit and I am sure that Logan will also agree.

Downstairs in the kitchen greeting me, is a plate of eggs, bacon, and toast; all positioned into an awkward smiley face. Normally food doesn't appear on my plate in any particular fashion, which makes this unnecessary arrangement make me feel like the child who needs their fork to sound like an incoming airplane in order to eat what's on it. She really is outdoing herself today. *I wonder if dad knows...*

"I was thinking we could do either pigtails or curls. Or maybe even a nice braid," she says, as soon as she enters the kitchen with her comb and a bottle of hairspray. Seeing the items in her hands, I opt for the braid. There is no way that I am letting her give me pigtails.

Eating then becomes another challenge that I didn't expect, which immediately reminds me of the nightmarish experience I had while trying to get dressed with her unneeded assistance. My head whips from side to side as she struggles to make the perfect braid. I wave my bacon in the air like a white flag, refusing to eat until she is done trying to give me whiplash.

On the plus side, she allows me to brush my teeth in peace. For extra precaution, however, I lock the bathroom door just in case she decides to burst in again. There is no way that both of us can hold onto the toothbrush at once and I don't want to give her the chance to even try.

While in the bathroom, I avoid the mirror at all costs; because between my outfit and now my hair, I know I will not like what I see, so why bother even looking at myself. I simply gargle and spit my mouthwash into the sink, watching the way that the blue liquid pours down the drain, imagining myself going down with it.

The walk down the hallway and stairs takes me about ten minutes to complete. I move at the pace of a sloth, stopping every few seconds for nothing particular. When I eventually make my way to the foyer and out the front door, I spot my mom waiting by the car with a camera in her hand, *good grief.*

"I want a nice picture for your album," she says.

I stand still and give her a halfhearted smile. It's not sincere, but I don't think she is paying enough attention to notice. The camera produces a powerful flash and I blink in response. She smiles and promptly tucks it inside of her purse. And that's when I notice, that no one else is here beside her.

"Where is everyone?" I turn towards her.

"One of the horses got loose last night and they are out trying to find it. I am sure that everyone is upset that they couldn't come see you off this morning, but they will be here when you get back," she smiles hopefully.

But I refuse to leave without saying goodbye. I don't care that I will be back later. And I don't care if a horse has gotten loose. They should be here. They should want to see me off. It's almost like they have lost sense of their priorities, as selfish as that sounds.

I tighten the strap on my backpack and feel the pull against my shoulder. The weight of my school supplies and lunch all of a sudden feel a lot heavier than they did a moment ago. It takes everything within me to hold back from running out into the fields to find everyone. But my mom's pull to get me into the car is much stronger. I edge towards her car as though I am being forcibly dragged.

"Come on, you don't want to be late," she opens the door and ushers me in.

Reluctantly, I climb inside, still combing the fields for any sign of them. But I don't see or even hear anything for that matter; therefore, I give up hope. I accept that I am setting sail on this voyage with no proper departure. I just hope that at least they will all miss me.

With the start of the ignition, so does mom's desire to reminisce about her days in high school just as dad did last night. If I thought his football stories were bad, mom's memories prove to be much worse, sans the need for reenactments. She tells me about how she was the head of the cheerleading squad, going into full detail about her school spirit and pride. And to top that off, she slides in the fact that she was also school president and prom queen! "Oh, but no pressure," she says. *You're too kind, mom.*

About twenty minutes later, we pull into a long driveway, which circles around to the front of a large brick building. The front and sides of the school swarm with students, making my nervous heart want to beat right out of my chest. I look down at my clothes and see that no one else is dressed anywhere near, to what I am wearing. Most of the girls who look to be about my age are wearing shorts or sundresses. Today is already not starting out well. I don't even see any braids.

My hand reluctantly reaches for the handle before it slips away. Unbeknownst to me, my palms have filled with sweat. I look towards my mom with nervous trepidation, as the sweat begins to drip down the side of the door.

"You will do great," she says for about the hundredth time, as she leans over to give me a kiss on the cheek. I have no faith in any of her words, but I don't tell her that.

"I will pick you up at the end of the day, all right?" She says.

I nod and push open the car door. The gravel meets my feet and I practically have to force myself to stand upright. I hesitate between walking towards the school and diving back inside of the car. But my mom continues to push me along with her words of encouragement, forcing me to shut the door quickly before anyone overhears her.

It's here that I turn to face the school just as she pulls away from the curb. *The adventure begins,* I think to myself. *I just wish I had my co-pilot with me…*

Chapter Four

I am lost amidst the chaos and swallowed up by the stampede. A darkening veil has fallen over my eyes, reminiscent of last night's nightmares. I am stationary, paralyzed by an unwelcoming sense of fear, which only turning around and running home could alleviate. I try to remember the survival tips that Logan and I read about in a book awhile back, but none of what we read seems relevant for the jungle that I find myself currently in. There is no need for me to lie low, because I have a sneaking suspicion that no one even notices me. I can also easily escape through the small clusters of people and get to where I need to go, but, unfortunately, I have no idea where it is that I am even going, leaving me feeling completely helpless.

Without thinking it through, though, I randomly choose to follow a few people, believing that they might actually be heading in the same direction, as I should be. But none of them do—go figure. I slithered behind them unsuspectingly, gripping tightly to the straps on my backpack. But when they ended up dispersing into classrooms that weren't the one I was looking for,

I slunk back into the shadows waiting for someone else to possibly lead the way. However, after several tries of this, I decide to locate a bathroom and slip away inside. The door swings open before gracing my back as it pushes me into a presumably empty room. I decide that it's best just to hide out for the time being until the hallways start to clear.

The bathroom isn't exactly a first rate hiding option. And It really isn't a second rate option for that matter either. But the rows of never-ending hallways and lockers made me feel quite dizzy that I figured, a bathroom would be beneficial in case the effects of it all made me want to throw up. I turn towards the sink, gripping my hands tightly around one of the small porcelain tubs, before deciding to take the edge off with a few splashes of water upon my face. But just as I am about to turn the faucet on, I hear voices emerge from the other side of the room. My grip loosens as my hands fall fearfully to my sides.

Footsteps sound from behind the last few stalls, rounding the corner from the other side. My private domain has been entrenched, forcing me to retreat into one of the stalls. I slide the lock gently into the holder and steady my breathing as they approach.

I have no idea what I am doing or why I even feel compelled to hide; but my actions make me feel like a total coward as a result. Logan without a doubt would make fun of me for this; therefore, I make a silent pact with myself that when I tell him about my day, I will just have to leave this part out.

"Did any of you see Jordan yet?" One of the girls announces to the group. "Summer did that boy well; he got hot!"

"But didn't you already date him, Morgan?" Another girl chimes in.

"Yea, well, I dated a lot of guys here; what is your point? I was about to become a repeat offender sometime." The voice I assume to be of Morgan's, ends with a snobbish giggle.

"Well, I don't think you will be repeating with him anytime soon," says another.

"Oh, really, and why is that?" Morgan scoffs.

"Because he is dating Stephanie Richards, that's why. I saw them ride into school together this morning."

"Savannah, that doesn't mean anything. I ride to school with guys all the time. It doesn't mean that I am dating them."

"Maybe not, but they *were* holding hands," Savannah shoots back, before her voice suddenly distorts by the sound of a bell chiming through the loudspeaker above.

Through the stall door, I hear them scurry out of the bathroom with the door swinging shut behind them. The residual sounds of their heels clacking against the floor dissipate only seconds after they officially leave. And when that noise finally stops completely, I unlock the hinge on the bathroom door and find myself in a completely deserted room. I pull my backpack off my shoulders and grab my class schedule from outside pocket. *Where is the map to these classes?* I search through my bag only to come up empty handed. *How I am ever going to find my way around this place?*

That's when I remember that dad is friends with the principal, Mr. Harper. Maybe he can help me. But the only flaw in that plan is of me trying to find him as well. The school feels like a giant maze and I am the mouse unable to sniff out the cheese. I am probably better off just sitting by the curb waiting for my mom to show up at the end of the day to come get me. I am sure I can at least find my way outside if nothing else.

Left with no other choice, I swing open the bathroom door and find myself in a deserted hallway. I imagine seeing several tumbleweeds roll on by me. You would never guess that a minute ago, you could hardly walk down it without bumping into someone. I look back down at my schedule and see that I need to find room 205, but all the classrooms that I am passing are in the 100's. I am far away from the cheese at this point…

"Excuse me, young lady?" I turn around and see a short, chubby man with glasses approach me from the opposite end of the hall. "Are you lost or are you starting the year off early with a bit of hallway roaming?" He snorts with derision.

"I guess a little of both," I reply

"Well," he clears his throat, "what room are you looking for?"

"205," I say rather meekly.

"Mr. Howard's room; I will take you there."

He slumps down the hallway with a sluggish gait. There is about a foot or two between us, which seems to grow smaller whenever I take a step. But when he stops abruptly in front of a classroom door about five minutes later, I almost stumble into him in the process. He looks back at me as though completely unaware that he had something to do with it.

His hairy fingers ball into a fist as he knocks upon the classroom door. From the threshold, I see a man seated behind a rather large metal desk, whom I assume to be Mr. Howard. Instead of moving, I wait hesitantly by the door until the chubby man ushers me into the room and asks me for my name.

"Emma," I squeak. My nerves shoot through my body like a makeshift pinball machine.

Without looking at me, Mr. Howard scans his seating chart and points me off into the direction of an empty seat. As I walk towards my desk, I can feel the eyes of the other students glare upon me, which restarts my nervous sweating again. The class schedule moistens and sticks to the inside of my palm like flies to a trap. I peel it off like a Bandage as soon as I sit down.

I would like to say that the rest of the morning only got better from here; but of course, it didn't. I was late to almost all of my classes, besides one, which I accidentally stumbled upon when I was looking for another bathroom to hide in. Aside from that, no one really has said anything to me, besides the teachers during attendance. And I am not quite sure how I feel about that yet. *Oh, how I wish I had Logan here with me.*

Lunchtime, however, is a completely new experience for me. I am so used to eating at the kitchen table with Logan talking about who knows what, whereas here, I find myself completely out of my comfort zone. There are no assigned seats, yet everyone knows exactly where they are sitting; but of course, I don't. I end up just sitting by myself at a small table in the back, slowly chewing away at my lunch, wishing that I were anywhere else but here.

The only plus side to my chosen seating, is that it provides me with a great view around the cafeteria. It's kind of like sitting far enough away from the cows and horses and being able to watch them behave naturally without human interference. And with the last bite of my apple just as the lunch bell rings above, I toss the remainder of my lunch into the trashcan, and head out to find my next class. According to my schedule, it's called, "study hall," which is surprisingly a few doors down from where the lunchroom is. Once I make my way inside, I notice the instructions on the blackboard telling us that we can talk quietly amongst ourselves. Everyone by the looks of it seems excited by this; I, however, keep to myself—no different from any of my other classes.

I rest my body into my desk chair feeling it mold around the wooden backing. Looking around the room, I notice that there are about twenty other students, all of whom appear to be from different grades. In front of me, however, there's a group of good-looking guys and girls, which me make me wonder if they are part of the 'popular crowd' like mom once belonged to.

The first girl I notice has blonde hair and blue eyes; but not like the blue eyes that Logan has; hers have a dull grey coloring to them, making them for lack of better words, dull. She is talking with a few girls beside her, all of whom are perfectly dressed. With every word, I watch as they flip their hair from side to side like rolling ocean waves hitting the shore. It is unnecessarily repetitive and I don't see the need for it. If their hair is bothering them that much, they should probably just tie it back. At least, that is what I would do.

One girl in the group of hair flippers, with dark brown hair and brown eyes, checks on her makeup in a tiny silver mirror every few minutes. She plays at her eyelashes and puckers her lips as though something changed from the last time that she checked on them. She is entirely overboard with her personal vanity.

I then direct my attention over towards the two guys sitting with them. They look very clean; much different from the guys that I am accustomed to seeing around the farm. They smell as though they have never set foot outside. My nose turns up at this. And from here, I can't detect any noticeable dirt lines underneath their fingernails to suggest that they have ever done any manual labor either. They are as clean as the girls beside them are—weird.

"Morgan, do you have any lip-gloss?" The brown haired girl asks the blonde sitting beside her. In a weird way, my day feels like it has come full circle with me being able to place a name to a face. I watch as Morgan hands the girl a tube of pink shiny liquid without taking her eyes off the boy beside her. She bats her eyelashes at him and continues to move closer whenever she laughs. She reminds me of what my mom does when my dad surprises her with a bottle of wine on their anniversary. Only Morgan's behavior appears borderline pathetic.

Lost in my thoughts, as my eyes begin to glaze over, I am unaware that I am in fact, staring. I only end up finding this out, however, because the blonde girl, Morgan, turns around and stares directly at me. Her eyes like sharp knives cutting through my gaze.

"Do you have a staring problem or something?" She barks at me.

My face burns red, forcing me to turn away. I have no idea what to say or do. Where is a bathroom when you need one?

"I said," She repeats herself a little louder, "do you have a staring problem?"

I know that I need to say something, but I have no idea what *to* say. My eyes widen and my palms begin to sweat again. Forcibly, I make myself clear my throat and croak out a *no*. I watch as her eyes survey me up and down, before she releases a chuckle through her shiny lips.

"Nice clothes," she smirks with disdain.

"Very little house on the prairie," chimes in another.

I look up at the front of the classroom in hopes that the teacher is seeing what is happening, but he is too busy playing around on his computer to notice. I am almost half-tempted to punch Morgan in her face, but I have to remember to stay calm. My farm etiquette probably wouldn't work here.

"Well, with her red hair and that shabby braid; she kind of looks like Pippi Longstocking to me" The brown haired girl pipes up.

"You are right, Savannah! She does!" Morgan continues to laugh even louder.

"Leave her alone," one of the guys they are sitting with, butts in. He has dirty blonde hair, a pointy nose, and oddly shaped ears. Still, even with all that, he isn't too bad to look at. A sigh of relief takes over me, as he thankfully comes to my rescue. But my mouth displays a smile too soon.

"What? Are you saying that you like the way she looks? Maybe I should start dressing like her?" Morgan jeers towards him. I watch as her eyelashes continue to flutter like tiny butterflies stuck to her eyelids. I imagine smashing them in with a flyswatter.

"Gosh, no," he chuckles back, looking at me. "It's just that I would much rather you pay attention to me than her," he says in a flirtatious tone. I almost want to gag. *So much for being rescued...*

After the final bell rings for the day, I head out of the building, as fast as my feet will take me. My legs move in the same hurried pace that they do when Logan chases me. I stop at the tip of the sidewalk and wobble back and forth looking for my mom. It takes me a good minute or two to spot her, considering all of the busses congregate in front of the school, blocking the view to all the arriving cars. I have never been so relieved to see her.

When I spot her, I take off across the front lawn and veer to the left where she is parked. Hearing the car door unlock, I quickly climb in and throw my bag over the seat. The contents spill out everywhere, but I don't care enough to pick them up. My day was absolutely terrible, so why shouldn't it end that way as well?

"How did your first day of school go?" She smiles towards me, oblivious to my despondent entrance.

"Don't make me go back," I plead into her shoulder. "People are so mean here!"

"Are you sure? Maybe you are just misinterpreting—"

"—Were you not listening to me? I think I understand the difference between people being nice and people being mean. And they were being mean! If you loved me, you would not make me go back," I cut her off, while folding my arms angrily across my chest.

She begins to say something, but I end up not paying any attention. I stare out of the car window as she pulls away from the school and heads home. I have no desire to say anything more, primarily because, all I want to do is talk with Logan. I want to tell him about my day and see if he knows what I should do. He is the only one that I trust in this world. I mean, it's not that I don't trust my parents; it is just that no one gets me like he does. And he definitely wouldn't second guess on whether or not I knew if people were being mean to me. He would take my word without question.

The farm greets me and I am relieved to be back home. I can care less about the clothes that I am wearing, before I head off into the pasture, calling out Logan's name. I can hear my mom trying to call me back to change, but I ignore her. From the corner of my eye, Logan appears out from inside of the barn and greets me with a sheepish look on his face. He is covered in dirt from head to toe and from this distance; I can make out a streak of mud across his left cheek. It almost fills up his trademark, making it level with the rest of his face.

I run up to him and wrap my arms around him. I don't even care about him ignoring me at this point. I just want a hug. The gesture even surprises me, considering we don't normally hug outside of the holidays, but I don't care. "Oh, it was awful," I say, pulling away from our embrace in tears, which I try my best to conceal.

"That bad, huh?"

I nod, "Worse than bad."

"Hey, listen, I am sorry for ignoring you. I have had a lot on my mind lately, and I just wanted to be left alone," he says to me unsolicited.

"That's okay. I am just hoping that my parents don't make me go back."

"Well, did you make any friends?" he asks me as if it were even possible, although, I do detect a hint of jealousy in his voice.

"No, people made fun of me. They made fun of the way I dressed and—"

"I told you to just dress like you normally do; didn't I?"

I shrug, "Maybe. But my mom practically forced me against my will. What was I supposed to do?"

"Just tell her that you want to be yourself." He hangs his finger off his belt loop.

"I don't think she'll listen."

"Tell her that the original is far better than the remake."

"Huh?"

"Think about it, with movies, the originals are far better than the remakes, but people feel compelled to change them because they don't appreciate leaving them as is. If it's not broken, don't fix it. And you Emma, you are not broken, and you definitely don't need to be fixed. Your original is by far better than any remake the world would want to do to you."

Chapter Five

It begins with a few snowflakes and then, before you know it, the ground and fields cover in this enormous fluffy white blanket. It's the kind of blanket that inspires you to have fun, while you use it to create snowmen, angels, and makeshift hills, which allow you to get a proper sled ride in or two. Then, when that's all done, you are greeted where the white blanket ends, and the front porch begins with a nice cup of hot chocolate and marshmallows. Because all it takes is just one tiny sip, before it warms you up from your ears to your toes; a sort of, recharging if you will, before you head back outside for another round of nostalgically thrilling winter games.

For the past few days, I have returned some normalcy back into my life being that I am able to spend more time around the farm. As soon as school concluded for winter break, I found myself instantaneously eager for my usual routine. Every morning as well as this, I hightail myself out of bed to go feed the animals during the wee hours of the morning. Sleeping in was never a perk to me. A perk to me is embracing the rising sun as my feet scuttle through the morning dewed grass to begin my day's work. Now, I just enjoy watching my feet make imprints in the snow instead. I love the way it crunches underfoot and envelopes the tops of my shoes.

Logan also appears to be happy to have me around more, or at least I think he is. He is more willing to do some of the things that I want to do, whereas before, he would just give me some sorry excuse not to do them. Mom, on the other hand, shares with me on occasion about Logan's progress with school. Apparently, he is doing exceptionally well. She even gloats to me about how he is a terrific speller and a history buff, which of course, has to be the two things that I struggle with the most. I think he excelled at those things just to spite me. Although, I am not doing too badly in school myself; I am able to keep my grades up and even made the high honor roll several times. Mom was so excited that she decorated the walls in the kitchen with my certificates. But a part of me feels like she is doing it to cover the parts of the walls where the wallpaper is tearing.

As for student life, I am either ignored or teased in some way, shape, or form. Dad told me over dinner one night that I cannot succumb to bullying after I admitted to him that I wanted to punch another girl in the face. Mom just sat back in her chair in disbelief. She never thought her daughter had any violent tendencies. She is just lucky that I don't act on any of them.

Today, however, after a morning of snow angels and talking about building an igloo, Logan and I separate around 11:00 am so that my mom can take me out to Syracuse to do a little Christmas shopping. I have been looking forward to this day for a few weeks now. It's one of my favorite days of the year.

"You ready to go?" She asks as soon as I head upstairs to change out of my damp clothes.

"Yep, just have to change first," I yell back down to her. The frozen snow melts with the warmth of the house. Behind me, I see a small icy trail begin to take shape.

Every year mom and I go Christmas shopping a few days before the holiday. She gives me a set amount and I am able to go and buy presents for her, dad, Mr. Solway, and of course, Logan. The amount always fluctuates, so I am hoping that this year I get a little more to spend with than I've had in the past.

When we arrive at the mall, mom parks the car in the underground garage, which leads us directly into a fairly decent sized department store. She hands me my money and lets me shop around the store without her. It is a small step into the world of independence, but I take what I can get from her.

"How about we meet in the front of the store in let's say, half an hour?" She looks down at her wristwatch.

"Sounds good," I say, before taking off into the opposite direction.

I am not much of a shopper, but I do love buying presents for other people and this year, I am hoping to outdo the ones that I bought for last Christmas. For mom, I find her a new apron, because she has a tendency to ruin hers rather quickly. This one is comprised of a stain resistant fabric that doesn't allow stains to seep into it. The tag even says that it stands up against spaghetti sauce, so I know that she will like it. Along with that, I find her a nice necklace in the same department store with an angel on it. I actually think it's made of real gold and to think, it will only cost me $10.00!

For dad, I buy him a solar-powered watch. It's such a great gift that I can't help but buying a second one for Mr. Solway as well. And with ten minutes left to spare before I have to go meet my mom, I quickly pay for my items and head over to the entrance of the store to wait for her. But just as I am about to make my way over, something catches my eye. Under the fluorescent lighting of the store glistens a red, shiny telescope, which I know immediately is the perfect gift for Logan. I can't help but to dart right towards it.

Taking a box down from the display, I carry it up to the closest checkout counter and wait for the girl to cash me out. I watch as she shines the price scanner over the barcode on the box, which excites me even more. *I can't wait to give this to Logan!* But when she tells me how much I owe and I go to count the change I have left, I realize that I am short.

Not believing in the amount that I have left, I count it again. I look up and watch the clerk peer over the counter at me, while she chews at her gum. Her long fingernails tap upon the box as though she has better things to do than wait for me to recount my money for the third time. Thankfully, my mom comes up to the counter just in time to prevent me from having a panic attack.

"Is everything alright, dear?" She asks, as she sets her shopping bags down on the floor beside her feet.

"I am $3.25 short," I say, revealing the money that I have left.

"Well, you know the rules Emma Rae. You get a certain amount of money every year to spend on gifts, and it is up to you to spend it wisely."

"Yes, but mom, this is the perfect gift for Logan! I swear that I will work the money off if you give it to me, please!" I beg her.

"Are you going to buy this?" The girl behind the counter asks with another chomp of her gum. The red telescope looks back at me as though pleading not to let me walk out of the store without it.

"Please mom," I beg again. Behind my eyes, I feel a layer of wetness form. Even though I am desperate, I hate to cry, so I do my best not to allow the tears to become too visible, although, they might actually work in my favor.

"You promise to work this off?" Mom asks as she waves the five-dollar bill at me.

"Promise," I say. I really don't care what I have to do. This present is perfect, and I can hardly wait until Christmas to give it to him.

* * * *

The house fills up with holiday music and the smell of honey ham with all the fixings. Mom has been busying herself around the house for several days, decorating and getting everything ready for the big Christmas Eve dinner that she throws every year. Family used to come in town to join us, but for the last few Christmases, the weather has been downright dreadful, making no one want to bundle themselves up and make the drive. Mom's brother Hank is usually drunk by the afternoon and his wife Shirley, never wants to make the drive on her own. Although for the rest of the family, I think the farm smell has something to do with their decisions to stay home too.

Dad comes downstairs in his normal holiday sweater. It's red with green stripes and from years of wear, you can make out small tears along the seams. But he loves the sweater regardless. And not to mention, he has a tendency to be rather nostalgic towards the weirdest things. Mom on the other hand, is wearing a new dress that she bought when we were out Christmas shopping. She looks great in it; she rarely ever buys herself new things.

"You look pretty," Dad exclaims entering the kitchen. Mom pulls herself away from the oven and hugs him.

"Thank you; you don't look too bad yourself," she smiles.

I love watching them together sometimes. They really do love each other, which makes me understand the sadness that Mr. Solway must feel. I wonder if he loved his wife just as I see my dad love my mom. And I am curious to know what it takes to love someone like that, because the feeling is so unfamiliar to me, but I admire it nonetheless.

As for me, however, I don't have to dress up. Mom lets me wear a pair of blue jeans and a Christmas sweater that she had picked out the day we went shopping. It's not over the top and cheesy, which I am grateful for. It has a subtle pattern of snowflakes on it; and besides that, I find it rather warm and comfortable. It beats still having to wear the dress that I wore to church this morning.

Something about the holiday season always puts me in a good mood. I head down into the kitchen with a slight skip to my step, but just as I am about to peek into some of the covered food dishes, I hear a knock at the front door. Standing outside are Mr. Solway and Logan, both holding a few bags that I know are filled with presents. I open up the door and let them inside, leading Logan to the tree so that he can begin unloading the bags.

"Merry Christmas," I hug Mr. Solway. His musty cologne billows up like a cloud of dust from old furniture.

"Merry Christmas young lady; where are your parents?" He says in reply.

"In the kitchen," I point.

He heads off towards the kitchen carrying one of the bags probably filled with a few of his famous apple pies. I never liked apple pie until he made me try his. It's sweet with a tiny of burst of cinnamon with each bite. He also says he uses a special ingredient to make it taste as good as it does, but he refuses to tell any one of us what it is. It still doesn't stop me from guessing every time that he makes it though.

After Logan is finished unpacking the presents, I turn to him. "I bet you don't know what I got you!" I tease him.

"I bet you don't know what I got *you*." He teases back.

Strangely, our gift giving this year feels like a competition. And if it is, I am sure to win. The moment I laid eyes on that telescope, I knew that nothing else in this world would make him happier than it would. I anxiously await his reaction. I know he will be the only one who understands my reason behind this gift though. To him, it will be much more than a telescope.

A little while later, mom calls out from the kitchen to tell us that dinner is ready. We scramble into the dining room noticing that mom has everyone's place set and all the food on the table. My mouth salivates at the smell of the honey ham. I love ham, so does Logan. He and I take our seats and anxiously wait for permission to dive in with forks and knives at the ready.

Once dad says grace, the food travels from one end of the table to the other. Logan and I both take a large helping of ham and several buttered rolls, before dad ends up slapping some veggies on our plates as well. We don't say anything as we continue to plow through our plates. We both know what awaits us in the living room, so we try our best to hurry the meal along in hopes that the adults will eventually match our pace.

From the French doors of the dining room, the Christmas tree with all of its decorations, tinsel, and lights, reflects off the surface like a shiny beacon over the presents. Staring at it makes us hardly able to wait to tear through all of the gifts—childish, I know. But it's not until the kitchen is cleaned to mom's liking and dad warms up the pies that we all gather together in the living room to exchange our gifts. This has been a tradition of ours for so many years. Christmas mornings are strictly for Santa and presents from mom and dad, but I find this to be much more exciting in comparison. Especially since I figured out Santa Claus was a fake when I saw mom and dad bringing presents down from the attic when I was about seven. As soon as I could, I had to tell Logan what I saw. I thought I was doing him a favor; but instead, he blamed me for ruining Christmas, forever.

The first present passed is to my mom and dad, which is from Mr. Solway. He has given them a new welcome sign for the front door with our last name of 'Jensen' hand painted on it.

"It's lovely," mom says, holding it up in the air for all of us to see. "I will hang it up first thing tomorrow morning."

My parents then give Mr. Solway a new teapot; because he broke the one he had chasing his cat out of the kitchen a few weeks ago. It's white with a blue outline of a cow. I never knew Mr. Solway liked tea, but Logan says every evening he unwinds with a cup or two. I guess it's better than whiskey, which my uncle Hank, mom's brother, guzzles down every evening after work.

Then it's my turn. I hand out my gift to Mr. Solway. He opens it and admires the watch with curiosity. "This will definitely come in handy. Thank you Emma," he says.

I nod, not caring about his reaction, because his reaction is not the one that I am waiting in anxious anticipation for. But just as my hand reaches for Logan's gift, he intercepts it and hands me the gift he has for me instead. I am put off slightly by this, but I tear through the packaging anyways and reveal a rolled up stack of quarters. I hold them out in my hands, allowing the stack to roll to the tip of my fingers back to the edge of my palm, but I don't bother asking what they are for. Instead, I toss them to the side and hand Logan his gift instead.

He, like me tears through the wrapping paper and uncovers the telescope. His eyes grow wide with excitement, before he rips open the cardboard box and in his hands, revealing the telescope to everyone. It is just as red and shiny as it looks on the box. I am quite pleased with myself. His reaction is just as I hoped it would be.

"Let's go outside and look at the stars!" He shouts, getting to his feet.

"It's ten degrees outside son, why don't you wait until the weather breaks?" His dad tries to stop him. But I know that look on Logan's face. When he is determined about something, there is no stopping him.

"We will wear our coats and boots!" Logan exclaims, yanking up the telescope to his chest.

Joining him, I quickly get to my feet, looking over at my parents to make sure that it's okay. They don't say anything, so I chase Logan out of the room, where we begin throwing on our snow gear. And once were bundled up, we head outside.

The night welcomes us both into its shivering embrace and the only hint of light guiding our way across the street is from the clouded moon and the porch light emitting from my house. It reflects off the surface of the snow for only a few feet, just before our steps become darkened by the rapidly approaching night. And when we reach our normal stargazing spot, I am surprised at how I am not paying the grey house any mind.

"This is the best gift ever!" He says to me with the biggest grin on his face.

"I am glad you like it."

He sets up the telescope and immediately looks through it. He is having so much fun that I don't want to interrupt him. Instead, I plop down into the snow and look up at the stars as we normally would do; but then without warning, he pulls his eye away from the telescope and frowns at me. I detect a small imprint of a circle around his right eye.

"I feel bad," he says.

"Why do you feel bad?"

"You gave me this awesome gift and all I got for you were those quarters. I feel like such a lousy friend," he sulks.

I pull the roll of quarters out of my pocket, revealing them as though to the world. A simple gift, yes, but knowing Logan, he would never just give a gift without any thought.

"They are lovely," I summon my mom's description to use on Logan's gift. I really can't come up with anything else to say.

"Lovely?" He says, plopping down in the snow beside me. "That's not an Emma's word." *He always catches on so quickly.*

"Well they are," I say.

"Just so you know though, I did have a reason behind *why* I gave them to you."

I look towards him, finding it funny that he and I both put extra care in our gift selections this year. "What's the reason?" I ask curiously. I stare down at the quarters, waiting for the simplicity of them to change into something remarkable.

"I just thought that whenever you need someone to talk to during school, like when you are having a bad day or something, I would only be a phone call away."

I look down at the quarters in my hand and smile. We really know how to make each feel better sometimes.

Chapter Six

The snow doesn't fade, but my days away from school begin to. The simple joys of life back on the farm are enough to make me feel like I am whole again. It is here that I belong without any question; and most importantly, I get to spent time with best friend again. And the thought that all of these good feelings are sadly numbered, depresses me greatly. Yet, I am the only one who seems to notice.

The morning back to school arrives and unexpectedly, my rooster alarm clock actually releases a pitiful crow. It almost sounds as though it has been under held water and somehow resurrected back to life. I decide to ignore it though and remain in bed. I have no desire to get up and face the day, because I know what to expect. To me, going back to high school is like purposely walking into the lion's den—to be devoured.

"What's wrong with you?" Dad asks, opening the door to my bedroom. It creaks open, inviting in the smell from the farm.

I pull the covers back over my head. "I don't want to go back," I say. "I want to stay here."

"I know, but you have to get an education." He pulls them back, revealing my face.

"What about Logan, isn't he getting an education here?"

"Well, yes, but it's different for Logan."

"How so?" The idea that Logan and I could be different baffles me.

"Well for starters, you are my daughter, and he isn't."

"Well of course he isn't your daughter dad," I laugh, "he would be your son."

For a change, my dad decides to take the morning off and drive me to school. The drive is much more relaxing, because mom has a tendency to stress me out without even knowing it. With dad, he just talks about the farm the entire time, which calms my nerves considerably.

"You know, there is more to life than the farm." He says, turning the corner off our street. "I chose this life after I had tried other things; and that is what I want you to do; try other things. It's a way for you to determine what is best for you by getting out of your comfort zone—it's the only way you will ever know."

"Well, what if I already know what is best for me? It would be foolish to waste everyone's time and mine; trying out a bunch of things that I know isn't what I want." The window fogs against my breath, I am unable to face him when we talk about this.

I see that he looks down at me from the corner of his eye. "I know you are still young now, but one day, you will understand why I am pushing you to do more with your life."

I know that he is trying to tell me something, without actually telling me. Much like when Logan apologizes to me without actually apologizing. I do however; ask him if he feels like he could have done more with his own life. Diverting the conversation seems like my best option at this point.

"I had a great job in the city, Emma. Your mom and I both did. But we got tired of the stress and the lifestyle, which brought us here. And yes, there are days that I wonder if I gave up on that life too easily. Maybe all we really needed was just a good vacation, not another life. And I know your mom misses the way things used to be—at least, the glamorous part."

His words startle me. *Does he not want this life?* For so long, I thought he was happy. He worked tirelessly day after day on the farm and never once did I ever suspect that he wasn't entirely happy doing it. "But I love this life," I finally say. "And I am perfectly content with not knowing any other."

He smiles at me, "I was sure that you would say that, but please for me, give high school a chance. And if you don't want to continue your education after you graduate, then you don't have to go to college, all right?"

My eyes widen in shock. Wasn't that the whole purpose of me going to high school in the first place? His comment makes me think that there is no point in all of this. No one seems to understand how troubling this is for me; and the fact that I have been separated from my best friend, makes it even worse. And to think it's probably for no reason at all, makes it hurt even more.

* * * *

In I walk through the metal doors, caging me in against my will. The only lifeline I possess is tucked safely away in my backpack pocket. It's nice to know that Logan really is only a phone call away. The only problem I see with this, however, is the fact that he is never home. I guess he didn't really think his present through.

The only positive part of my return to school is that some of my classes changed with the new semester. I am beyond relieved to know that I no longer have to deal with Morgan and her obnoxious friends during study hall. I hope in my case, I never see them again.

Upon the commencement of fifth period gym class, however, I am surprised to find how completely uncoordinated I really am. The gym teacher sets us loose to play a couple games of indoor soccer and I am having a hard time kicking the ball effectively. No matter how hard I try, the ball never quite goes where I intend to kick it to; it either heads in the opposite direction or I end up tripping over it.

For being just a gym class game though, I am finding that many of my teammates are getting upset with me. Most of them, I learn are on the varsity soccer team, so their standards of playing are of course, a lot higher than mine. But I have never really played the game before. The sportiest thing I do, is throwing around a football with Logan. We don't even play the game properly, we just like the way that the ball spirals into the air and how we tackle each other trying to catch it.

"Emma, you need to kick the ball like this," one of the soccer girls pull me aside to show me how it's done. I can tell by the frustration in her voice that she had enough of my lack of talent. I watch as she begins to demonstrate the way that her foot meets the ball and how it elegantly glides into the goal. She makes it look rather easy. Something that I know I will not be able to replicate.

"I am sorry," I say through another one of her demonstrations, "I have never played this before." I am hopeful that it will excuse my lack of skill, but the expression on her face suggests that she doesn't care. At the blow of the teacher's whistle, the game resumes. I try to implement the moves that she taught me as best as I can; but then I decide to avoid the ball altogether, which seems to make everyone a lot happier in the end.

* * * *

The white fluffy blanket begins to melt, just as spring peeks its head around the corner. It's almost as if I can smell the flowers well before they even begin to blossom. I am anxiously waiting for summer to get here, so that life can go back to normal for me. For almost a year, it felt sporadic and unfulfilled. My purpose, in itself, felt questioned. And the only thing that kept me going was knowing that there is a possibility of Logan coming to join me sophomore year. The finish line appears in the horizon of my mind.

Sitting in English class today, I envy Logan. There he is enjoying the farm on such a beautiful day, while I am stuck inside this building for most of it. I imagine us lying side-by-side down by the river with the cool air surrounding us, while we listen to the sounds of the river rolling on by. The water is still without question, cold; but I still envision our toes sampling out the temperature to be sure. A few rocks are thrown with a clunk into the water and Logan tries his best to skip a few. I watch them hop across the surface of the water before plummeting to the bottom of the riverbed. I immediately feel happy at the thought of these simple delights. I smile with a sense of bliss.

Coming to, I notice Mr. Jorgenson, my English teacher, walking towards the front of the classroom giving us instructions on our class assignment for the day. He is an egotistical man who has self-proclaimed himself to be some kind of literary critic. Every book we have read this year at his request is followed up by a lengthy speech pertaining to his personal opinions and interpretations of it. His eyes appear hallow and empty like a shell. And when he calls on you during class to answer any off the wall questions he wants, he judges you well before you even provide an answer. I am so looking forward to ridding myself of him after this year.

"All right class, I want everyone to turn to page 156 in your textbooks. I am going to assign you into groups where I want you to discuss the key points I wrote on the blackboard."

My group consists of a boy named Henry who has braces and glasses; and fumbles over his book as though he is unsure as to whether it belongs on his desk or on the floor. His hazel eyes appear skittish like a cat, making him unable to make eye contact with anyone for more than a few seconds. Then there is Stacy; the class clown. Hardly a minute in class goes by where this girl doesn't crack a joke out loud. She can be funny sometimes, but during others, she can be rather annoying. Today she is a mixture of both. Mr. Jorgenson is openly not fond of her and I have a feeling that my group is already doomed well before we even begin.

"So what are we reading?" She pushes back her bushy blonde hair away from her face.

Henry muffles a response to her from behind his book that neither one of us can decipher. She looks at me for help, but I just shrug my shoulders.

The idea of group activities always sets my teeth on edge. And when I open my textbook, I feel a twinge of pain in my lower abdomen. I know I am nervous, but the pain doesn't sit well with me, so I do my best to try to calm my nerves in hopes to diminish it. But no matter how many deep breaths I manage to release, nothing helps. The cramp sensation increases regardless of me moving or remaining motionless in my seat.

Stacy then turns over to one of her friends behind us and blurts out a joke, which then causes Henry to snort and me to laugh at Henry. But as soon as the laughter escapes from my tightened lips, I feel a weird sensation. Something has happened. *Did I just pee my pants?* I can feel all the blood leave my face.

Embarrassed, I squeeze my legs together tightly and pretend to drop a pencil on the floor to see if I can spot any evidence—but the floor is clean. Nervously, I pull my cardigan off and nonchalantly tie it around my waist for extra precaution. At this moment, I am thankful for my mom forcing me to wear it this morning, even though I said I was warm enough without it.

For the next few minutes, all I can think about is getting to the bathroom. From here, I know that it's down the hall and to my right, but the distance seems like too long of a gamble for me. I am afraid to get up. The last thing I want to be known as is 'the girl who peed her pants'. I have never peed my pants! Okay, maybe once, but I was six! And Logan made me laugh when he knew I had to go, so really, it was all *his* fault.

The best I can do for myself right now is to continue squeezing my legs tightly together until they feel like they have formed into one. I am afraid to move; but I have to do something. Nervously, I move one of my hands towards the lining of my skirt. Maybe if I try to feel between my legs, then I will know, but I am afraid of someone seeing me. None of this makes any sense. *I didn't even have to go to the bathroom in the first place!*

Thankfully, everyone's eyes appear as though glued to their books, while I try my best to keep a lookout for any unsuspecting eyes. Pretending to adjust my skirt, I trace the outline of my underwear and pull my hand back towards my lap as fast and inconspicuously as I can. Looking down, all I see is red—blood.

Paralyzed by fear, I can barely move and my face feels as red as what I uncovered from down below. Once the bell rings, I wait until everyone leaves so that I can make my way to the bathroom as fast I can. It is there that I stuff a half a roll of toilet paper in my underwear to prevent an even bigger miss. And when I am done, I find the nearest payphone and fish through my bag for the stack of quarters that Logan gave to me for Christmas. Pulling a quarter out from the stack, I slide it into the coin slot just as I begin to dial the number for home.

"Mom?" I breathe into the phone.

"Hi sweetie, what's wrong?"

"I think you may need to come get me."

"Why, what happened?"

I look around to make sure that no one can overhear me. "Um," I hesitate. I am embarrassed and scared beyond comprehension. "I am…bleeding."

"Did you cut yourself?" She asks.

The line goes quiet for several seconds until I hear a sudden gasp on her end. "I will be right there," she says, right before I hear nothing but a dial tone on her end.

I place the phone back on the receiver and make my way towards the front entrance of the school. There is no way that I am going back to class to wait for my mom there, so I opt to wait outside instead. I feel horrible and all I want to do is lie down; but mom is a good twenty minutes away and it will take an additional twenty minutes on top of that before I even see a bed in my future. A thousand and one things are zipping through my mind as to what is going on, but the longer I obsess over the possible reasons, the more nervous it makes me as a result.

When my mom's car finally pulls up to the front of the school, she runs up to me and gives me a hug. "Everything will be alright sweetie," she says in a calming voice. I relate the connection to the same tone of voice she used when I had my tonsils out a few years back, as well as when I went into the hospital for a bladder infection. But something tells me that my situation is not good. She must be trying to keep me calm for a reason.

Once I stand up, she practically walks me to the car as if I somehow forgot how to use my legs. Opening the door, I look down, noticing that she had laid out a towel for me to sit on.

"It's fine sweetie," she says to me with a smile. "Sit down."

Apprehensively, I sit down as she rounds the car and gets in.

"This is completely normal," she begins, as soon as she pulls away. "This is the start of you becoming a woman." I detect a soft smile emerge onto her face.

I am having a hard time grasping the concept and am slightly annoyed that she never once thought to tell me about this, especially when she knew that it was bound to happen in my near future. Shouldn't I have had a warning so then perhaps, I wouldn't have thought for the last hour and a half that I was dying?

When we get home, I carefully step out of the car in fear of what may happen. Logan appears from inside of the barn, but I don't stop to say hi to him. Instead, I make my way quickly inside as I hear my mom explaining to him that I don't feel very well.

"Does she need soup?" He asks, hoping to be of any help.

"No, she just needs some rest. She will be better in no time."

I sincerely hope she is telling the truth.

For the next hour, however, I endure a lengthy lecture of how to use feminine products, which include maxi-pads and panty liners as visual-aides. I curl my lips in awkward embarrassment and wonder just how red my face has become. It feels like absolute torture.

And once she is through or maybe just tired of repeating herself, I ask to be left alone so that I can rest. Besides mom in small doses, there is really no one else that I want to see, which sadly, includes Logan. Therefore, I seclude myself inside of my bedroom until further notice or until this supposed natural catastrophe runs its course.

No matter how many times I toss and turn (gently, I might add) my mind somehow will not escape the looming echo of mom's words, *you're becoming a woman now.* But I see no difference in my reflection when I stare into my bedroom mirror. And if I am now this "woman" and Logan is still the same boy, then what does that mean? Sadly, with these turn of events, I feel my days of digging up treasure in the backyard are pretty much over.

Chapter Seven

The end of the school year approaches and I can already smell the sweet scent of summer in the air as it pushes spring completely out of the picture. I can hardly wait to join Logan back on the farm. And with it finally being the last day of school, I begin to make a mental list of all the things that I want to do with him when I am finally free from this prison. One item in particular is of us attempting to have another sleepover in the tree house. I do make note, however, that will need to have a talk with my dad to see if he can place something in the windows to prevent another bat episode from happening. That way, Logan will actually make it through the entire night without breaking anything. He is such a big baby sometimes.

I run out of the metal doors towards my mom's car with a burst of excitement. The sun heats my face with a welcoming embrace. The smell of freshly mowed grass tickles my senses and I can't help but grin from ear to ear. The entire year felt like a marathon and I have officially crossed the finish line. I figuratively tear my body through the ribbon and hold my hands out for the trophy that is summer; that is Logan—and that is home. And with all my final tests completed, the only things that I have to worry about now are my chores around the farm and I couldn't be happier.

Logan greets me as soon as my mom pulls into the driveway on our way back from school. "How did your last test go?" He asks, putting his arm around my shoulder while trying to tackle me to the ground. My book bag falls into the dirt and I just leave it there without a second glance. I don't have to worry about it or anything inside of it for a few months. Therefore, I will just pick it back up when that time comes.

"It went fine." I finally say, fake punching him in the stomach.

Since my apparent step into womanhood, my interactions with him have been somewhat guarded and apprehensive. The rough housing we normally engage in has been taken down a notch, which Logan seems to have not noticed in the slightest. Regardless of everything that has happened to me this year, I decide to push it all aside. It doesn't matter, because I feel like the same person as I always was and with that, why act any different? I am home now; I am with my best friend again; and that is all that really matters.

* * * *

Summer picks me up and gently moves me along with the breeze. I float around the farm like a blown dandelion; and for the first time in months, I feel carefree. I don't worry about what it is that I am wearing and how much attention I may draw at school. I don't care how my hair looks in the mirror, and I am definitely pleased with the fact that it isn't frozen to my head by all of the hairspray that mom would spray into it in the morning. I do however, wonder how many bottles of that crap she went through this year. It was always such a pain to wash it out the next day.

I am back in my work clothes in the matter of a few days after school ended. I make my way through the opening of the pasture when Mr. Solway exits out from the barn, carrying a couple of buckets of fresh milk in each hand. "Where is Logan?" He asks me.

"I don't know," I say, "I was just about to go look for him."

He sets the buckets down and itches at his beard. He is a tall man, much bigger than my dad is, and every time that I see him, I wonder if he is how Logan will look when he gets older. I can barely picture Logan with a beard without smiling.

"Well, I wanted to talk with you both, so when you see him, you can pass this message along, alright?"

I nod as my posture straightens, giving him my undivided attention.

"This summer, I want no trouble. No holes in the pasture to dig for treasure; no setting the brush on fire because you are both convinced that there are prehistoric creatures hiding amongst it; and most importantly, you will understand the laws of gravity. This means, you will not create any device with sticks or anything else you two can find to help you fly. So please, stay off the roofs," he smiles, even though I know that he is being serious. "Your father and I just fixed one of the barns' roofs and still have no idea how there came to be a giant hole in it," he peers down at me. *Oh god, he knows…*

The image of Logan and I trying to jump into a pile of hay surfaces into my mind, but I quickly wipe the thought away in fear that my deception will become visibly apparent.

"Yes, sir," I finally say, clicking my heels together as I salute him. Considering how he was once a Marine, I always thought this was a way of showing him respect.

"Why do you do that?" He chuckles.

"Logan says it a sign of respect, which you like."

He laughs again. "Just run along and stay out of trouble, do you hear me?"

I nod and take off.

I find Logan down by the river, no surprise. He is lying down on the grass with his eyes closed. His hair glistens in the sunlight, making each strand appear as though they are comprised of diamonds. For a moment, I catch myself almost admiring; but I quickly remove the thought from my mind and sit down beside him.

"What are you doing?"

"Just thinking," he says without looking at me.

"About what?"

"George called today. Dad wouldn't speak to him as usual. He said that he wanted to come home again, but dad just walked out saying that the cows needed to be milked." He stops, as a small breeze blows through us. "I just miss him and I want him back, but I don't think that dad will ever forgive him."

I look up at the sky unsure of what to say. I only look back down when my eyes begin to burn from the sun.

"I just want to tell dad that he should let him come home, but I don't want to upset him. I just don't know what to do."

"Try telling your dad how you feel. He can't get mad at you for that."

"I guess."

I lay down beside him still unsure of what to say. Part of me wants to say that George deserves to never come home again, but the other part of me, feels bad for Logan and wants him back just as much as he does. But what can I do? If Mr. Solway doesn't want George back, there isn't anything that anyone can say or do to change his mind. But George was so young when he decided to leave. *A child's decision that is being punished like an adult*, my mom would say.

"Hey, you want to have a campout in the tree house?" I ask, changing the subject. I watch as his eyes open and peer over at the wooden box high in the tree above us.

"What, like, tonight?" He sounds uninterested.

"Yea or whenever—at least sometime this summer."

"Maybe," he says, getting to his feet. "How about we use my telescope and stargaze tonight instead."

For the first time in awhile, a sense of adventure runs through me. Even though Logan and I are only stargazing, it's a small piece of my childhood that I feel like months ago I was forced to leave behind. I am perfectly aware that there will be no treasure this summer or even any dinosaurs for that matter, but that didn't mean he and I still couldn't have fun. We will just have to reinvent the way we have it. I am a woman now, so I get it. Or at least, I think I do.

The night pulls itself in faster than the day was around. It comes with a gentle coolness and after dinner, I sit on the front porch enjoying every minute of its arrival. The sky is darkening and I can make out a few of the stars already. I wonder if Logan wants to talk to his mom tonight, ask her for advice about George. I guess it's not a bad thing, but I don't think that I should be included in the conversation. A part of me feels like it should be private.

A short distance away, I hear Logan's front door creak open. Underneath one of his arms is his outdoor blanket and underneath the other is the telescope. The red shiny surface twinkles under the porch light, signaling to me that it's almost time to head across the street. But it's early. Much earlier than when we normally go stargazing, but I have a feeling that he is desperate for an answer. And if this is his only way for him to get one, than as his best friend, I will follow without question.

I greet him as I exit the porch and take the blanket out from underneath one of his arms. "I didn't expect you for awhile," I say.

"I was bored," he says, trying to keep the telescope from sliding down his arm. "Why, did you have plans?"

"Perhaps," I smile.

I catch the shadow of his dimple appear, as he shuffles his feet with a smile. But as he's about to inch his way towards our normal stargazing spot, I stop him. "Did you hear that?" I say, pretending to hear a noise off in the distance. I lean my ear in towards the pretend sound. A burst of childish excitement hits me without warning and I am eager for him to play along.

"Hear what?" He asks visibly leery. Logan has always been somewhat of a scaredy-cat, even though he never admits to it. Sometimes, I like to play into his fears to get a rise out of him.

"That noise," I hesitate to pretend listen, "You didn't hear it."

"No," his tone worries.

I close my eyes as though concentrating on hearing the noise again. I peek out from beneath my closed lids to see that Logan is trying to do the same.

"What did it sound like?" he asks.

"Like running," I say.

"Running?" He looks over at me confused.

"Yea, running."

He listens all around him, but looks back at me as though still confused. "I still don't hear anything," he says to me. "Maybe you were just hearing things." He shrugs it off.

"Perhaps," I say, right before my foot lifts a couple of inches into the air and stomps down hard upon his shoe.

"Hey!" he yells back at me as I take off running.

"Chase me Logan Solway!" I yell to him as I head across the street. In the short distance that divides us, I can hear the sounds of his feet rapidly hit the ground behind me. "I hear the sound now!" I call out.

"You are a buffoon," he calls out to me.

"Maybe, but I would rather be a buffoon than a horse's ass." I smile, as he grabs a hold of the back of my shirt, forcing us to go tumbling to the ground.

From the corner of my eye, however, I see Logan lose his grip on the telescope as it flies out from underneath his arm. Desperate not to let it go crashing down, I reach out and grab it. My elbow then bangs hard against the ground, just as my hands tighten around the main tube, bringing it in towards my stomach to protect it. It almost impales me as a result.

"That was close," I say, handing Logan back the saved telescope. I wince as my elbow stretches. There will no doubt be a bruise there by tomorrow morning. I rub at it gently to try and soothe the pain.

"Yea, close," he breathes out a sigh of relief, "you all right?"

"I'm fine. I will heal," I peer down at my elbow. "But if it were the telescope, no amount of rubbing it would be able to fix it."

Logan gets to his feet and begins prepping the telescope as I roll out the blanket. He points out his mom to me and then peers at her through the eyepiece. As for me, I pretend to spot a few fireflies off in the distance and chase after them, leaving him alone so that he can speak to her in private.

I dance around the darkness reaching out towards nothing but the air that surrounds me. My imagination, it seems, has turned it nothing more than a way for me to create white lies. I guess it's not a bad thing to use it that way, because I did get Logan to chase me; and now, I am pretending to preoccupy myself while I give him some privacy. I try not watching him as he presses his eye firmly to the telescope. I also try not watching him as his lips move slowly in conversation with his mother. I pretend to be oblivious to these things. But since when has my imagination become my reason to escape the reality of situations in this way? And for what reason? I just wish that one day this summer, my imagination will be put to better use, maybe to fight off an evil pirate or something; anything but this.

* * * *

I awake in the early morning hours, throw on my work clothes, and head towards the barn. Logan is already feeding the animals, as he hands me a bucket to go and finish feeding the rest. Mr. Solway has hired extra hands this summer and Logan and I have been told to take it easy, but it's hard not to be involved like we normally are, especially Logan—this is his father's farm after all. He has a tendency to follow around the help and critique their work. Several times, Mr. Solway had to remind Logan of his place.

"I want a campout for my birthday," I say, taking hold of the bucket. My hand grips around the handle to steady it.

"We have all summer to campout," he huffs.

"My birthday is at the end of July. We still have plenty of time," I point out. "Wait, you are not still afraid are you? It was just a bat, Logan."

"You realize that bats carry rabies, right? I am not going to get bit by one. You can, but I am not."

"Well, what if I ask my dad to cover the windows somehow, would you then?"

"Maybe, but I will have to inspect his work," he smiles, making me want to stick my finger into his cheek crater. "Race you to the river!" He yells.

We dash out of the barn, startling a few cows along the way. This summer, unlike any other, looms with a ticking clock. I can't hear it or see it, but I know it's there and every day that comes and goes, I know that it's bringing me closer to the day that I will have to separate from Logan again. But this time, I refuse to let that happen. Yet, somehow, the clock still ticks on, which reminds me; I still haven't told him what my father said. I make a plan to bring it up as soon as we cross the finish line.

Down by the river, we sit cross-legged and pull at the grass. Logan talks about random things and I do my best to listen and nod where appropriate. When he is through with talking, I bring up school. "This could be the year you join me," I say as though he has something exciting to look forward to, "you can finally experience the joys of high school." My tone echoes back to me sarcastically.

"I don't know," he throws some grass off to the side.

"What do you mean, you don't know?"

"I mean, I don't know if I want to go. Sounds like you hated it."

"Yea, but it wouldn't be so bad if you were there with me."

He says nothing, as he continues pulling at the grass. I can actually hear him tearing handful after handful up from their roots. He pauses just before he throws it all off to the side," I don't know; I will think about it," he finally says, as the small pile of grass scatters around us.

I want to shake some sense into him, but I hold myself back. Sophomore year will be upon me very soon and it didn't seem so bad because I thought I wouldn't have to go back alone. I hate being alone all the time, and I know that I made a pact with myself that I wouldn't make any new friends, but a part of me feels like I will almost have to, in order to survive, that is. That's only considering whether or not people would want to make friends with me.

"You know," he begins, holding out a few blades of grass in his hand to me, "These almost match your eyes."

"Well, I am glad you didn't hold out dirt in your hands," I joke.

"Ying and yang," he smiles, blowing the few blades out of the palm of his hand. "I am the sky and you are everything below."

Later that day, I make my way home for dinner, wash up, and sit at the kitchen table. I wait for dad to come in and once he takes his place beside me, I ask him about covering up the windows of the tree house.

"I don't see why I couldn't, but aren't you two a bit old to go up there?"

"No, why would be too old for a tree house? I take a large sip of my milk.

"Well, it's mainly a kid thing, and you are no longer a kid."

I turn to my mom, hoping that she did not reveal my change into womanhood with my dad. She nonchalantly shakes her head back. The redness cools from my face.

"You know," he changes his voice to a more serious tone, one that he uses when he wants to punish or scold me for something. "Your mom and I have been talking a lot about you and Logan lately," he begins, taking a bite of his dinner. He chews slowly as though still thinking about what he wants to say on the matter. I assume he wants to talk about school and just as I am about to voice my desire for Logan to come along with me, he cuts me off.

"You guys are getting older now and spending nights together is no longer appropriate."

"Appropriate?" My fork loosens from my grip.

"You're of that age now where you two are getting older," A helpless expression weighs heavily on his face as he looks to my mom for help.

"Yes," she speaks up. "You two are of that age where boys and girls start to," she pauses, "notice each other differently and we think it's best if you two limit your time together—"

"—Notice each other how?" I butt in.

She now looks to my dad for help.

"In a romantic way," he says.

I look back and forth at them confused. I do not think of Logan that way and I am entirely certain that he doesn't look at me that way either. "Well, he promised one last sleepover in the tree house for my birthday," I say affirmatively, because there is no way that I am letting Logan get out of it, even if the reason is circumstantial.

"Well, then it will be your last," my dad says back.

"You don't make any sense," I say to both of them. "Logan is my best friend and just because we are getting older, you feel the need to punish us for it? Is that why you sent me to school? You wanted to begin to separate us?" I stand up from the kitchen table unable to sit still any longer.

"No sweetie, that was not our intention," mom responds calmly.

"I am not hungry," I say, storming out of the room. My feet pound up the wooden staircase just before I slam my bedroom door. On the other side of it, I wait a few seconds, believing that one or both of my parents were going to come up and yell at me, but I hear not a sound.

What makes them think that I would ever look at Logan as anything more than a friend? If anything, he is more a brother to me than anything else. I can barely wrap my head around their need to curtail our time together. What have either one of us done to show them that we cannot be around each other? Did Logan say something? Have I missed something? I seriously have no idea…

During the next few days, however, I can barely bring myself to talk about what the conversation I had with my parents with Logan. He acts the same as he usually does and I find no suspicious behavior from him at all to suggest he has any idea. I don't even talk with my parents for that matter. Meals are silent and I do my best to avoid coming home for anything. If I have to use the bathroom, I go and use Logan's instead.

I do, however decide to talk to Mr. Solway about Logan coming to high school with me. I figure, if Logan doesn't do it and my parents want us apart, than I have to take matters into my own hands.

"I think it will be good for him," I say to Mr. Solway when I finally get him alone.

"Well, I know, but he can still get an education here with your mom. Not to mention, he is a great help to me around the farm."

"He is not riding the tractor now, is he?" I ask brusquely.

"I plan on training him soon, yes," he says.

"Well, what about me?" I whine.

"You will have to ask your parents and if they agree, then I will train you too."

Oh, great, just what I need, to talk to my parents. "Could you at least think about it? Wouldn't you want Logan to have access to better opportunities than he would get being homeschooled?" *Gosh, I sound like my parents now.*

He peers down at me as though considering, "Can I think about it?"

I nod. Thinking about it is much better than a flat out no, so I take it, and run.

My silent treatment with my parents surprisingly doesn't stop my dad from finding the time to install a few glass inserts into the tree house windows. I only know this, because just now, as I dart through the brush, I stumble upon his handiwork.

Immediately, I climb up and inspect the new windows before Logan does. Once I am inside, a flood of memories hits me all at once and I almost lose my balance because of it. Closing my eyes, I try to pinpoint when everything started to change for us. The only thing that comes to mind is school. It's the root cause of all my issues it seems. And I would do anything to go back to the way things were before. But I can't turn back time nor can I change what has already been done. The only thing I can do now is to convince Logan to come with me, but I have a feeling that nothing I do or say is going to work.

Chapter Eight

For my birthday, mom makes my favorite dinner of spaghetti and meatballs, which strangely feels more like an apology dinner than a celebratory one. Wearing her stain resistant apron, I see splatters of sauce upon it. The sight excites me, because it's the first time I have seen the apron being put into action. Although, according to the instructions, the stains will remove in the wash. I guess I will have to wait around and see if that is really the case.

On the far back counter, beside the bowl of fruit, sits a perfectly iced red velvet cake with strawberry flavored frosting. The sweet smell drifts over to me and I am almost half-tempted to stick my face into it and claim the entire cake as my own, but I don't. Logan would kill me if I don't at least save him a slice. He loves cake.

"Turning fifteen this year", mom turns to me. She says it as though I had no idea what age I was turning.

I nod with a sad excuse for a smile and make my way into the dining room where dad is already sitting and waiting for us.

From the corner of my eye, I watch her untie her apron and set it off to the side. She brings in the bowl of spaghetti and sets it down beside the garlic bread on the dining room table. As soon as she sits down, she hands me a box to open. But Considering this is the most interaction we have had in awhile, I feel slightly strange for opening it. "How about we eat first and then I will open it?" I say, hoping that it will give us enough time to diffuse the tension in the room.

But it takes two servings of spaghetti, the Happy Birthday song, and for dad to cut himself a second slice of cake before there is any noticeable difference. I reach across the table for the present feeling my mom's twinkling eyes watching me as I slowly tear through the paper. I am paying more attention to her than on the present; and when I look down, I realize what I have just opened, a box of…makeup.

"When I was your age, my mom let me start wearing it. I thought it would be a fun tradition to pass down to you. We can experiment with all the different colors and shades to find what will look the best on you," she takes the box out of my hands, pointing to the various eye shadows and lipsticks inside. "I will even paint your nails!"

I don't wear makeup and have no intentions of wearing it either. I don't even care that most of the other girls in my grade already wear it; I have no use for it. Still, I try to muster a fake smile of gratitude, but I am kind of repulsed by the gift, which is the only expression my faces wishes to bear.

"You don't like it?" Mom inches the box back towards her.

"It's not that I don't like it, it's just that I never saw myself wearing any of it."

"You don't have to, if you don't want to. It's just if you choose to, now you can."

The smile wipes clean off my mom's face as the twinkle in her eyes start to dim. I didn't intentionally try to be rude about the gift, but I could have appreciated something more useful like a new fishing rod or permission to have tractor lessons with Mr. Solway instead.

What tension erased from the room quickly returned tenfold. It is so quiet that I can actually hear the clock tick away in the living room. And for the remainder of time that we are all seated at the table, we do so in an awkward silence. Dad tries to go in for his third slice of cake, but mom intercepts and tells me to take the rest for when I go on my camp out with Logan in a bit. I can see that dad has the same disappointed look in his eyes that mom does, only I can live with why he is upset. His could easily be solved by more cake.

When I am finished playing with the remainder of my food, I put my dishes in the sink, and make my way up the stairs. I gather what I need in my backpack and call Logan on the walkie-talkie to come meet me outside in ten minutes. The box of makeup gets thrown into a dresser drawer with a bang. Picturing lipstick on my face is like picturing Logan with a beard, I can't help but to laugh. But just as I am about to make my way out of my room, I hear a knock on my door. *Please don't be mom…*

"It's just me," dad announces his presence through the wooden barrier.

"Come in," I say. My backpack slides off my shoulder to the floor with a thump. He walks in only a few steps and stops before me. "Are you looking for more cake?" I ask.

He laughs, "No, I just came up here to see if you were all right?"

"Yea, I am fine. Why?"

"Well, you seemed pretty upset about the whole makeup ordeal. I thought it was best if I just checked on you."

"Did mom send you?" I glare over at him.

"No, but she probably will want me to come talk with you anyways," he clears his throat. "Listen, you don't have to wear that stuff if you don't want to. Your mom though it would be a nice gesture; same thing her mom did with her at that age, that's all. Keep it and who knows, maybe in the future you will be curious enough to try it out," he smiles. "Although, I don't mind if you stay away from it forever. I kind of you like you the way you are," he nudges my shoulder. "You have fun tonight," he says, before making his way back out of my room.

"Dad?" I stop him.

"Yes?"

"If you want another slice of cake, meet me in the tree house around nine."

He turns around just as his feet grace the threshold of my bedroom, displaying the smile quickly sweeping across his face. Seeing this, a smile instantaneously generates onto mine. And without having to say another word, all is forgiven between us. I like that about us.

The door shuts behind him and in his wake; I make my way out of the house with the leftover birthday cake, drinks, my sleeping bag, and pillow. Logan carries about the same, minus the food. Although, when I get closer to him, I notice that he brought something unexpected along with him. I roll my eyes as soon as the object comes into focus.

"What's that for?" I point at the baseball bat in his hands.

"Protection."

"You're going to kill a bat with a bat? How clever."

"Better than nothing; dad wouldn't let me take his shotgun."

Side by side, with a baseball bat between us, we make our way down the pasture, until we reach the bottom of the tree house. I am the first to begin climbing up, "No more bats," I say to him below. "My dad fixed the problem, so will you relax?"

He nods, as he continues to ascend the ladder. From the corner of my eye, I watch as he grips tightly to the bat as though ready for possible combat. He looks just like I do next to the dark grey house.

When we are both inside, it doesn't take long before we set up our sleeping bags and I reveal the cake from my backpack. Logan's eyes widen, and I tell him that the extra slice is for my dad and if he doesn't come down at nine to get it, then it's all his.

"I have something for you too," Logan says, opening up his backpack and handing me a small wrapped box. The wrapping paper is simply a lunch bag that he cut to fit around his gift.

"Is this my birthday gift? I ask.

"Of course it is—what else would it be?"

I open it up and reveal several pieces of strange items. There is a cracked bell, which was once used on one of the cows, various fur, hay, grass, and a few of the flowers currently growing beyond the pasture, "What's all this?" I ask.

"It's a box of the farm. Whenever you are at school, and you find yourself missing this place, I thought it would be nice if you had a piece of the farm with you," he smiles.

I stare down at the contents before returning my gaze back onto Logan. Against the moonlight I detect a sudden somber expression occupy his face. And when I go to hug him, he doesn't reach up to meet my embrace. He remains strangely silent and still.

"What's wrong with you? " I say, punching him softly in his shoulder. "Then again, this strange behavior of yours is becoming somewhat of a norm for you."

"I am fine," he says.

But I know that he is lying. His head cocks to the side as though afraid to face me. Did my parents talk to him about us spending less time together? I am infuriated at the thought.

"Did my parents talk with you?" I wait a half-second and don't give him a chance to respond. "Geez, I am so sorry. It's ridiculous really. I have been trying to think of a way to talk to them about it. To think, that just because we are getting older we can't hang out the way we used to. What do they think we want to do up here?" Then the thought hits me. I know exactly what they are thinking. I have seen enough movies to realize what goes on behind closed doors. Or in this case, behind tree house walls. My cheeks go up in flames.

Logan's mouth is gaped. He stares at me and after he tries to respond, I realize that he had no idea. "What?" He asks. I see him inching a bit farther away as though to tell me that he doesn't think of me that way. I inch myself away from his as well, until pretty soon our backs are almost against the tree house walls as we stare at each other uncomfortably. *Can you say, awkward?*

"They don't want us to hang out like we normally do?" His face puzzles.

"Well, we can't have sleepovers and things like that."

"Oh," he says as though somewhat relieved. I think it has something to do with him not having to sleep in the tree house anymore.

"So what is bothering you then?" I ask, changing the subject.

"Grandma Jane called dad today, said that grandpa is getting worse."

"What's wrong with him again?"

"All timerz?"

"You mean Alzheimer's?"

He nods. His grandma Jane and grandpa Charlie are Mr. Solway's parents (not the grandparents that George went to go live with in Denver). I have only met his grandparents a few times. Grandma Jane is really strict and told me once that my place was not running around the farm with the boys. I should be inside with the women. I don't know what she meant by that, but I never listened. She thinks I am a bad apple, according to Logan. But I love grandpa Charlie, he is so much fun! And Logan and I love hearing the stories that he tells. Someone always ends up being blown up in the end, so I think that's why we like them so much.

"I just can't imagine forgetting things like that. Grandma Jane even mentioned that he is starting to forget her. It upsets me," Logan sighs.

"Do you think that it will happen to us when we get older?"

"I don't know, but do we want to take that chance?"

"What do you mean? What could we do about it?"

"Well, we should make a list of things to remember about each other; so that in case we lose our memories, we never forget, because it's all written down."

"That's brilliant!" I dive into my backpack to see if I have anything to write with; I end up uncovering two pens and an almost filled notebook. I Hand him a piece of paper and one of the pens, "hmm," I begin, "what should I write about me..."

"No, I think I should write about you and you should write about me, that way we are completely honest."

"I will be honest."

"No, you won't," he smiles.

Not wanting to argue, we spend the next forty-five minutes engrossed in our lists. I write about Logan in as much detail as I can. I talk about his stubbornness and the way that he gets distant whenever he is upset. I talk about how his eyes remind me of skies and the way that he always calls me a buffoon. Thinking that I have created a long enough list, I tell him that I am done.

"You cannot be done," he says, setting his pen down.

"Well I am," I affirm.

"Well, the idea of us writing the list tonight is just a start, it should take us a few more years before we actually finish."

"A few more years?" I gasp.

"Yes, because we haven't yet become the people we will be for the rest of our lives."

"But I will always be me," I say.

"Maybe," he says, "but I won't always see you that way."

The next morning I awake to find the tree house deserted. Logan took all of his things and crept out without even waking me up. I wiggle out of my sleeping bag and slide on my shoes. The scent of birthday cake emits from my backpack, making my stomach gurgle with hunger. I can't help but to wonder how long he has been gone and what made him leave so soon. After a good yawn and stretch, I gather my things and climb down to find that he is sitting at the bottom of the tree. Apparently, he didn't go too far.

"What are you doing?" I ask, once my feet reach the ground.

"Just climbed down and needed a rest."

"A rest? Did you not get enough sleep last night? Or were you up on bat watch all night?" I smirk.

"I am not tired, my leg is. I tripped climbing down and banged it up pretty badly." He shows me what looks like the start of a bump by his knee. Beside it is a small cut, which I take a napkin out of my bag and blot the blood up for him.

"You all right?" I ask, examining the bump. "It doesn't look that fresh."

"I am fine, and you don't know that."

I pick up his backpack and walk with him through the field and to his house. I tell him to go put some ice on it and if he wants to do something later, to let me know. But I don't end up hearing from him for a few days.

* * * *

The nights of summer brush by me faster than I could have ever anticipated. And not one of them consisted of unexpected invites to stargaze or even for some casual small talk through our walkie-talkies. There was nothing but the silence and the refusal on my part to accept the situation. No matter how many times I brought up school to Logan, his answer never changed. But I refuse to accept it because he is my best friend and I can't seem to wrap my head around why he would not want to be there for me. And with my parents thinking that I am poking my nose around in business that isn't mine, my only potential ally in these matters, is Mr. Solway. I just hope that he could talk some sense into Logan, get him to see reason.

I linger in anticipation on my front porch steps, waiting for any sign of Mr. Solway. Having learned his schedule pretty well, I am able to stumble upon him "accidentally" almost perfectly. He seems none the wiser, but with my scripted tone, I think I may have given myself away.

"He doesn't want to go," I whine.

"If Logan doesn't want to go, then there is no point in making him," he rounds the corner, but I continue to follow him.

"Well, *I* don't want to go, but my parents are forcing me. Shouldn't you be doing the same with Logan?"

"It sounds to me like you may need to be having this conversation with your folks. I already talked to Logan about going with you, but he doesn't mind staying back here. Give him some time, maybe in the future he will come around."

"But this *was* the future I was looking forward to! I thought he would be joining me this year, which made everything easier on me. I thought I would be coming back with my best friend," I sigh.

"I can understand how you feel, but you two spend an awful lot of time together. I think it might be nice to have a little break from each other, don't you?"

"Ugh, have you been talking to my parents? What is it with you all?" I storm off.

The field of grass whips across my ankles and provides an almost stinging sensation, which anger helps me ignore. I continue pounding my way through it, unaware that I am actually disturbing the cows as they graze. I look back, hoping that neither Mr. Solway nor my dad took notice, but thankfully, I don't see either one of them. And with a quick turn of my head, I charge my way through the brush where I stumble upon Logan. He is napping under the shaded area from the tree house.

"Get up!" I yell, as I approach him. He stirs slightly, until I bend over and push at his shoulder. "Get up!"

"Geez, what is your problem?" He yawns.

"I want to know what is *yours*," I demand.

"Well, that's easy, I don't have one."

"Oh yeah? Then why don't you want to come with me, huh? Why is it that you have the chance to come to high school with me, and you refuse—tell me that?"

"I just don't want to go, that's why."

"That's not a good enough reason Logan Solway. Why wouldn't you want to go with me? Why wouldn't you want to be with your best friend?" I watch as he rubs at his calf where he fell a few days ago. His face cringes. "Leave it alone," I say, "You're going to make it hurt worse or give yourself a bigger bruise."

"Don't tell me what to do. Why do you have to be so bossy about everything?"

Bossy? His word take me aback. Since when does Logan think I am bossy? I have always been this way and never once did he ever complain or have anything to say about it; and besides, he can be bossy at the best of times too, but I don't hold that against him. "I am not being bossy," I finally say. "I just want you to come with me. Do I have to beg you or something?"

He sits up and rubs the sleep out of his eyes again. I can see small blades of grass sticking sporadically around the back of his head and shirt. "I don't want to go Emma. I want to stay here and work on the farm and have life the way it has always been for me."

"But it's not the same life. I am not here," I say. Why is he not getting this? Am I not explaining this right?

"Yea, I know, and it sucks, but it's better than going to high school where I know I don't belong. I belong here."

A catch in my throat releases and I feel the swelling form behind my eyes. Some crazy, unknown feeling erupts within me that I can't name or even place. I try to talk myself out of crying, but nothing I am saying to myself is working. The swelling continues to build and before I know it, the first tear releases and I can't seem to hide it fast enough.

"Your fake crying is not going to work," he says.

"I am not faking," I get angry as I wipe the falling tear aggressively away from my cheek.

"Let's just drop this okay?" He looks at me as though the words will make everything better. "I belong here and here is where I will stay."

I am almost half-tempted to tell him that he is wrong, because he belongs with me; but instead, I turn away in anger. I leave him by the river and swear off any contact with him for the next few days.

* * * *

So here, I am, a few days into avoiding Logan, staring at the four walls of my bedroom, trying hard not to go stir crazy. Several times, I have tried to muster enough courage to contact him via walkie-talkie, but unfortunately, my stubbornness wouldn't allow such a thing. Not to mention that I am perfectly aware of school starting in a week and of the time I have been wasting in unnecessary solitude. But if Logan doesn't want to be my friend then why bother being his? Of course, I blame him for this. I mean, where else would I have picked up the skills on being so stubborn?—him of course…

Then again, maybe I should just go over to his house and talk to him. There is no need to place myself on house arrest just because he doesn't want to go to school with me. I can't stay mad at him forever for it, so I might as well head next door and end the argument for good. But just as I am about ready to climb out of bed to do so, mom walks into my room, shouting, "School shopping day!"

The only response I can give to her is a loud unenthusiastic groan. I am in no hurry to get out of my pajamas, regardless if it is almost 2:00 in the afternoon; especially when I know, the reason is for shopping.

"I need to go talk to Logan," I say as she practically drags me out of bed, but she doesn't seem to listen or even care about what I am saying. She simply throws an outfit onto my bed and tells me to hurry up. I guess Logan will have to wait, I just hope I still have enough courage to talk to him when we get back.

The first store she ends up dragging me into is the large department store where I bought all of my Christmas presents last year. Instead of shopping, however, she sends me off into the dressing room where I am to wait to try on everything that she picks out. She throws so many items of clothing over the door at me, none of which I would want to wear. One item in particular is a form fitting dress that hugs my body like a suction cup. Mom clasps her hands together like always and turns me around several times in front of the mirror, until I begin to get dizzy from all of the spinning. "You look stunning!" She says to me several times before spinning me back into the dressing room to try something else on.

An hour and a half later, I feel like I have tried everything on in the store. That's until much to my surprise, she throws over several pairs of bras for me to try on as well, which makes me feel like my day has taken another turn for the worse. Holding one in my hand, it looks like a double-sided slingshot and I am almost half-tempted to let her buy it, so I can use it to throw rocks over the river. "What's wrong with the sport bras I have been wearing?" I ask, tying the bra into a knot.

"You need more support," she says very motherly to me. "You can't wear those types of bras all day every day. You need to act like a lady, so try them on." As another one comes flying over the door and hits me in the head.

"Is this part of becoming a woman too?" I snarl under my breath.

I slip off my sports bra and try the first contraption she threw over the door to me. The back clasp feels like a puzzle and it takes me several minutes before I am able to put it on successfully. I stand in front of the mirror and for the first time I realize, *holy shit, I have boobs.* Before, my sports bra would kind of squish them into my chest, making them not as noticeable. Now they look like two round balls sitting on my chest and I cannot have that. *I definitely cannot have that.*

"How does the first one fit?" Mom asks through the door.

I hesitate, "Doesn't fit," I lie.

"Let me see," she says. And before I get the chance to lock the door, she bursts right through. There she is staring at me and I know exactly what she is thinking, *Holy shit, my daughter has boobs.*

Thankfully, when there is nothing left to try on, she brings up all the clothes to the register to purchase. I straggle behind looking around at several rows of clothing, some of which I know mom will actually approve of, but I don't want my curiosity to become too obvious. Knowing her, she'd make me turn back around and try them all on.

My hand runs along the various textures of fabric, some silky, soft, and some not so comfortable against my skin. For a second, I catch my mind wondering what I would look like if I actually dressed like the other girls in school. The idea of not being ridiculed for my normal attire sounds rather intriguing at the moment, but I am not ready for such a drastic change.

Therefore, I quickly walk away from the racks, before my consideration reads upon my face.

We leave the mall soon after with several bags of clothes. Mom doesn't seem too happy with my selections, but I have the sneaking suspicion that she bought a few of the outfits that I turned down anyways. As for our next stop, mom needs to run into the grocery store and when we get there, she asks that I go pick out some snacks for school.

I roam down the aisles, but nothing looks good. My appetite has been off for a while, compliments to my situation with Logan. And for that reason, I decide to make my way over to the magazine aisle and waste some time there. When I round the corner, I see a few girls about my age, hovering over a fashion magazine. They stand there pointing and smiling until someone calls their names out from the next aisle over. Curious, I walk over to see what they were looking at as soon as they leave. The magazine cover has a picture of a beautiful girl, wearing some kind of pantsuit with a plunging neckline. She is showing way more cleavage than one would in a bra. *Oh geez, the last thing I want to think about is bras.*

But curiosity takes the best of me again. I slide the magazine out of the holder and skim through the pages. It has everything inside regarding how to wear makeup, what the best shoes to wear for the fall and winter are, what bags match what outfits (didn't know you needed more than one), and pretty much how to dress from head to toe. In my opinion, it kind of acts like a bible for women, to know how to be, well, women—how appropriate. I quickly shut the magazine and put it back down, just as I see my mom inch her cart down the aisle.

Part Two

"Growing apart doesn't change the fact that for a long time we grew side by side; our roots will always be tangled. I'm glad for that."

-Ally Condie

Chapter Nine

The scent of summer passing goes unnoticed. It came quick as an unsuspecting breeze and left before I had the chance to even feel it, or in this case, smell it. I didn't bask in the summer sunlight or listen to the flowing river. I didn't reminisce about passing times or spend my days wishing that I could experience some of those moments again. I simply shut myself completely off. I locked myself up in my bedroom and lived amongst the quietness. I counted the number of flowers on my pillowcase. I organized my dresser drawers. I even tried fixing my rooster alarm clock, but all I think I managed to do was make the whirring sound much louder. I ended up just tossing it into a box of junk in my closet, which I ended up digging back out an hour later because I missed it.

A part of me does regret the fact that I chose to isolate myself. My isolation was strictly due to avoidance, which subsequently had me missing out on a lot. One of the things that I unfortunately missed out on, was the farm. Again, I blame Logan for this, of course. This entire thing is his fault really. He had a chance to be there for me; but instead, chose what he thought was more important. He chose to keep things the same for him with absolutely no thought to how his decision would make me feel. After school shopping the other day, my desire to go and speak to him quickly dissolved when we returned home. I guess if I wanted to, I could walk out of my room right now to go and talk with him. But where would that get me? It's too late. School will be here in the morning, with or without him.

The morning of my first day back to school arrives, as I awake to the strange ambiance of silence. I slide the covers down and inch my way to the foot of my bed. It is here that I await the sounds of my mom breaking down my bedroom door, before she snap opens my blinds with some musical introduction to start my day. But nothing happens of that sort. Embracing the carpet threads are my feet as they hit the floor in unison. And when I finally open the door and exit through the threshold, she isn't even in the hallway to greet me with her bottle of hairspray. Should I be alarmed at this?

Then, as I descend the staircase, gripping tightly to the banister in order to steady my balance, I can hear sounds coming from the kitchen a few feet away. Mom's voice emerges when I round the corner, where I see her having breakfast with my dad. I am still in my pajamas rubbing the sleep out of my eyes. I am not even close to getting ready for school, partially because I am in shock to have not received any forcible help.

I pour myself a bowl of cereal and sit down beside dad. The only logical conclusion that I can come up with for mom's behavior, is that they finally came to their senses and will let me stay home this year. The cereal begins to dissolve in my mouth as I await the reality of the situation.

"Good Morning; excited for your first day?" Dad asks, setting down his newspaper.

"There are hardly any words," I respond disappointedly.

"Have you picked out what you are going to wear?" Mom asks over her coffee.

What, she didn't pick out my outfit already? Once again, I am shocked. "Not yet," I reply. I watch as she peers over at me with a slight twinkle in her eye—*I see where this is going.* "Do you want to help me pick one out?" I ask with a noticeable lack of enthusiasm.

Immediately, the twinkle comes alive in her eyes, regardless of my tone, as she bolts out of the kitchen and up the stairs. "I know just the outfit," I hear her call from a distance.

I turn to dad and he just smiles. "Thank you," he says, "She loves this kind of stuff."

"No problem; but she is not doing my hair," I simper.

I wonder if I like torturing myself sometimes. Last year, I let her dress me on the first day and I ended up being picked on for it. Do I subconsciously want to endure the same thing again this year? Maybe being tormented on the first day will become a tradition of mine. Luckily, this time around, the wardrobe selections are more catered to my taste minus the few outfits that she purchased without my permission. Unfortunately, dad hinted at the fact a few nights ago that he saw mom uncovering a couple bags of clothes in their room. I just hope that he was mistaken. But when I rinse my bowl off in the sink and make my way back upstairs, I see my mom holding out two different outfits, both of which I have never seen before. *Damn it!*

"I can't decide," she says, as soon as I approach her. She doesn't even acknowledge the fact that I have never seen the two outfits before and doesn't think to provide me with an explanation as to why that is.

One outfit is a simple sundress with no pattern and is navy blue in color. The other is a pair of shorts paired with a loose fitting blouse. I decide to go with the lesser of two evils. "The shorts and blouse are fine," I say.

I head to the bathroom to shower, brush my teeth, and get dressed without mom's help. She surprisingly keeps her distance while I complete these tasks, but when I open the door to meet her out in the hallway, she shakes her head at me and turns me right back around. "Where are the bras that we bought?" she asks.

"I don't know, in my closet?"

She leaves me in the bathroom as she walks across the hallway to my bedroom. I can hear my closet door creak open as she yells out my name. "Emma! They are still in the bags with the tags on them! You can't wear these; they haven't even been washed!"

I slither over and linger apprehensively in the doorway. "I am sorry," I say very unapologetically. Although, I am glad to have extended the life of my sports bra for another day—my mom, however, doesn't look too happy about it though.

"Why didn't you give them to me when I washed your other clothes?" She asks as though it will make any difference. Her fists begin to dig into her hips and I wonder if steam will begin pouring out of her ears as well.

"I don't know; I forgot?" I lie.

She grabs the bras from the bag and throws them into the hallway hamper. "I will just have to wash them later," she huffs.

Perhaps her disappointment in me makes her forget to address my hair, which is okay by me. I quickly blow dry it and throw it back into a loose fitting ponytail, no different than how I would normally wear it, and then follow her down the stairs. The entire way she shakes her head and mumbles words underneath her breath. A few times, I catch her saying that I am purposely trying to be difficult or something. But I just ignore her. If anything, she should be happy that I let her pick out my outfit this morning.

My bare feet slide across the wooden floor, before they knock into the edge of the foyer carpet. It's here that I locate my shoes and put them on by the door. They are a pair of sandals that mom found on the clearance rack at the same department store we did my school shopping. I have a feeling, however, that by the end of the day, my feet will be festooned in blisters and red marks, since they were not properly broken into yet. My work boots look rather enticing at the moment.

As I bend down to put my shoes on by the door, I notice several cuts on my legs from my attempts at shaving the night before. It took me almost two hours to shave both legs and when I was finally done; my legs looked like I walked through barbed wire to escape the confines of the bathroom. But thankfully, most of the cuts are not too noticeable now, besides the few hovering above my ankles, resembling the pattern of a spider web.

With my shoes securely fastened, I walk over to the coat closet to grab my book bag and find that the hook where it called home for the entire summer is empty; I turn around and see mom holding out a leather messenger bag in her hands. "What's that?" I ask.

"It's your new school bag," she says, handing it over to me.

The leather is cool against my skin. I admire the bronze colored buckles, wondering just how expensive this bag must have been. Surely, dad would have never approved of spending a lot of money on such a frivolous item.

"It was your dad's," mom continues, as though she knew where my thoughts were lingering. "He wore this when he worked for the insurance company in New York City; it was his travel bag. But we both thought it would be the perfect size for your new school bag," she smiles. "Beats collecting dust in the bottom of our closet; almost forgot we had it."

Up close, I can now see some of the aging within the leather fibers. But it's done so beautifully, which seems to only add charm and character to what I still assume to have been a very expensive bag. "It's really nice; thank you," I say, running my fingers along the buckles.

"Don't worry; I put everything that was in your book bag into this one. You're all set," she says, before exiting out of the front porch and down the steps to start the car.

In her wake, I open up the flap on the bag and reach my hand inside. I feel around for a particular item and once my fingers graze the top of it, I pull it out. It's the box full of random items from the barn, which Logan gave to me for my birthday. Even though I haven't spoken to him in a week, it still means a lot to me. I would never disregard such a thoughtful gesture out of spite or even anger. This has to be one of the best gifts that he has ever given to me, quarters included, which I actually hope to put to use this year.

Once I leave the house, I immediately notice that not only are my parents waiting by the car, but so are Mr. Solway and none other than the horse's ass himself. I make my way down the steps and try my hardest not to make eye contact with anyone, even though I can feel Logan's eyes burning holes into the back of my head, but I do my best to ignore the sensation.

"Why don't I get a picture of both of you?" Mom asks, pointing to Logan and me. Is she that oblivious to the fact that Logan and I haven't been speaking? Apparently, the tension between us is not as palpable as I thought.

Logan releases a groan as he slumps over to where I am standing. I don't want to give him the satisfaction that I heard him, so I just keep quiet. And when the camera finally flashes and the adults begin to talk amongst themselves, I am surprised when Logan turns to me and apologizes. "I am sorry," he says under his breath. He can barely look at me.

"What?" I purposely have him repeat himself. Logan never apologizes, so the words sound rather sweet to my ears.

"I said I am sorry. I didn't know you would be this upset," His right foot shuffles across the gravel. The sound it produces fills our awkward silence.

"Well, I am," I finally say.

"Are we still friends?" He asks, still unable to make eye contact with me. His foot slows in anticipation of my answer.

I turn to him now and nod, "Yes, but I am still mad at you. You knew how hard school was for me last year and how much I wanted you to be there with me."

"Well, I am sorry," he pauses briefly. "You can make new friends if you have to."

"I *may* have to," I say back, just as my mom calls me over to the car so that we can head out to school. "You won't like it if I do though," I begin walking away. My threat feels empty to me, but I don't give that away to him.

"Probably not," he almost whispers in response. Although, neither one of us realizes how prophetic our words will eventually become.

I don't know why heading off to school feels like a goodbye to me. I am completely aware that I will return at the end of each day, but the time in-between feels like nothing more than a tortuous separation. I climb into the car and buckle myself in. Turning back, I see my dad, Mr. Solway, and Logan, waving me off as mom pulls out of the driveway. Focusing only on Logan, however, I can see the sadness in his face. Does he regret his decision to stay? With his unexpected apology, I feel better about the situation. The boy never apologizes for anything, so I don't want to discourage him from doing it again in the future. Not to mention, how I may have to make friends this year. I can't help but to find that aspiration to be farfetched and unrealistic. But a slight part of me feels excited at the prospect as well. I will just have to keep an open mind about it; either way, I still have Logan and always will.

* * * *

The metal doors swing open and I am once again, thrown into the jungle of a massive student body. The only plus side, is that I am more aware of my surroundings and feel no need to cower into any bathroom that I pass along the way. What ends up being a total surprise, however, is that I actually end up locating my locker with about fifteen minutes left to spare before homeroom commences. The only thing I worry about now is that I hope that it doesn't end up being the highlight of my day.

Turning the combination clockwise then counterclockwise, and then clockwise again, I turn the lock until I hear the click and push up on the handle to release the door. The locker, although, quite small, greets me with a welcoming hello and I can't help but to smile in return. I shove my supplies inside and only leave out what I need for the morning. When I am finished with the sorting, I hang the strap of my bag on one of the metal hooks and admire how nice it looks inside of its new metal walled home. I admire how the leathery scent emits out of its new confines.

But as I am about to shut the door to my locker, I hear a voice from behind me. "Emma?" I turn around and see Henry, the boy from my English class last year, although, he looks quite different. He no longer has braces or even glasses for that matter. The color of his skin reminds me of the initial summer glow that Logan gets whenever the weather breaks. And his hair appears to have been styled differently from the last time I have seen him.

"Henry?"

"Hi," he says, shoving his hands uneasily into his pockets. We make eye contact for a second, before he turns his head away and begins staring off into the distance.

"Are you all right?" I ask. I am asking because for one, he seems rather nervous. And for two, he is talking to me outside of a classroom project.

"Yea, I just wanted to say hi." He mumbles under his breath.

"Hi," I say.

But before either one of us says anything more, he turns and makes his way down the hallway until he is completely out of sight. I have no idea what just happened; but at any rate, I decide to count it as an attempt on my part to make friends. The only question is—will I tell Logan about it?

The idea about making friends, however, still baffles me. I never thought I would ever need anyone more than Logan. And I am not entirely certain if I actually need any more friends anyways. But having a friend here would be nice. It definitely would make things a little less unbearable for me.

As for the rest of my day, overall isn't too bad. In gym class, we did nothing but aerobics that thankfully didn't require much skill on my part. Lunch, however, is the same as it was last year. My usual table awaited me and I spent the better half of my time, surveying the room around me again. Although, I did come to the realization that my lunchtime solitude was never once shared with my parents. I guess I just didn't want to upset the captain of the football team and the prom queen, when they realized that together, they created an antisocial daughter.

At the end of the day, however, when mom comes to pick me up, I don't feel the need to plead into her shoulder about not making me go back. I am indifferent about the whole experience for some reason. I didn't hate or love it today, it was just a normal day. I found all of my classes within a reasonable amount of time; I found my locker before homeroom even started; and someone actually said hi to me. Could this then have been a perfect day? Maybe not, but it feels rather close to being one.

"How was your day?" Mom asks, as soon she pulls the car away from the curb.

"It was good."

"Really?"

"I mean it wasn't spectacular or anything. I still hate it there, if that's what you're asking—but it was alright."

"Well, it sounds like you are making progress."

I roll down the window and rest my arm on the edge. The fading heat from the passing summer sun beats down upon it, but I barely feel any warmth against my flesh. Not even the air that flows into the car smells like anything in particular. It's more or less the scent of limbo between a summer that went by too fast and an autumn, which is vastly approaching.

My thoughts of summer and of the new school year stay with me until we reach home. Dad is in the driveway greeting us with a wave. From inside of the car, I see that his clothes are glistening. "Tractor needed an oil change," he says when we approach. "Got most of it on me, I'm afraid," he looks down.

"Don't you dare come into the house with those clothes on; I will put something for you to change into on the porch," mom announces as she makes her up the porch steps.

"Sorry honey," he calls out to her with a laugh, "but I don't think the neighbors want to see me in my underwear."

"I will shut the curtains," she smiles, shutting the front door behind her.

I set my school bag down on the front porch steps and make my way over to the barn, but Logan isn't there. Next, I head over to the river beyond the brush to check for him there, but come to find it deserted. Finally, I enter through the side door of his house where I eventually spot him. He is doing something that I have never seen him do during the day—watching television.

"What are you doing?" I ask, walking into his house without knocking. From the corner of my eye, I can see Mr. Solway in the kitchen making his afternoon tea.

"Watching T.V; how was your first day back?" He asks.

"It was fine," I say, sitting down beside him on the couch. I catch the smell of the wind in his hair, the fields of grass, and what dad calls the mixture of 'hard work and fun' radiate from him. It is the perfect combination of smells, but only Logan seems to possess them all. I can't help but to inhale deeply.

The silence between us however, is once again awkward, which I thought his morning's apology would have dissipated. As he sits beside me, he flips through channel after channel, watching nothing in particular, yet too focused on the television screen than on me. I am as apparent as a couch pillow or the throw blanket I am sitting on. If it weren't for my breathing, perhaps I could be mistaken for the couch itself.

Unsure of what to do, I stare off towards the clock upon the fireplace mantel as it ticks away. Ten minutes go by until I finally decide to share with him the highlights of my day with the hope that it will spark up a conversation between us; but sadly, I am met with the same silence as before. The clock is contributing more to this conversation than he is. *I am really getting tired of this boy's mood swings.*

"Someone said hi to me today," I say over the television noise. My outburst, although unpremeditated, renders a surprising response from him.

"That's nice."

"Yea, he was in my English class last year. I was surprised he even came up to me."

Logan turns to me, "He?"

"Yea, his name is Henry," I look back at him.

He mutes the television. "Henry?"

"Yes, his name is Henry," I repeat myself.

He nods his head and peers over at me in a very peculiar way, "Henry, eh?"

"What's the matter?"

"Nothing."

"You mad?" I tease. I can't deny that I am partially excited at the hint of jealousy exuded from his tone. But I don't know why he even frets. No one will ever take his place as my best friend. And I certainly shouldn't have to tell *him* that.

"I'm not mad," he takes the television off mute. "I told you to make friends."

"That's right, you did," I affirm.

He goes silent once more and I feel the tension between us resurface again. Doesn't he know the unspoken bond between us? Even if I were to make friends, he should never have anything to worry about, and I would only do it to make high school more bearable for me—something he could have prevented if he just agreed to come. "No one will ever be my best friend," I say to the side of his head, "but you."

The background noise of the television fills the space between my words. I hesitate on whether it is pointless for me to say anything at all, but remaining silent doesn't seem like the best option for me either. "Besides," I continue, "there is only room for one horse's ass in my life," I laugh.

Slowly, his head turns towards me as a smile creeps up on his face. Seeing this, I can't help but to smile back. No apology needed.

Chapter Ten

I am patiently waiting for the leaves to turn into those beautiful saturated colors of red, orange, and yellow. My sense of smell prematurely picks up on my mom's pumpkin pie and various autumn scented candles that she lights around the house during the fall season. I am anxious for the season's arrival and apparently so is Logan, whose dad is allowing him to go turkey hunting with him this year. Something I never thought he would ever be interested in doing.

He shows me the new shotgun his dad bought for him over the weekend. For some reason, he makes me uneasy with it in his presence. Seeing Logan holding that big piece of metal in his hands doesn't sit very well with me. I prefer a water gun in his hand, if I had to choose. But he tells me that it's a "man thing" and that all men have to learn to hunt. I just tell him that he had better go and find a man to shoot that thing.

"It's been that way since the beginning of time, Emma," he says, bringing the shotgun back inside of the house and handing it over to his dad to lock up.

"Yea, well, what about women?"

"They were gatherers. Don't you pay attention in school?" He laughs.

"Listen, if you think that I am going to spend my days gathering who knows what in the fields, while you are off hunting everything that comes your way; you are sadly mistaken."

"Then stay inside or call up Henry," he jokes.

I just roll my eyes.

When Monday morning rolls in, mom bursts into my room and opens up my bedroom blinds in one quick and fluid motion. "Good morning," she says.

"Good morning," I yawn into my pillow.

"We need to talk," she says, sitting down at the edge of my bed.

Rubbing the sleep out of my eyes, I pry my head off my pillow. She sits a few feet away from me, with a sour look on her face. And when I look down into her lap, I see the evidence as to why that is.

"Why aren't you wearing these?" She holds out one of the bras in front of me. It sways angrily in the air at me.

I shrug, "I don't know."

"You are a young lady, and you need to start wearing the proper undergarments. Now, I am leaving them on your bed, and I trust that you will wear one today for school." She says, before getting up and leaving the room.

Once again, what is the big deal? I was able to get away wearing what I wanted to wear for about a month now without her none the wiser. What, is she monitoring what I put in the hamper now? Who cares about proper undergarments, because if I really had it my way, I probably wouldn't wear anything at all. Doesn't she remember how long it took for me to wear the sports bras in the beginning? She should have expected that this wouldn't have been an easy transition.

I climb out of bed and pay the garment no mind. Instead, I need to think about what it is that I am going to wear as I head off to the bathroom. In the shower, I linger much longer than normal under the warm rain of the faucet until my fingers and toes start to prune. I am perfectly aware that my parents hate it when I waste water, but staying in the shower is the only thing keeping me from what is lying and waiting on my bed.

When I finally climb out, dry off, and slip on my bathrobe. My first stop is my closet, but I don't have anything bulky enough to wear. I have a few sweaters, but it's either not that cold out or I have worn them to work, which mom will not approve of me wearing to school. My only option is a loose fitting long sleeved shirt, the rest of my clothes are sadly, in the wash.

But before I get dressed, I decide to engage in a little initiation ceremony with the evil garment. I take two rolled up pairs of socks and walk over to one of my bedposts. I loop one of the straps through one post and hold on to the second strap in my right hand. Then, I use my other hand to place one of the rolled up socks into one of the cups, before pulling back and releasing it into the air. It flies about two feet out in front of me and I challenge my distance with the second pair as well. After I am done, I take the strap off the post and put it on me instead. Once again, finding the hook to meet the clasp is about as hard as trying to put on my socks without any hands—difficult and almost impossible.

While I get dressed, I avoid the mirror. I don't need to look at my reflection to know what I look like. Most importantly, I don't want to subject my eyes to the embarrassment. Quietly, I make my way down the stairs to the muffled sounds coming from the kitchen. Mom and dad are having their morning coffee and I am almost tempted to skip breakfast and just wait in the car. But mom sees me and ushers me into the room where she has prepared some French toast for breakfast.

As quickly as I walk in, I sit down. I avoid eye contact with both of them and instead focus on the short stack of French toast cooling on my plate. I slouch as much as I can. *Gosh, this is so embarrassing.* Lucky for me, however, dad greets me without looking up from his newspaper and heads out of the kitchen without really paying attention to anything but his solar powered watch that I bought him last year for Christmas. I just hope that now I can get through the day at school with everyone not looking at me as well. Then again, they never do anyways, so perhaps, I really have nothing to worry about…

After breakfast, I throw on my jacket, which I contemplate wearing all day as a form of camouflage and meet my mom outside by the car. Thankfully, no one else is outside so that I am able to slip into the car without being noticed. But just as I am about to descend the final porch step, Logan rounds the corner and runs up to me.

"Hey Emma! I was going to ask you—" he stops dead.

"Ask me what?"

He is unable to formulate a response as he jumbles his words together in no particular coherent pattern. "Um," he hesitates, before rubbing his hand down the back of his neck. *Do I detect small beads of sweat on his forehead?*

From the corner of my eye, I see mom get out of the car. But I am too focused on Logan's reaction to pay her any mind. I know exactly what is happening here and it's all her fault. Therefore, if she wants me to wear this thing, then she will have to endure the consequence of her desire.

"What's going on?" She asks, as she approaches Logan and me. "We have to get to school."

"Logan here was about to tell me something, but it seems that he is unable to speak—any idea why that could be?" I peer over at her.

Mom looks down at Logan, who tries to look up towards the sky. "What's the matter with you dear?"

He brings his attention to her before accidentally looking back onto me at the place that has him apparently tongue-tied.

"It seems that Logan is the first to witness the magical workings of my new bra," I say very sarcastically. "I can see why you want me to wear this. Maybe I will have all the boys in school shut up before the day is over—great idea mom!" I hop towards the car and climb inside.

She stands by Logan and tells him to run off, before she charges back to the car to scold me.

"You don't talk like that young lady," she scolds, shutting the car door.

"Well, you're the one who made me wear this thing. Now look what you have done, my own best friend can't even look me in the eye or even look at me at all! I can't imagine how he will react during one of our sleepovers," I sneer.

"Emma!"

I get to school and decide to leave my jacket on. I find that if I button a few of the buttons, it conceals what lies beneath quite nicely. Mom isn't too happy with me, but I don't care. This would never have happened if she just let me wear what I want to wear, so in a way it's almost payback—although, I am partially paying for it too.

My temper cools as I plow through the groups in the hallway towards my locker. I grab what I need and slam the door shut, feeling better as the remaining anger dissipates.

"Hey Emma," I turn around and see Henry walking up to me.

"Hey," I say, feeling my books loosen within my grip.

"I see that you are in the same lunch period as I am, and I know you like sitting by yourself and all," he hesitates, but I take notice to how his words don't jumble together. "I was wondering," He starts again, he doesn't look anywhere but in my eyes and then at my locker. "I was wondering if you would like to sit at my table instead?"

The unexpected invitation takes me aback. For a second though, my mind hovers over the possibility of there being a motive behind his offer. But Henry has never struck me as being a mean person and he doesn't hang around with Morgan and her catty friends either. I revel in the offer and feel an unfamiliar excitement hit me. "Sure," I say. *What could it hurt?*

"Great!" He says. His nervousness wanes. "I will see you then."

I turn back around and make my way towards my homeroom in what feels like a haze. My eyes provide a tunnel vision effect to the hallway around me and I don't notice anything but my breathing. Have I really made a friend? Not on purpose, I might add. I wasn't even the one who approached Henry or asked him to come sit with me at lunch, he asked me! I can hardly contain my excitement and to be quite honest; I don't want to.

During English class, an hour or so later, my teacher assigns us a project that we have to collaborate with another student in the class. And against my wishes, work outside of the classroom on it too. It is a project on *To Kill a Mockingbird*; and when the teacher, Ms. Perkins, begins to pair us up, I am reminded of the last project that I had in English class, which turned into an unexpected mess. Thankfully, I am much prepared for such occurrences now. *Thanks mom…*

"Hey, looks like I am your partner," Jessica Rockingham, a junior in my class, whom I have never spoken with, sits down beside me. She is pretty and wears the same kind of clothes that would make my mother proud. And by the strap peeking out of her shoulder, I can tell she wears the appropriate bras too. "Well, since we have to work outside of the classroom on this, how about you come over to my place tomorrow night. We can switch on and off from there," she says, biting at the end of her pen.

"Sounds good," I reply.

My mind begins to race, *Have I made two friends today?* Logan had better be careful or I may end up leaving with a whole crowd of them before the day is over. I grin from ear to ear at the very thought.

For the first time, I am surprised with my ease of conversation. Jessica and I not only talk about our project, but engage in a little small talk as well; and before I know it, we are exchanging phone numbers as we make plans for tomorrow after school.

"My mom usually picks me up," I say.

"That's fine. I have my license; you can just ride with me and I will drop you off after."

"Sounds good," I say.

With the arrival of the afternoon, so comes lunchtime. I grip tightly to the brown paper bag until I start to feel small tears form along the fold. I make my way into the noisy lunchroom and begin to survey around the room for my new table. My previous table in the far back glistens under the fluorescent lighting and I am a half-second away from just retreating back to my place of comfort, right as I feel a tap against my shoulder.

"Emma?"I turn to see Henry behind me. "We are over here," he points to a small table about eight feet away.

I follow him over, feeling my palms begin to sweat. I fear that my lunch bag will tear open and the contents will go spilling onto the floor. I decide to hold it from the bottom just in case. He pulls out a chair for me and I sit between him and a girl I have never seen before.

"This is Emma," Henry announces to the group. "She was in my English class last year."

Everyone says hi to me and I nervously reply in return.

As soon as my lunch bag hits the table, I am immediately bombarded with questions from everyone. Most of them have to do with growing up on the farm. But the girl beside me, named Maggie, seems more fascinated in the idea of how I was previously homeschooled and how I still wish to resume that original arrangement.

"Don't you like high school?" A boy named Kevin asks me with a bite of sandwich in his mouth. He wears a graphic t-shirt and styles his hair like I have seen on Logan when he wakes up in the morning.

"Not really," I say. "Freshman year wasn't exactly fun for me."

"Why's that?" asks another.

"I wasn't use to dealing with assholes on a daily basis," my sarcasm takes me by surprise, and I wonder for a split second if I have offended anyone at the table. First day not eating alone and already, I am ruining my chances of sitting with them again. But against my initial gut reaction, everyone starts laughing.

"Ain't that the truth!" Kevin announces through everyone's laughter.

"Yep, if you are not part of the popular crowd, then you pretty much don't rate anything," Maggie announces. "But you see," she says, leaning into the table. "No one is going to care who you were in high school after you graduate. While they are off shopping at the malls, we might be the ones discovering a new medicine or working on the next great American novel." Her black framed glasses side a half an inch down her nose as her small almond shaped eyes peers around the table for support. "They will still be here pretending like they are still in high school, while we will be the ones who got out and made a difference in the world." She sits back into her seat and quiets herself with her can of soda.

"So let them peak now!" Kevin roars, "I refuse to let these years be the best years of *my* life."

"So are we like the nerds or something?" I joke curiously.

"No, actually, we are cooler than the nerds, but that's about it," Henry says with a chuckle. Maggie turns to him with a smile.

For the first time since starting high school, my peanut butter and jelly sandwich never tasted better. I laughed and told stories about some of the adventures Logan and I had on the farm, which they all seemed to love. And when the bell rings to signal the end of the lunch period, we all grab our things and exit the lunchroom still laughing. Words can't describe how I am feeling inside right now and the only person I care to share this with, is Logan, but something tells me that he won't be as happy about it as I am.

When I leave school for the day, I immediately jump into my mom's car to tell her about my day.

"I told you; you would like it," she smiles.

"Well, let's not get our hopes up. I just had one good day; that's all. I still hate the place—don't forget that."

"Why don't you join an afterschool activity or something; you might make even more friends that way."

"Maybe," I say, which reminds me of the project I have with Jessica. I tell mom about it and let her know that she doesn't have to pick me up tomorrow from school.

"I don't know about that," she says. "A young girl with her license; there's no way that she is at all an experienced driver. And I don't know how I would feel about you getting into a car with her either; I will have to talk this over with your dad."

"Well, I have a project to work on with her and she drives to school, don't you think it would be rather stupid of me to drive separately?"

"I just want you safe, that's all."

The car screeches into the driveway and I see Logan ride up through the pasture on the tractor. I am seething inside at the sight. I want to learn so badly, but dad says that I can't until I get my license, but I thought that riding the tractor would be good practice for me. All he said to me was that he would have to think about it. Apparently, he is still thinking…

When I open the car door, the tractor meets my ear with a loud roar, making it hard for me to process a clear thought. I am trying to come up with a good speech to give my dad about me riding home tomorrow with Jessica. But if mom gets to him first, my chances of persuading him might be slim.

I run inside of the house and see that he isn't there, so I storm back out and make my way towards the barn. It is here that I find him screwing a hook into the wall to hold one of the buckets, while the previous hook lies broken into pieces on the ground.

"Dad, you busy?" I ask, fully aware that he is.

"Not for you; what do you need?"

"I would like to talk to you about my day," I say, shuffling my way into the barn. A few stray nails scrape underneath my shoes.

Surprised, he turns and sets the screwdriver down. "Well, I would love to hear about it."

"Well, I made some friends today," I say as though the announcement in itself will prove to my father that I am not the ant-social loner that he feared I would remain.

"You did? That's great!"

"Yea, I was asked to sit at a lunch table with a bunch of people, and I ended up making a friend in my English class, her name is Jessica."

"I am so proud of you. See, you were always meant to fit in and make friends. I never doubted you for a moment," he turns back to fixing the hook.

"Well, there's more," I stop him. "You see, Jessica and I have been paired up for this English project on *To Kill a Mockingbird* and—"

"I read that," he says, interrupting me. "It's a great book."

"Yea," I say, "well, we have to make this presentation on the symbolism of the book and—"

"And you need my help?" He asks. "I don't know; it's been awhile since I read it."

"No, I haven't read it yet either. You see, she asked that I come over after school so that we can begin to."

He nods as he peers over at me, "And?"

"And mom doesn't need to pick me up because Jessica will take me in her car and bring me home when we are done working."

"I see," he says in a tone resembling mom's, "And is Jessica's mom driving?"

"No," I hesitate, "She is; she has her license." And before he can voice another question or reply, I cut him off. "She is older than I am, about a year. We are in an advanced English class together, well, advanced for me. She is a junior."

"Have you asked your mom?"

"Well, I talked to her about it and she doesn't think that I should be riding around with an inexperienced driver. But she has been driving for awhile, and I don't want her to think I am a loser, having my mom drive me instead of just riding with her."

"Can I think about it?" He says to me.

I nod, slowly making my way out of the barn. I just hope that he doesn't take as long thinking about this as he is about the tractor.

Chapter Eleven

I allow the evening to pass without any need to share my day with Logan. When it is time for dinner, the subject of me riding home with Jessica tomorrow, becomes the center of an unexpected heated debate. My head bounces back and forth as though I am watching a tennis match unfold, which only reveals that neither one of them are on the same page over this apparent issue. Until I am finished with my plate, however, I sit here thinking that maybe they should have had this conversation in private; but then again, it at least allows me to know if my request even stands a chance.

The morning is here and I crawl out of bed. After I get ready, I make my way down the stairs and into the kitchen. As usual, dad is reading the paper and mom is enjoying her coffee. I clear my throat and enter and immediately my mom's jaw opens and crashes to the linoleum floor. The twinkle in her eye bursts like tiny fireworks, as she stands up from the table and makes her way on over to me.

"Is this?" she asks, surveying my outfit.

"The outfit that you bought for me—yes," I say halfheartedly. I decided to wear one of the skirts she had bought without my permission as a way to help me along in this battle. I really hope that my plan works because I am sure I look as ridiculous as I feel.

"You look so nice," she smiles, embracing me in a hug. "Ted, doesn't she look nice?" She calls dad's attention over towards my outfit.

"Are you going to a school dance or something?" he teases.

"Actually, now that you mention it, the homecoming dance should be here soon. Are you going?" Her eyes widen even more.

"I didn't put too much thought into it."

"Well, now that you have friends, you should ask them if they are going. Oh my, we will have to buy you a dress!" She dances away from me, rambling aloud a to-do list of what I will need to do to be prepared. I shake my head at my dad who only mouths out a *sorry* to me in reply. It's not much of a consolation for what I am probably going to have to endure for his remark.

My attempt at getting a positive answer on the Jessica driving situation has, unfortunately, opened up an entirely different can of worms that I didn't anticipate. I slump into my chair and chug my orange juice in defeat. I almost want to stay home sick.

"Why the long face?" Dad asks when mom leaves the room.

"Please don't use any of mom's trigger words please," I beg. "You know how she gets."

"I will try to remember for next time," he laughs.

I get up from the table after I finish my bowl of cereal and go rinse it off in the sink.

"Emma?" Dad catches my attention. "Will you do me a favor?"

"Sure," I say.

"When Jessica drives you to her house afterschool today, will you call me so that I know you have arrived to her home safely?"

I drop the bowl into the sink and rush over to give him hug. "Thank you, thank you!"

When I enter into my English class later today, I see that Jessica has saved me a seat beside her. Feeling the confidence erupt in my stride, I make my way over and sit down.

"So are you coming over afterschool?"

"Yes, if you still want me to," I respond.

"Of course I want you to," she smiles.

Jessica, just by looking at her, is nowhere near like me. She wears makeup for one. Although, the way she wears it, makes her look nice. Not how I saw that one girl, Savannah, last year cake it on. I try to recall the box of makeup that mom bought me for my birthday, wondering if what is inside of it is enough to create the same look Jessica did. Then again, what am I thinking? Me—makeup—I wouldn't dare.

At lunch, I bring up the subject of the homecoming dance, partially because my mom stuck the idea in my head earlier this morning and because the entire cafeteria is already decorated with banners and signs to announce its pending arrival.

"Are any of you going?" I address the table.

"Nope," Kevin grimaces. "It's just an event where a bunch of cliques gather to compete on who dresses the best and not to mention, a place where ridiculous fights break out."

"Over what?" I ask, taking my sandwich out of the bag.

"Like who dances with whose boyfriend and stupid stuff like that. Instead, I am inviting you all over to my house for pizza and a *Lord of the Rings* marathon."

"I will bring the energy drinks!" another kid shouts out.

"You wanna come Emma?" Kevin chomps down on his sandwich.

"Well, it does sound better than the dance. I will let you know."

Leaving the lunchroom, Henry stops me. "Are you really going to go to Kevin's?" he asks.

"I don't know," I say, "I told him that I would think about it."

Just then, Maggie walks up behind us, "You should really consider coming with us instead. We always have a lot of fun, right Henry?" she smirks into his direction.

He nods," absolutely."

"So you are both going?" I look to both Maggie and Henry.

"I haven't decided what I wanted to do yet, so I thought maybe whatever we decide we could do together?" Henry answers.

"Okay," I answer slightly bewildered.

Maggie steps back, "Yea, we can all do together," she smiles, before walking away.

The day drags on and my habit of staring at the clock only makes it drag on even more. The minute hand ticks loudly, but it doesn't seem to move. The hard wooden chair digs into my backside and I feel like I have been here sitting long enough to have given my seat butt prints. And when the last bell of the day finally rings gloriously throughout the halls, I practically skip my way to my locker before I go meet Jessica in the student parking lot. This is the first time I ever went over to a girl's house and even though it is just for a school project, it feels like a sleepover party to me.

When I meet up with Jessica, she leads me through the parking lot where her white Toyota Camry waits. Inside, it smells like peppermint and I see that she has decorated the dashboard with various flower stickers as a form of self-expression. "I like your car," I say, buckling myself in with the seatbelt. It clicks with the sense of freedom.

"Thanks! My parents bought it for me for my birthday last year. When do you get your license?"

"Well, I turn sixteen July twenty-second, so sometime after that, I guess."

"Let me tell you, life has been great since I passed my driver's test. I don't have to rely on my parents to drive me places. The only thing that stinks is that there is that stupid driving curfew at 10:00pm. Other than that, I am free as a bird."

"Must be nice."

"Oh, it is."

In comparison to driving around with my mom or dad, Jessica drives as though we are about to embark on an adventure. The excitement I used to have for digging up treasure or fighting off dinosaurs emerges within me; although, I don't speak on it. I hardly doubt someone of her status would understand where I am coming from and the last thing I want is to make her think I am a nerd. It is not as if driving has anything to do with those things.

The car breezes on by various large homes outlying the banks of a decent sized lake. Down the road a little further, she turns into the driveway of a large white house where several expensive looking vehicles are parked. The house descends a small hill where the back deck almost kisses the shore of the lake we've been passing the entire time that we left school. It is quite breathtaking. I can't even begin to imagine what the inside must look like.

Jessica pushes open the front door and throws her backpack on the entryway bench, right after she takes out her English notebook. I slide my shoes off, just as her mother rounds the corner greeting us with a plate of snacks and a couple of sodas. Jessica takes the plate and hands me the drinks to carry up to her bedroom. I mumble out a *hello* to her mother and follow up the stairs at Jessica's lead. I hope my introduction wasn't too awkward.

Heading down the hallway we stop at the only door decorated in clippings from fashion magazines. She bursts through it and at her wake; I admire how different her bedroom looks in comparison to mine. Her walls are plastered with posters of guys, bands, and a few supermodels. Various items of clothes decorate every inch of the room, as well as framed pictures of her and her friends. On her bedside table, however, there is a picture of a boy with dark brown hair and brown eyes.

She hands me her cell phone so that I can call my dad and after I hang up with him, I find myself admiring the picture of the boy by her bed again. "Is that your boyfriend?" I point.

"Yes, isn't he cute? His name is Dan. Do you have a boyfriend?" She asks as though it were even possible.

I shake my head. The idea of having a boyfriend never crossed my mind. "I don't really date."

"Really, a pretty girl like you doesn't date? That's crazy!"

I stumble at her words, pretending it's because of the shoe on the floor. No one has ever called me pretty outside of my parents and family. Logan my best friend has never even uttered the word to me, so I always assumed I wasn't, as sad as that may sound. The word is almost as farfetched as the idea of me making friends; then again, I am making friends, am I not?

"Although, you could use some makeup and a new hairstyle," she says, bringing me over to her vanity. The entire surface is littered with bottles and tubes of the stuff, which would make the makeup aisle in my local grocery store blush. "Oh—my—god, I have the best idea, ever!" She exclaims, sitting me down on her vanity stool.

"What's that?" I answer apprehensively. The look in her eyes reminds me of my mom and I can't help but to fear what's about to come next.

"I want to give you a makeover!"

"A what?"

"A makeover, silly! — Imagine what you would like with a little bit of eye shadow or lipstick. Plus, I think I have some clothes that would fit you in my closet! I don't wear them anymore, so they are all yours!" She says, making her way over to the closet where she begins to throw whatever clothes she no longer wants, out. If my mom were here to witness this, her eyes would probably explode.

When the last item gets thrown out from her closet, she walks over and holds up a few of the shirts to my neck. "And with boobs like you have, well all the boys will notice you now!

You will have a boyfriend before the end of the week!" She clasps her hands together just as I have seen my mom do. The thought almost sickens me. Weren't we supposed to be working on our school project here? Or have I suddenly become the new project?

The evening ends with no more than a few words scribbled into my notebook about the book. I think we managed to read five pages all of which required a break after each one. Instead, however, I leave with several hair products to make my hair sleek and smooth, makeup on my face, painted nails, and the clothes that she so generously had donated to me, which makes me feel like nothing more than a charity case. *What was so wrong with the way that I looked before?*

Later that evening when Jessica drives me home, her nose turns up with disgust as soon as she heads down my street. "Ugh, how do you live with that smell?" She rolls up her window.

"You get used to it," I say.

"I don't think I could ever get used to a smell like that!"

Her car eases into my driveway right under the muted front porch light. My eyes survey around the badly lit perimeter for Logan, but I know that he is not outside waiting for me. Still, I can't help but to double check.

"Listen," meet me at the second floor rest room by Mr. Higgin's class tomorrow morning at 7:15am and I will complete your makeover there. Bring the outfit we talked about, okay?"

I exit the car with the bag of donated items and watch as she drives away. As soon as her car is far enough down the road, I wipe as much of the makeup off my face that I can onto the sleeve of my shirt. Even under the dimness of the porch light, I can see the colors of brown, black, and tan streak jaggedly across my sleeve. But I much rather prefer seeing the makeup on my clothes than on my face. And the last thing I need is for my mom to witness my willingness to try the damn stuff; otherwise, she will probably insist that I wear it all the time.

* * * *

The second go at a makeover takes place in the bathroom, ironically the same bathroom where I hid the first day of school. My hair is straight and smells like apricot from all of the products that Jessica is pouring into it. It leaves behind a cloud of mist that hovers in front of my face, making me want to sneeze. When my hair is finally styled to her liking, she twirls me around and begins applying makeup from a small pouch she keeps in the side of her bag. If I thought mom trying to get me ready in the morning was bad, Jessica is actually much worse.

The foundation feels like a heavy lotion being plastered upon my face, as she smoothes it into my skin all the way to the base of my neck. Powder comes next in various shades. The brush dusts across my face from right to left, then up, and down. And when she finally gets to my eyes, I struggle not to blink, but I have never had anything that close to my eye before. The pencil presses into the lining of my eye. It's quite a grueling process, if I do say so.

Catching a glimpse of myself in the mirror, I see that my eyes are outlined in a black color with a bronze shadow on the lids. I have to admit that my eyes actually look quite nice. The shadow makes the green in my eyes pop out. However, I have no time to check on the rest of my face, before Jessica practically pushes me into one of the empty stalls, forcing me to put on one of the dresses that my mom bought without my permission before school started.

"I can't believe you have never worn that," she says through the stall door. "If it were to fit me, I would totally take it from you."

"I never liked dresses," I groan.

"Well, you better start."

I throw my clothes over the stall door where Jessica catches them and sticks them into my messenger bag. I slide the dress up the length of my body feeling the uncomfortable tightness suction around my frame as though I am wearing a vacuum. I don't like this and I don't have to see myself in front of a mirror to figure it out. But when I open the stall, frown and all, Jessica ignores my apparent distaste and grabs me excitedly by the arm. She almost pulls it right out of its socket.

"You have a killer body!" She shrieks, beaming at me as though I am her equal.

I catch my reflection and feel a sickening feeling take hold of my stomach. *Who is this person staring back at me?* I look nothing like myself and I am infuriated by it. I want to tear off the clothes, mess up my hair, and scrub the makeup off my face. But Jessica doesn't seem to notice or even care, because she takes me by the arm again and practically throws me into the hallway for everyone to see.

It feels like one of those dreams where you are in a crowded room with people looking at you funny. You have no idea why until you look down and realize you are either in your underwear or naked. I am not naked, but I feel exposed and to me, it's pretty much the same thing. My body begins to move at a glacier pace down the hallway. I timidly reach the combination lock on my locker as I feel various eyes burn into my skin like the summer sun. Once I enter the combination, the locker pops open just as Jessica leans her back against the neighboring lockers with a satisfying sigh.

"I feel like everyone is staring at me," I bury my head in my locker.

"Well, they should be. You look amazing."

I look around me at few of the nearby onlookers. "It's not a big deal, right?" I primarily ask myself. "So, I am wearing different clothes and you did my makeup, no different than anyone else?" I try to convince myself at this point. My justification, however, doesn't convince myself of this dramatic change. Of course, they are staring; I went from looking like a girl who grew up on a farm to a girl right out of the city. This is almost as embarrassing as the bra incident.

"What's the big deal? Are you kidding me Rae?" Jessica decides to coin my middle name as my first, another thing I am not too happy with; I corrected her at least six times last night, but each time fell on deaf ears."I told you, you were a hottie; and with this makeover, there is no way that the boys won't notice. And I think *someone* will be asked to the winter ball this year," she smiles. "Or if you were in my grade, the prom."

"I don't dance," I say. I have no interest in going and if mom hears about another approaching dance, she will go crazy. I can't imagine what her reaction will be.

"I will teach you," she says, picking her back up off the lockers, "You are going!"

"So does that mean you are going to the homecoming dance next Friday?" I almost want to kick myself for asking.

"Yea, aren't you?"

"I haven't really given it much thought," *at least not as much as my mom probably has.*

"Oh, no you are going. I will introduce you to the rest of group at the football game tomorrow."

I turn to her, "football game?"

"I will pick you up at 6:00pm, so don't give me any sass!"

Chapter Twelve

A ghostly silhouette of myself follows me down the hallway. She cannot be seen, felt, or even heard, but I know that she is there. My reflection screams at me for my betrayal to change it. *What was wrong with me before?* First, it was with my mom wanting to change me as soon as I started school; and then, the first girl friend that I make, wants to give me a makeover. Does no one like me the way that I am? Then, I can't help but to think of Logan, who would never want to change a single thing about me. *Gosh, how I miss him.*

Walking into the lunchroom makes me tremble. I try to calm my nerves by counting the number of floor tiles it takes to make it over to Henry's table—eighteen to be exact. Eighteen square tile I uneasily travel across, hearing the sound of someone else's heels clacking against the floor in my wake. They are Jessica's heels, but they are on my feet. Even my walk is not my own.

I walk into the lunchroom and sit down at Henry's table. Even they begin to look at me as though I am no longer the same person, which only confirms to me why I liked the way I previously dressed. In this outfit, I feel like someone else, a complete stranger; I just feel like I can't be me. And amongst them, I stick out like a sore thumb.

"What's with the get-up?" Kevin asks, pointing to my outfit and makeup. He chomps away at a handful of chips in his mouth.

"Yea, it's a little too much, I know. But Jessica wanted to give me a makeover, and I have come to the conclusion that she can be a little pushy at times," I take a bite of my sandwich. In my mouth's wake, it leaves behind an imprint of my glossy lips. *Gross.*

"Jessica who?" He continues to ask.

"Rockingham," I reply.

"Rockingham?" Maggie butts in.

"Yea, Jessica Rockingham."

"Are you kidding me? She has to be one of the most popular girls in this school. She dates the captain of the football and Lacrosse team, Dan Stevens. How do you know her?" Maggie asks behind her black framed glasses. She surveys me up and down several times before I respond.

"She and I are working on an English assignment together. I went over to her place last night to work on it and she apparently wants to hang out tomorrow at the football game," I pause, "and the homecoming dance," I groan.

"She asked you to come with her?" Maggie's face expresses apparent disbelief.

"Yea, what's the big deal?"

"The big deal? Jessica is like one of the coolest people in this school and if she likes you; then you are "in" and if you are "in" you won't be hanging out with us much longer," she sits back into her chair, looking around the table for affirmation.

I am staring down at my lipstick stained sandwich, bewildered by Maggie's comment. What does hanging out with Jessica have to do with whom I hang out with or whom I sit with at lunch? Shouldn't I be the one who decides that? Then again, would I even be brave enough to stand up to Jessica if the moment presented itself where I had to choose? I could barely tell her that I wanted no part in this makeover, now look at me.

Henry clears his throat and we make eye contact for a moment. His feet shuffle under his chair as though perturbed by the thought of my inevitable status change.

"Well, by me hanging out with Jessica it does not dictate who my friends are." I finally say, taking another bite of my sandwich.

But no one seems convinced.

* * * *

Throughout the entire drive home from school, mom doesn't shut up about the way that I look. She pets my straight hair as though I am a dog and talks about how perfect the dress looks on me, which makes me want to exit the moving vehicle. So that by the time we get home, I don't even wait for her to stop the car before I unbuckle my seatbelt and get ready to depart.

Off in the distance, Logan is pushing the wheelbarrow into the shed, just before he makes his way over to me. When I step out of the car, I notice that his mouth is open as though he wants to say something, but then he quickly slams it shut.

"What's all this?" He finally says, looking at me from head to toe. "Makeup, Emma? Really?" His tone is a mixture of disbelief and sadness.

"Why does it look bad?" I worry at the thought. Of course, it looks bad; I was just kind of hoping he didn't mind it too much.

"Well, it doesn't look like you, if that is what you are asking. I thought you said you would never paint your face with that crap?" He points at my face. "You look like a clown."

Mom's footsteps sound in the distance as she makes her way inside of the house, and shuts the door. My face follows her steady departure until I turn back to face Logan. "Yea, well," I begin, as I close the car door, "my new friend Jessica wanted to give me a makeover, said I would look better." I try to act as though I am okay with what she did, but I have a feeling he will see right through my act.

"Well, what kind of friend is that?" He says rather disgruntled.

"What do you mean?"

"What I mean is, shouldn't your friends like you for who you are and what you already look like? They shouldn't want to change you to suit their needs." He says very matter-of-factly. "Friends don't do that."

I stand there with no retort. *He is right. How can I argue against that?*

He reaches into his pocket and pulls out his handkerchief, "wipe that stuff off your face," he hands it to me. "I am going to have to revisit your list."

"What list?"

"The things we are writing to remember about each other, duh."

"Oh," I say through the handkerchief. It smells like it could use a good washing, but I don't tell him that. "And why's that?"

"I am going to have to remember that you are going to need someone to keep you in check."

"You mean you?" I chuckle.

"Well, I don't see anyone else up for the job," he smiles, taking the handkerchief back and sticking it into his pocket. "Someone has to keep your original intact."

* * * *

The night of the football game arrives. Dad dances around the kitchen reenacting plays again. He tosses an apple into the air and catches it, while explaining to me about how he had to run so many yards to score the winning touchdown. But all I see is him knocking into the kitchen table and spilling my glass of juice everywhere.

"I want to see the shape the team is in since I left," He says, plopping back down into his chair. "We were state champions, you know."

"I am sure they are doing just fine without you," mom smiles.

"Charlotte, I was incredible back in the day. Maybe later I can dig up my old pictures, and I can show you. I am sure they are somewhere up in the attic."

My eyes narrow at the thought. I am just glad that I won't be home for another round of reminiscing.

Making my way to the foyer, I grab my coat and shoes and decide to wait on the front porch for Jessica to arrive. This is my first school event and I feel almost as nervous as I did before the very first day of school. I don't know what to expect. I don't even know how to act under these circumstances. The only plus side is that I won't be going alone, which makes things a little easier on me. Still, I hardly know Jessica and I haven't actually figured out how to act around her—I am sure she will probably end up telling me how to do that too.

As I continue waiting, however, out of nowhere, Logan walks on over and sits down beside me on the front porch steps. His cool icy stare freezes me to my spot.

"Going out or something?" He asks. I catch him looking at my face for makeup. The only giveaway of my attempts at experimenting is the glistening effect my lips have under the porch lights. For all he knows, it could be Chap Stick.

"Yea, I am going to a football game," I hesitate, "with Jessica."

"You have been spending a lot of time with her lately," he points out the obvious.

"Yea, she is really nice. You would like her," I look off to the side, digesting my life, but there is an aftertaste of phoniness filling up my mouth.

"I doubt it."

The silence between us remerges. It rolls in and lingers like a glooming fog, which saddens me deeply. How is it that he and I have been so disconnected lately? I guess I could have asked Logan to come along, but since Jessica was the one who invited me, I didn't know if it was my place to extend the invite. I know that Logan doesn't understand and seeing the sad look in his eyes right now, makes me want to stay back and be with him instead. I miss him, but I can't turn back now. I need friends.

And if memory serves me correctly, didn't he tell me to make them?

"We haven't stargazed in awhile," he says looking up at the sky.

"I know. I was just thinking about that the other day."

"How about we do it tonight," he says rather hopefully. "You can come get me when you get back."

"I am not sure what time I will be back," I say. "It might be late."

"What about tomorrow night?"

"Maybe," I begin to recount my schedule in my mind.

"Well, when can you pencil me in?" He snarls sarcastically.

"Huh?"

"Well, with your new friends and life it's like you don't have time for me anymore."

"Oh, stop it, Logan. You are the one who didn't want to come to high school with me this year. Not to mention, wasn't it *you* who advised me to make friends?"

"Yea, well, I didn't think you would forget about me," he stands up.

"I haven't," I say.

"Sure feels like it to me."

Just then, Jessica pulls into the driveway and honks on her horn. Mom comes down the porch steps and over to her car to meet her. I can hear her gushing about the makeover that Jessica gave to me the other day. But I don't move; I remain by Logan's side. Something within me is finding it hard to breakaway.

"I haven't forgotten about you," I say. "This doesn't mean anything." I loosely point over to Jessica's car. "It's just a football game."

"Yea, whatever," he says, taking off.

"Where are you going?" I yell out to him.

His boots pound at the ground as he charges from me. I want to chase after him. I want to make things right, but I can see Jessica waiting for me in the car and I know she wouldn't understand my need to go after him. I would skip the football game if I didn't think she would never ask me to hang out with her again. But I don't know much about her to take that gamble. I will just have to make amends with him when I return; it's all I really can do.

I crawl my way to the car and climb in. The scent of peppermint greets me, temporally erasing the smell of the farm as well as my thoughts for Logan.

"Who was that guy next to you?" She peers out into the darkness. Logan is nowhere to be found, but I have a good idea on where he went.

"That was my best friend, Logan. He lives next door to me."

"He is really cute. Is he single?" She laughs, which makes me think she is joking.

"Yea, he is." I say, slightly apprehensive at the sudden label.

"Well, if Dan and I ever break up, I know where I will be coming to hang out," she smiles. But this time, I don't think she is joking.

* * * *

The nighttime ambience silhouettes the school, intriguing me in a way that daylight could never do. I grip tightly to the handle releasing the latch, before climbing out of the car. The scent of a cool night mixed with the mystery that awaits me, excites the blood in my veins. I walk around the car and stand beside Jessica, feeling that excitement wane. I look down at my sneakered feet and then at her heels. The perfect example of two people from two different walks of life. She walks with a sense of entitlement and pride. Her nose instinctively shoots up into the air and her hips sway ever so slightly with each step that she takes. With me, on the other hand, I totter behind her, digging my hands into my pockets, completely unsure of myself and why the hell she even invited me along in the first place.

The cheering crowd amid the stands roars into the parking lot and inspires a rather awkward skip in my step. Jessica doesn't seem to notice this, because she appears much to focused on waving towards a small group of people congregated by a black jeep. I follow close behind her as she introduces me as "Rae" to everyone. I wish to correct her, since I prefer my real name of Emma, but she leaves no break in her introduction for me to do so. Thus, giving everyone permission to call me, Rae.

The first person she introduces me to is Megan. Her tight skirt and patterned tights gleam against the parking lot lights as my eyes travel to her cheetah print boots. Her long dark hair is slick and straight like a bone and it hangs over her face covering one of her eyes. She smirks a half-smile into my direction and snubs me thereafter. I can already tell that she and I will never be friends.

Next is Pete, who is currently dating Megan, which she seems to be put-off by his need to want to hold her hand. "I am trying to check my phone," She whips her nose into the air. He backs off and starts talking with the guy next to him, who I am introduced to as Joe. He is drinking something out of a paper bag, which he then begins to pass around to everyone. Watching the brown paper bag float from person to person, prompts me to ask if they serve drinks at the concession stand.

"Then you guys wouldn't have to share," I continue. I hear the paper crinkle against Joe's grip.

For a moment, there is a palpable pause felt amongst the group, before they all burst into a fit of laughter leaving me quite confused as a result. I retract my previous comment back into my mind unable to determine what I had said to set them off, but then Joe announces, "Yea, but they don't serve alcohol!"

*Oh, so they are drinking…*I shove my hands into my pockets feeling the sweat begin to pour through my palms, subsequently filling my pockets up like makeshift water balloons. *I was not prepared for this…*

"I am taking homeschooled Rae and making her cool," Jessica smiles, taking a sip if whatever lies beneath the brown paper bag.

As I watch her take a sip, I am somehow reminded of Logan and the brown paper bag he used to wrap my birthday gift.

I wonder what he is doing right now. I can't imagine how alone he must feel. I star up into the night sky wondering if I can see his mom from here. She is probably so upset with me right now or is at least reporting back to Logan on what it is that I am doing. I almost catch myself from wanting to yell up towards her, saying, *I am not drinking Mrs. Solway!* Still, I feel the stars staring down at me like judgmental eyes. And if the strangers amongst the starry crowd are judging, I know for a fact that she is as well.

"What is this, a movie or something?" Megan bursts out laughing, as she lights up a cigarette. My eyes pull into her direction by the flicker of her lighter.

No one on the farm smokes so the smell is quite unfamiliar to me. It smells worse the cow mess I pick up every morning. It's pungent and makes me cough. And the fact that she is sticking it into her mouth, makes me cringe.

"Well, I am going to go find a seat. I promised Lindsey I would go sit by her and Rebecca. I will see you all later," Megan announces, as she sets off towards the field, with Pete dragging himself behind. He kind of reminds me of the Solway cat who follows everyone around on the farm by their coattails, begging for attention which it never gets.

"Do you want a sip?" Jessica asks, leaning the paper bag towards me.

Apprehensively, I look towards it and ask, "What is it? Wine?"

"No silly, it's just a little vodka and cranberry juice. Joe here mixes up drinks for us before every game. Although, I don't drink a lot because I tend to always be the designated driver," she whines.

"No, thanks," I say. I can smell what I assume to be the vodka emitting from the bag. My stomach slightly churns. I can't imagine how it would react if I actually took a sip. I turn my face away.

Regardless of my reluctant beginning, however, the football game turns out to be a lot of fun. I cheer along with our school team and occasionally allow Joe to explain to me what is happening out on the field. I pay close attention to everything he says, hoping to impress my dad later when I get home. However, even through all of that, I still look up to the sky, letting Logan's mom know, that secretly, I would much rather be with Logan instead. I feel her star twinkle with forgiveness.

Chapter Thirteen

I am hungry, tired, and my clothes are stretched out from constant removal. My limbs limp under the fluorescent lighting of every single dressing room that I have been dragged into, only to come out empty-handed. Nothing that I have been forced to try on turns out to be the dress that mom has envisioned in her mind for me to wear. None of the twenty stores we scoured through from top to bottom has what she is apparently looking for; and when I try to be of service, she turns her nose up at my selections and walks away.

A hundredth yawn releases just as a bright blue dress falls over the stall and drapes across my head. I pull it down and hold it out in front of me with no expectations. I slide into it and open the door, picturing my mom's scrunched up face as she tells me to try something else on. But instead she greets me with a screech—hands clasped and all.

"This is the one!" she beams.

She yanks my arm and the rest of my body out of the dressing room and moves me over to the main mirror so that she can get a better look at me. "Look at how nice your figure looks in that dress," she exclaims, "I wish I had that body when I was your age."

I have a look of excitement on my face too, but it's not because of how nice I apparently look, it's because shopping is finally coming to an end. *I just want to go home already.*

We return home around dusk, dad is in the kitchen serving up whatever mom left simmering in the Crockpot all day. I could care less what is inside of it; I would eat my shoes if it were possible. The least she could have done was allowed me to get a snack or something while she held me hostage, but all I was offered was a lousy stick of gum.

"Your back," dad says, not believing in how long it took us to go shopping for a dress.

"We had to find the perfect dress," mom says.

I just roll my eyes. At least dad knows that I would have tried to come home sooner if it weren't for mom's need to treat me like her own miniature Barbie doll.

The next day at school, everyone is talking about the dance. Girls congregate and talk about their dresses and everyone bounces around ideas for what they are doing after. At lunch, Kevin brings up *The Lord of the Rings* marathon again and gets the final headcount for all whose attending.

When he turns to me, I say, "I am actually going to the dance with Jessica and her friends, but thank you."

"Yep, she is officially one of the cool kids now," Maggie announces to the table.

"But," I chime in, "I wouldn't mind coming over after."

Kevin looks as though he is wavering on my offer. "Well, we might be partially into the second movie by the time you get to my house. But I guess it's okay," he says, taking a bite of his sandwich.

Henry looks over at me, "I didn't know you were actually going to go to the dance, but I am glad you are going to come over to Kevin's after."

I catch a smile begin to form on his face. *Since when do people care about what I am doing?* I get Kevin's address from him and make a note to myself to tell Jessica to drop me off there after the dance.

When I come home from school today, Logan is nowhere in sight. I haven't seen him since our most recent fight and when I tried to go over to his house after shopping the other day, Mr. Solway told me that he was sick and didn't want any visitors. But

I know Logan, he is a real big baby when it comes to him being sick and the last thing he wants is to be left alone; so I know there is no way that he is *really* sick.

When I walk in the house, however, mom greets me in the kitchen with every piece of makeup and hair product that she owns. "Go shower," she orders.

"I showered this morning."

"Shower again. Don't you want to be fresh for the dance?"

While I shower, mom orders a pizza, which she never does. I slip into my bathrobe just as I am being dragged down into the kitchen by the smell of tomato sauce and melted cheese. I find this an unfair advantage on my mom's part. She wants to keep me in the kitchen for as long as she can and she knows that pizza will do it.

I chow down about four slices and almost putting my father to shame. I am about to reach for my fifth, until mom intercepts. "You are not going to fit into your dress if you keep eating this way. You will bloat," she commands.

"Charlotte, let her eat another slice if she wants it," dad sides with me. "She is obviously hungry."

"No, it's just that she eats just like you."

And for the next hour, minus the fifth slice of pizza, mom does my hair and makeup. She curls my hair so that they cascade down shoulders like waves. And of course, to keep them from falling, she sprays what feels like a half of a bottle of hairspray in my hair.

"I invited Logan and his dad to come see you off to your first school dance," she says, pinning a few short pieces of my hair away from my face.

"You did?" I ask surprised.

"Yes, why is there something wrong?"

I sit silently in the chair unable to articulate the thoughts and feelings erupting within me at the sound of Logan's name. Doesn't anyone notice the lack of time that he and I have been spending together? Or even the awkwardness that surrounds us whenever we come face to face?

"You know," mom begins, interrupting my thoughts, "I know something is wrong. I can see it all over your face." *Okay, maybe she does notice.*

"It's probably the makeup," I joke.

"What is going on with you two?"

I really don't want to talk about it. Most of my issues stem from me having to go to high school in the first place. It brought on this huge continental divide between Logan and I, which only continues to grow bigger—something that I never thought would ever happen. The simple things that have once accessorized my life have become lost amongst the things that I don't truly want. I don't want to be this girl that my mom, Jessica, and the rest of the school wants me to be. The clothes, the makeup, the attitude, and social aspects that come along with it, are not enhancing the girl I thought I was inside; why can't I just wear my sports bra, work clothes, and be homeschooled again? But no one seems to want that for me. My parents wanted me to get a different form of education, which unbeknownst to them filled me with the pressures of having to live up to their previous accomplishments. And what about Jessica? The girl who never noticed me until she put makeup on my face? The girl who changed me into nothing more than an accessory, that hangs on her arm. The thoughts circulating throughout my head are making me second-guess this entire thing. I don't want to go anymore. I want to stay here where I belong.

"Sweetie?" Mom reels me back in.

"Yea?"

"Are you going to talk to me?

"Sorry," I say. "Logan and I just haven't had time to hang out in awhile with everything going on with me and school. I don't think he likes it." I beat around the bush.

"Well of course he doesn't like it. It's always been just you two. But he will get used to it and soon understand that these things happen in life. It doesn't make either one of you wrong."

Then why do I feel like I am the one who is in the wrong? But I don't tell her that.

Soon, mom sends me upstairs to get into my dress, before Jessica is set to get here in a half an hour. I battle my previous thoughts again when I ascend the stairs. How angry would Jessica be if I called and told her that I wasn't going? Better yet, how angry would mom be? Either one of them, I don't exactly want to face if I chose to back out the last minute.

I slide into my dress and stand in front of my dresser mirror for a good twenty minutes, before I finally make my way back downstairs. Mom, dad, Mr. Solway, and Logan, are all in the kitchen, waiting. I hesitate between the front door and the threshold of the kitchen. If I move fast enough, I might make it halfway through the pasture before anyone notices that I took off. But just as I am about to see that plan through, the floorboards creak underneath my feet, prompting Mr. Solway to turn around and usher me into the kitchen.

"Well don't you look nice, young lady," he says, just like a proud parent would.

Mom clasps her hands to her chest, while dad holds his finger down on the camera's flash button. The flash becomes a single ray of light as he takes about ten pictures in the process. Logan, on the other hand, sits uneasily at the kitchen table. His fingers drum along the wooden surface unable to face me. "You look nice," he finally mumbles.

I want to go sit beside him or be the one that chases him into the fields to get him to smile, but as soon as I set foot into the kitchen, Jessica is knocking on the front door and any hopes of doing those things, quickly slip through my grasp.

* * * *

The homecoming dance is not what I expected. Actually, I don't know what I had expected. Opening the car door, I can hear the loud music roaring all the way outside, forcing my prior thoughts to rear their ugly head, but it's too late to turn back now.

"Who are you going to ask to dance with you first?" Jessica yells above the music as we pay for our tickets at the front table.

The thought never crossed my mind. Dancing never crossed my mind. I was behaving under the assumption that it was simply a social gathering, like the football game, completely leaving out the social convention of dancing and awkward interactions between boys and girls. I never allowed myself the chance to practice alone in my bedroom. I hate to admit, that I, Emma Jensen, have never danced—even at weddings. I usually just hang around where the food is, without any desire to step foot upon a dance floor. But here, there are no food tables to keep up with my routine, which sucks.

Behind Jessica, I follow her through the gymnasium doors to the massive crowd of students dancing in small-congregated groups, which somehow interlock into a cluster of nonsensical dancing. There is no pattern or similarities to their moves. There seems to be routine to follow, which is slightly relieving. But even so, my arms and legs do not know how to move in conjunction to my hips, which everyone seems to be swaying. Observing from a distance, their hips move in ways that mine only know the familiarity of when inside of a hula-hoop. Some dancing I see, make me blush under the heat of all the breathing and disco lights. Girls rubbing against boys in ways that I thought were only ever appropriate behind closed doors or when you were married. Apparently, being overly sexual is the way to express a talent in dance. Although, I personally wouldn't call it dancing. It has more similarities to that of dry humping—*I watch enough movies, remember?*

Without warning, Jessica yanks me by the hand and drags me over to a group of her friends, all of which are dancing somewhat towards the back. I wonder why they have chosen such a spot, but when I see Megan reach up her dress for a small flask inside of her garter, I realize that the purpose is for them to drink.

There they go again, passing around the communal drink. When it gets to Jessica, she takes a sip and then hands it over to me when she is finished. The flask weighs into the palm of my hand, just as I see a boy with dark brown hair and brown eyes come up behind her and wrap his arms around her waist. He leans down and kisses her on the cheek—this must be Dan.

"Come on take a shot," she says, hitting the flask in my hand.

"No, that's all right," I hand it back.

"Come on, how else are you going to have fun and let loose?"

I was not operating under the assumption that fun could only be had with alcohol. "I have never had any before," I cower into admittance.

"Any vodka?" Jessica yells confused.

"Any alcohol before." I correct her. My voice is loud above the music. A few people in the group scan the crowd for any unsuspecting eavesdroppers.

In disbelief, she laughs into the air, announcing my confession to the group. "Well, honey after the dance, we are going to show you the meaning of letting loose."

"But I am going to Kevin's, remember?"

She turns away and hands the flask back over to Megan, who quickly conceals it back inside of her garter. I can't imagine walking with that between my legs.

The group soon heads towards the dance floor, where they break off into partners. I sway nervously off to the side, before Jessica pushes me into Joe, forcing me to dance with him. I stand uneasily before him, trying my hardest to replicate what I am seeing the other girls do, but just as soon as I think that I have the hang of it, the song ends, leaving a slow one it's place.

Joe places his hands on my waist and my arms go around his neck. The dance is easy since all we have to do is sway from side to side, which was what I was doing before he came along. I feel like an idiot, but no one seems to notice. They also don't notice how red my face has become. *Thank goodness for horrible lighting.*

After the dance, Jessica and I leave with the rest of the group. I remind her again that I promised Kevin that I would partake in his gathering, but she still won't listen.

"Rae, you are coming to a party with us," she says to me. Her tone reminds me of the one mom uses when she orders me around to do something. There she goes again, pulling me by the arm like a ragdoll.

The entire car ride, I try to persuade her to drop me off, but we end up going to the party instead. Again, she drags me inside where I have no choice but to make-do of the situation. With a heavy sigh, I plop down on the living room couch, feeling horrible for standing up Kevin and his friends. Looking around, I notice that everyone is drinking and stumbling around the house like idiots. The music is blaring almost at the same volume that was at the dance. I can hardly hear myself think. *I want to go home.*

"Here," Jessica rounds the couch and hands me a red cup filled with a pale-bronze colored liquid. "It's beer."

Apprehensively, I take the cup into my hands and watch as she just stares at me. I am not in the mood to try it or even become one of the idiots I see stumbling around the house. But as she drinks from her cup, she keeps her eyes solely on me as though watching and waiting for me to do the same.

She says to me again, "You need to have some fun and it will loosen you up." She gently taps the bottom of my glass, forcing the rim of the glass to kiss my lips gently.

I don't want to and I do try my best to fight her on it. But my defense is no match to her offense, which leaves me almost forced against my will to take a sip. "If I take a sip, will you take me to Kevin's then?" I consider the wager smart on my behalf, but unbeknownst to me, she is much smarter.

"How about I take you to Kevin's after you drink what is in your cup."

"All of it?" I look down inside the cup, which to me looks a never ending well.

"All of it," she confirms.

I take a deep breath and slide the rim through the opening of my lips. Her eyes widen as though she is about to experience a miracle. And when I finally feel the first drop roll down the back of my throat and hit the pit of my empty stomach, she smiles deeply at me. "I am proud of you," she says. "Now drink up and let's have a good time."

Time escapes and I feel like every time I set my cup down, more beer magically appears. Jessica keeps telling me that I am overreacting, but with every sip I take, I am nowhere near to the bottom of this intoxicating well. One sip equals two more in waiting. *I will never get through this cup.*

I stand up to go and use the restroom, and for a moment, the room slightly spins. I sit back down to recover, motioning for

Jessica to come over. The sound of my voice seems distorted and slurred. I have no idea what is going on, but strangely, I don't care either.

"You are wasted," she smiles at me.

And sadly, that's the last thing I remember.

* * * *

The rising sun blasts through Jessica's blinds and hits me like a ton of bricks. I feel like I have come down with the flu with a mixture of an intense stomach bug. I slowly get on my hands and knees, using the end of her bed as support to get up. My dress is crooked and stained. My hair and face look like a Halloween nightmare and when I look down at the bed at Jessica, she looks just about the same.

"Jessica?" I whisper across the bed at her. She doesn't move so I repeat myself again.

With as much energy as my body can muster and as slow as I can move without wanting to throw up, I walk over and try to wake her.

"What?" She growls from beneath her pillow, where she then slams down upon her head at the touch of my hand.

"What the hell happened last night?"I ask. Of course, I know that I drank too much and am now paying for it. I also know that she tricked me into getting drunk, which I am not too happy about either, but I choose not to say anything at this point. Instead, I ask that she bring me home.

"I need to sleep." She says to me. "I will bring you home later."

"I want to go home now," I say.

She throws her cell phone from her bedside table over to me, which lands on the floor. Slowly, I bend down to pick up and dial home for my parents.

"Hello?" My dad answers the phone.

"Dad?"

"How was the dance?" He asks, oblivious to my sickly tone.

"It was fun, but I think I caught a bug or something. I started to feel sick last night, but now it's worse. Can you come get me?" The smooth lie that creeps through my beer stained lips, sickens me more than what is brewing in the pit of my stomach. Where did such skilled deception come from? I have never outwardly lied to my parents and here I am becoming a master of the art before my very own eyes.

Jessica remains in bed when I go downstairs and wait for my dad. No one is home, which is a good thing. I am able to sit in the living room in peace, trying to collect my thoughts, while trying not to throw up on what looks to be a very expensive couch. Resting my head upon the side of it, I feel my stomach churn with the contents that I am not so thrilled to have consumed. The only question that arrives within the confines of my pounding head is how does the room go from hot to cold then from cold to hot, so fast?

Unable to keep whatever it is that is so desperately wanting to come out, I rush to the bathroom around the corner and throw up. My body heaves over the toilet seat until I feel like the pressure from it tries to fold me in half. I feel terrible. Thankfully, no one hears me. I crash to the bathroom floor and rest my head upon the carpet until my dad's car horn sounds from the front of the Jessica's house. Gradually, I steady myself, wipe my face on a few pieces of toilet paper and make my way slowly outside. How soothing the fresh air feels against my tear and vomit stained face.

"You look terrible," Dad, says when I open the passenger side door.

"I know."

He buckles me in, because I am unable to do so. My body is weak and I have the sneaking suspicion that being inside of a moving vehicle might make things worse, but I do my best to keep my eyes closed and focus on my breathing.

When we arrive home, dad puts the car into park and turns to me, "What's been going on?"

Oh my god, he knows about me drinking last night. I try to remain calm and just look at him as though I am perplexed by his question, which thankfully prompts him to continue.

"I know," he says, "about you and Logan not getting along. I had a talk with him yesterday after you left for the dance, and he seems to think you don't have time for him anymore."

"I do have time," I say, wiping at my face.

"Do you? When was the last time you set aside time to be with him? I thought you two were best friends?"

"We are."

"Then maybe you need to think about how you would react—if the tables were turned."

We climb out of the car without another word. I look over at Logan's house, knowing that he is probably somewhere inside. I do miss him terribly. Have I really been that horrible of a friend? I know that I need to make things up to him, but I need my rest first. After today, I promise to set things right. Logan should be all that I need, so why surround myself with people that I don't?

For the rest of the day, however, I sleep; and the only time that I pull myself into an upright position is when mom comes into my bedroom to bring me some soup. It cools on my bedside table instead of being devoured. I think I only took a few spoonfuls before my stomach said it didn't want anymore. The only thing that it did want was the water and ginger ale that my mom kept refilling for me throughout the day. *Gosh, this is horrible.*

Thankfully, when Sunday arrives, I feel so much better. I make a vow never to drink again. And I am surprised that neither one of my parents suspected anything. But when I come down into the kitchen, both are sitting there, not eating, but waiting. I celebrated too soon.

"Good morning," I say, heading over to the pantry to grab a box of cereal.

"Good morning," they respond in chorus.

"Something wrong?"

Dad clears his throat, "I didn't want to say anything to you yesterday—"

"We were afraid that the message wouldn't sink in." Mom cuts in.

I place the box of cereal on the counter and linger fearfully by the fridge, unsure as to whether I should grab the jug of milk or stay put. I decide to stay put.

"Have you smelled your room?" Mom asks.

Still I say nothing.

"It smells like old alcohol. Normally people, who get the stomach virus, do not emit those kinds of smells."

I have two choices here. I can lie, which will not work in my favor, considering they already know the truth. Or two, I can just tell the truth, while begging for misery in the process. *I will go with begging.* "Okay, okay. After the dance, Jessica took me to this party, and I didn't want to go," I begin, leaving the cereal box on the counter and making my way over to the table to sit down. "I tried to tell her that I made plans at Kevin's like I told you both, but she wouldn't listen."

"So why didn't you call us? We would have come and got you." Mom takes a sip of her coffee.

"Because I didn't have a way to call you; it's not like I have a cell phone or anything."

"So, none of this would have happened if you had a cell phone?" Dad peers over the table at me.

"I am not sure," I hesitate between words. "Anyways, like I said, I kept telling Jessica that I made plans to go to Kevin's to watch the movie marathon, but she insisted that I stay at the party with her. Then, she tricked me into having one cup of beer before she would take me."

"All you had was one cup?" Mom asks with a suspicious undertone.

"Well, I thought so at first, but every time I set my cup down, it magically refilled."

"Refilled?" Dad asks.

"Yea, she tricked me. And the last thing I remember is waking up on her bedroom floor."

"And you don't remember how you got there?" They speak in a chorus again.

"No, but Jessica's car wasn't there in the morning, so I know that she didn't drive."

"That is very irresponsible and not to mention, dangerous. Your father and I for the first time need to think of the appropriate consequence for your actions. I will say this,

Jessica and you are not going to be hanging around as much if this is what happens when you two are together."

"Well, I still have that school project to work on with her. Keep that in mind," I say, standing up from the table.

I leave them alone in the kitchen to talk amongst themselves and even though my stomach is empty and yearning for nourishment, I still leave the house and make my way next door to find Logan. I only care about making him feel better right about now, not me.

The crisp chill in the air hits my face as soon as I step down from the front porch. The pasture is blanketed with a slight frost on the ground; yet, the cows continue to graze unaffected. As I walk over to Logan's house, I can't help but to think about how much has changed in such a short period of time. And even though I am upset with Jessica for what she did, I can't decide if whether or not I am mad enough to stop talking to her. She wasn't trying to be mean; she just wanted me to have a good time. The funny part is; I can't remember if I had a good time or not, which makes the aftermath of it all seem not worth it.

I knock on the kitchen door and Mr. Solway opens it. He is having his morning cup of coffee. The knock even surprises me since I never do it.

"Good morning Mr. Solway, is Logan inside?" I peer around the corner.

"Good morning," he smiles at me, "yes, he is upstairs. How was your dance the other night?"

"It was alright"

"Not much of a dancer?" He chuckles as I make my way inside.

"No, not really."

I walk out of the kitchen and quietly make my way upstairs. As I continue to climb stair after stair, I can hear Logan's voice coming from down the hallway. From the top of the staircase, I can see his bedroom door cracked and the cord from the hallway phone stretched through the opening. I linger a few feet away and eavesdrop quietly.

"I miss you though; are you really joining? Did you tell dad?" Logan's voice seeps through the crack in the door. "If dad knows you are, maybe he will talk to you. He was once in—" Even though I can't hear the caller on the other end; I know it's George. And with that, I know he cut off Logan, which he tends to do whenever he gets defensive. Logan told me it's a habit of his. "Well, there is something else that I wanted to talk to you about. It's about Emma," he continues.

Suddenly my desire to eavesdrop doesn't feel right anymore. The change in conversation makes me want to back up slowly and make my way back down the stairs. But I feel paralyzed by the sound of my name. It roots me to where I am standing and I hang on to every word that follows behind it.

"She has changed, George. Do all girls go through this? Will she ever change back?" Logan goes silent as he now listens to his brother's response. I wonder what George is telling him. "Do I?" Logan's perplexing tone increases in volume—*does he what?* "I don't know how to answer that? Do I like her? Of course I like her, she is my best friend!"

Then, he goes silent once more. I shouldn't be listening to this. I shouldn't be eavesdropping on a conversation that was not intended for me to hear. My feet begin to glide backward down the hallway, producing not a single sound or creak in their wake. And as I reach the top of the stairs to turn around, I hear him speak again. But I am too embarrassed to let his response register in my mind, because his response wasn't intended for anyone's ears but George's.

Chapter Fourteen

"You were totally in your element at Jake's party after the dance," Jessica exclaims with a nudge on my shoulder. "I told you once you get a few beers in you, you would loosen up."

I catch a whiff of her flowery perfume as she rests her back against the neighboring locker. The cool mint of her chewing gum, tries its best to conceal the scent of what I presume to be of cigarettes, which faintly releases into the air after every few words.

"What do you mean I was in my element?" I shut my locker with a startling bang. Jessica's head perks up and she looks at me. *How could she not think that I wouldn't be upset?*

"Well, I definitely wasn't as drunk as you," she laughs my reaction off. "I did scurry off to be with Dan—if you know what I mean."

I head off down the hallway, hearing Jessica's heels clack after me. "Rae, wait up!" she calls, but I continue walking faster, until she reaches my side, pulling me to a stop. "Listen, you were laughing, dancing, and just having a good time," she says to me with a smile. "And," she leans in closer, "I think Jake likes you." This bit of information releases from her lips with the expectation that it has the power to mend and forgive. It does nothing of the sort. But I do find myself somewhat intrigued regardless.

"Who is Jake?" I ask. I don't remember anyone by the name of Jake at the party.

"Jake Robertson? Are you kidding, you don't know who he is?" She appears flabbergasted.

I shake my head.

"Jake is one of the most popular guys in this school. And he is pretty damn good looking too, if I say so myself; not to mention, he is Dan's best friend, so we can totally double date!"

The thought of another outing repulses me, which also reminds me of my parents' wishes to have me limit my interactions with her. To appease her, however, I nod just to shut her up. "I've got to go," I say, before making my way down the hallway and out of sight.

When lunchtime arrives, I find that I am sitting amongst some unhappy looking faces. Kevin is noticeably irritated at me and made a point to say that if I am "too cool" to hang out with them afterschool than I am "too cool" to sit with them at lunch.

"It's not like that," I say, surveying my lunch bag for a way to bury my head inside, "Jessica wasn't exactly being reasonable at the time. I told her I had plans with you guys."

"So why didn't you call?" Kevin crunches on a couple of potato chips. *What are they my parents now too?*

"I didn't have access to a phone," I reply.

"What, you don't have a cell phone?" Maggie perks up. Her face lingers into Henry's direction as though he may have the answer instead of me.

"No," I say.

"You're joking, right?" She continues to pry.

"No, I am not."

Apparently, the idea of me not having a cell phone causes the entire table to roar with an uncontrollable fit of laughter. They all pull out their phones and argue over who has the better one. I am happy that all seems to be forgiven, but when I look over at Henry, he gives me a melancholic frown and turns his attention over to his sandwich.

Afterschool, I make my way to the car, bewildered by the day's events. Who knew that having no friends made things complicated; yet, having them, still made things that way? I slump into the passenger seat, just as mom advices me that during the day, my guidance counselor called.

"I don't know if your father will be able to go, but I will definitely be able to make it though," she says, as my face turns white.

"I wonder what it's about." I just hope that it has nothing to do with the events of this past weekend. I shudder at the thought.

"Well, we will find out tomorrow."

The car turns away from school and I just stare blankly out the window. I watch the passing houses and trees, wondering why so much of my life feels like a gigantic mess. Then, my thoughts drift to Logan. Since our argument before the football game, I really haven't spoken to him. As soon as he would see me coming towards him, he would take off into the opposite direction and avoid me altogether. I have had enough of his attitude, really. His stubbornness and willingness to avoid me, instead of talking out what he is thinking or feeling, is starting to wear thin. How am I supposed to know what is going on with him, if he doesn't tell me? I am not a mind reader.

When we arrive home, I find him sitting on the tractor out in the middle of the pasture. It's not running, but he is just sitting there as though he is doing something productive, wearing his working jacket and a pair of ripped jeans all covered in grass and mud stains. Alluring at best, which strangely pulls me like a magnet into his direction; I find the familiarity of the farm, quite enticing. I stare down at my own clothes wishing for the same kinds of stains.

"Hey, you want to come down from there?" I call up to him.

He turns to his side and looks at me with disbelief in his eyes, "I am sorry, who are you?" He combs back a few of his golden strands away from his eyes.

"Funny," I say, "now will you come down so we can talk?"

"I can hear you perfectly fine from up here."

What I had initially hoped as being a civil conversation with multiple apologies on my end turns out to be the beginning of yet another argument with him. I kick at the loose grass underneath my shoes, while asking him for a third time to come down. It's only when I turn to walk back home, do I hear him climb down from the tractor.

"What do you want to talk about?" He calls out to me.

"I wanted to apologize for how I have been," I turn back around.

From where I am standing, I can see him perfectly. His vibrant blue eyes pierce through me and for the first time, I stare at my best friend with a sense of longing. I miss him. I miss everything. But how can I tell him that without it sounding all mushy? Instead, I run up to him and give him a hug. I smell the combination of smells that only Logan possesses and his hug strangely feels like home to me. It grounds me back to the reality that I have somehow escaped from. "I am sorry for being a buffoon lately," I say.

"I would have said horse's ass," he smiles.

* * * *

The meeting with my guidance counselor has arrived. The suspicion I had towards the initial invite swells within me. I am finding it hard to sit still, as mom and I wait outside her office. When her door finally opens, a woman with long curly hair and brown eyes walks out. For a second she doesn't make eye contact with us, but after she looks at me and then up at my mom, her eyes widen with what looks to me like utter disbelief.

"Charlotte?" My guidance counselor asks, walking closer to my mom.

"Yes?" My mom acknowledges.

"It's me Cassie Baker, oh well, now Cassie Griffin."

"Oh my, how are you? You look amazing," my mom exclaims, getting up from her seat and hugging my guidance counselor. I watch as they begin to talk amongst themselves filling in the gaps when they last saw each other in the matter of seconds.

"—Yes, my husband, Ted and I purchased a farm outside of Syracuse where we have been living and working for the past ten years. We absolutely love it."

"That sounds great. Well, I moved out here about six years ago when I was offered this position—still close to our hometown of Syracuse though," she smiles. "Well, anyways, the husband got a job offer in Dallas and I was supposed to move out there with him once we closed on the house, but he ended up in a fling with his secretary," she whispers to my mom. "So, I am here, but enough of me, let's step into my office," she ushers us inside.

I make my way behind my mother, who takes the first seat quite comfortably. I sashay by her and sit down. The lingering small talk between them dissipates with an expected release of a sigh on my part.

I have never been in Ms. Griffin's office before. She has a few pieces of artwork and pottery, but other than that, no personal photos or memorabilia. Her desk is neatly organized. Beside her computer, she has a penholder, stapler and a few piles of notebooks. She is plain, simple, and I quite like that about her. Her hair, her face, and even her clothes, suggests a rather casual and normal life. She doesn't appear as though longing for big cities or weekend shopping trips.

"Well," Ms. Griffin begins, interrupting my thoughts, "I called you both in here today to talk about Emma's grades and progress. First, I am quite pleased to announce that Emma has made high honor roll ever since her first marking period as a freshman. Were you aware of this?" she turns to my mom.

"Yes, her dad and I have been quite pleased with her progress so far."

"Well, it will definitely open up a lot of opportunities for college. But what I wanted to call you both into my office today was to discuss graduation. Have you considered graduating earlier, Emma?"

I turn to my mother. Why was this piece of information left out? I had no idea that it were even a possibility. By the look that appears on her face, however, I guess that she didn't either.

"Graduate early?" I repeat the surprising fact. The tension ceases from my back, as I sit more comfortably in my seat.

"Yes, you can graduate next year alongside the junior class instead of the year after, as long as you meet the credit requirements."

"Yes!" I say, unfortunately simultaneously with my mom who says that she would prefer discussing this option with my father first.

The meeting soon ends with Ms. Griffin and my mom catching up again. "You know, the holidays are just around the corner, why don't you come over to my place on Christmas Eve? We always throw a Christmas dinner with our neighbor and co-owner of the barn and his son. Sometimes family joins, but you know how that goes." They chuckle in unison.

"Sounds lovely," she hands my mom her card and tells her to call her with the details when the time gets closer.

* * * *

I **watch the** first snowflake fall from the sky from my bedroom window. I breathe onto the glass, drawing pictures of whatever comes to mind. Mom is downstairs having lunch with my guidance counselor, Ms. Griffin, apparently waiting until the holidays to get together became an impossible task. The two have been calling each other every other day since the meeting.

"Echo Romeo," Logan's voice comes through my walkie-talkie.

I get up from my window and make my way towards it. "Lima Mike?"

"Who is that in your kitchen?—Over."

"My guidance counselor—over."

"Oh," he pauses, "you want to come outside?"

I walk downstairs and head out the door just as I see Mr. Solway walking up the front porch steps. He is dressed in his town clothes, holding a carton of fresh eggs in his hands. When I open the door to let him inside, he asks me where my mother is.

"She is in the kitchen."

"I am going into town," he continues, as if I didn't notice his clothes, "but wanted to drop these off first before I go," He holds out the eggs to me.

"I can bring them into the kitchen for you, if you would like," I offer.

But as Mr. Solway is about to hand over the eggs to me, mom makes her way from the kitchen and takes them instead. "Where are you off to?" She asks.

"To town for some paint; I think it's about time I paint the barn doors before winter is officially here."

"Charlotte, what would you like in your coffee?" Ms. Griffin makes her way from the kitchen holding the coffee carafe in her hand.

"Oh, just little cream and sugar. Cassie," she calls her back, "this is my neighbor and also the co-owner of the farm," her voice trails off as she begins introducing Logan's dad to my counselor. I walk out of the house not interested in hearing anything more.

A small layer of frost greets my feet, but I wish that there were more. Logan is bending down trying to make a decent pile in his hand, "It's not enough for a snowball!" I call out to him.

Realizing that I am right, he wipes what he has in his hand off onto his pants and walks up to meet me. "You want to go down by the river?" He asks, putting his arm around me. "Thanks by the way."

"For what?" I ask.

"For not wearing that crap on your face," he messes up my hair.

"Well, don't get too excited, mom is probably going to make me wear some for the school dance in February."

"Dance?" His stride slows.

"Yea, it's the school's winter ball."

"Well, just don't get drunk like you did last time," he smiles.

We walk side by side through the brush, where we sit down by the river. Even though it's quite cold out, we take off our shoes and roll up our pants, in order to stick our feet into the water. Once my feet break the surface, a chill runs up through my leg piercing my skin from below. The water is freezing, much colder than what we had anticipated, which forces me to pull my feet back out and frantically pat them dry with my socks.

Logan spins around to do the same and just as he is about to unroll his pants, I notice the spot where he fell over the summer, it lingers like a stubborn scar.

"Does that still hurt?" I ask, pointing to the mark on his leg,

He looks down, "Not all the time, for the most part, it doesn't bother me.

"Should it still be there?" I stare down at it.

"I don't know; are you a doctor? Do you examine my legs or something?" He teases. "You can if you want to," he wiggles his leg at me.

I just slap it away.

* * * *

A few weeks roll by and everything feels like as it did before. Jessica came over once or twice to work on our school project, which we handed in shortly after, both receiving a 90% grade. One of the times that she came over, however, Logan was coming through the backdoor to give my mom a couple gallons of fresh milk not realizing that she was there. I watched as she batted her eyelashes at him with a smile, which instantaneously made his face redden to the shade of an apple. I cringed at the sight and almost wanted to yell at them both. But for what? Jessica has a boyfriend and Logan wouldn't know what to do with a girl like her anyways. He never showed any interest in girls the way that Jessica has interest in boys. I think I am safe; however, the fact that his face reddened over her, made me unfamiliarly jealous. I chugged the remainder of my juice and walked him out the door.

The unfamiliar twinge of jealousy pulls me away from Logan for a few days, just so that I can work the feeling out or at least wait until it passes. There is no way that I can tell him how his reaction to Jessica affected me, because I can barely understand it myself. But within a few days, I finally hear from him; although, I was not prepared for the reason why.

"ECHO ROMEO!" Logan's voice roars through my walkie-talkie.

"This is Echo Romeo," I say into the mouthpiece.

"Did you have something to do with this? Why didn't you tell me?"

"What?"

"My dad is taking your dumb teacher out to dinner tonight!"

"My teacher? Logan, what are you talking about?"

"That teacher-counselor of yours; he is taking her out to dinner!"

"What makes you think I have anything to do with that?" The information comes as a surprise to me too.

"Are you trying to replace my mom or something? Since when is it any of your business to butt in like that?"

"Logan, calm down, what are you talking about? How is that my fault?" Through this unexpected heated debate, I realize that I am pacing the room. The carpet threads bear the markings from my feet, but I don't slow down. If I keep up this pace, I may be coming through the ceiling below.

"My dad was perfectly happy with the way things were," I hear a catch in his throat release.

"I swear Logan; I had nothing to do with it." But all I hear in return is static.

Chapter Fifteen

One million snowflakes fall to the fields below, but not any of them are used for snowballs, igloos, or even for a sled ride. After being released from school for winter break, I am greeted again by another separation from Logan, but this time, I have nothing to do with why he is mad. But he won't listen. And it doesn't matter how many times I have knocked on his door, called him on our walkie-talkies, or approached him in the barn, he just won't listen. *Happy Holidays, to me…*

The farm pulling in barely any profit these past few months becomes news to me. Mom only shares this piece of information when I ask her about Christmas shopping. *It's going to be a tight Christmas,* she said to me, which means that our shopping day is not going to happen. It's understandable. I just feel bad that I have no means to get anyone anything.

At church service, Logan sits a few spaces down from me, seething. Again, I have nothing to do with why he is so angry, but he is too stubborn to listen. Why would he think that I would want to meddle in with his father's personal affairs? Why would he think that I would want to replace his mother? That is not my doing and the fact that he refuses to look into my direction makes me angrier than he is at me. If he wants to blame anyone, blame my mother. She is the one who decided to introduce them.

The church service is like any other that I have attended in the past. I sit there trying to find what page the hymns are on and then lip the words back to the choir as though no one can detect that I am lip-synching. Dad is wearing his Christmas sweater again and when he reaches to put his hymnbook back into the book slot, I see a small hole tearing through the arm of his shirt. He notices it too, because I watch his finger trace along the perforated seam. He smiles down to me, "Favorite shirt," he shrugs.

I sit back into the wooden pews, trying to meet Logan's gaze again. I am so uncomfortable and it feels like my tailbone wants to merge with my spine. My eyes then find Mr. Solway and mom's friend Cassie sitting next to each other on the other side of mom. Their behavior doesn't suggest anything that Logan seems to be so keen on blaming me for. Maybe he is reading too much into this.

When the service is over, I pull Logan off to the side by his jacket. It pulls against his loosened button, forcing him to look down to make sure it didn't pop off.

"Listen, you need to stop being so mad at me all the time!" I yell. A few patrons turn to me and frown at my behavior in a holy place. I roll my eyes and turn my attention back onto Logan. "I had nothing to do with it. Maybe they are just friends?"

Mr. Solway doesn't appear to be looking at mom's friend Cassie in any manner that I have seen boys look at girls. I am no expert in the subject, but I really don't think that Logan has anything to worry about. But he just pulls his jacket away from me and stomps out of the church.

Later that evening, Christmas dinner becomes as awkward for me as church service was. And not because we have a new guest, but because the atmosphere feels tense and the gravy boat looks like it would better placed in Logan's lap than on the table. Cassie throughout dinner talks about her job (things I probably shouldn't be hearing), because she goes into great detail about the trouble she has with some of my peers.

"I mean, these kids think that having an education is pointless. I don't know how many of them I try to counsel, but it gets me nowhere. *Who needs high school? Who needs college?*, they say to me. They have no idea just how big the real world is.

They will get chewed and spit back out without some degree behind them. Nowadays you can't get anywhere without a college degree," she points very authoritatively with her fork.

"We believe strongly in education," my mom chimes in.

Mr. Solway digs into his mashed potatoes nodding every few seconds. He smiles towards Cassie who smiles back; Logan turns to me and scowls. I don't know how many times I have tried to explain to him that this isn't my fault, but he just won't listen. But as I see the interaction between his dad and Cassie, I realize, that I am doomed.

* * * *

"I want you to meet Jake," Jessica says, slamming her back against my neighboring locker. The hallway begins to fill, as does the commotion, which surrounds us like a cocoon. She doesn't look at me when she talks, she is too busy looking at everyone else. I think she likes to see if people are looking at her. She is entirely too vain for me to handle sometimes.

"I don't know," I say.

"Oh, come on, I want you to come to junior prom with us instead of the winter ball. And if he is going to be your date, then you have to meet him—which is why I planned a double date on Friday," she smiles.

I throw my books into my locker and turn to face her. "What?" I am flabbergasted. Who does she think she is? I have no desire to date anyone and here she is forcing another thing on me. Unfortunately, I still don't have the courage to stand up to her, so it looks like I am being pulled again into something I don't want to do.

When Friday rears its ugly head, Mom will not leave my room. Better yet, she won't leave my sight. She dances around and grabs every item of clothing out of my closet, holding it up to me as though trying to find the perfect outfit for me to wear. I roll my eyes, because no matter what I say or do, she is relentless. I just let her whip me around the room like a life-sized Barbie doll, because I really have no choice in the matter.

When I got home from school earlier today, I cornered Logan in the barn and made him talk to me about Cassie. He finally mustered up and apologized for getting so angry with me, but I just told him just to forget about it. I didn't care anymore; I just wanted to be done fighting. He left me shortly after to tend to a few chores, while I headed back home to great ready for this stupid double date.

"They are here!" Mom screeches, just as she hears Jessica's car pulling into the driveway.

As we make out way down the stairs, I see dad lingering in the foyer, "I want to meet this boy," he says.

"Ok," I say, putting on my shoes.

I walk outside feeling the coldness burn against my cheeks. I knock on Jessica's window and let them know to come inside. And as I stand there in the cold, watching the three doors open, I am surprised to see who steps out from behind door number three. It's the guy with the pointy nose and oddly shaped ears from my study hall last year. My heart drops to the pit of my stomach, *oh, no.*

As I lead them up the front porch steps, I hear all three of them gripe about the smell.

"She says you'll get used to it, but I have been here several times, and it still stinks to me," Jessica announces, just as my dad opens up the front door.

I don't know whether I should be more nervous about the lecture my dad is above to give, how mom's eyes won't stop twinkling away, or the fact that one of the first people who were ever mean to me at school, is my date. Does he not remember me? Then again, I really don't look like the same girl, but I still remember how rude he was. Makeup doesn't aide in forgetting, I'm afraid,

The date is the 7:00 pm showing of some action-based movie, which isn't exactly an ideal place to get to know someone. Jessica spends most of the movie making out with Dan, while I just watch the movie next to Jake. His hand is pretty much stuck in the popcorn bowl the entire time, which doesn't leave me much room if I wanted some. Thankfully, I don't.

"Awkward, eh?" he whispers over to me.

I jump slightly at the unexpected sound of his voice, "yeah, awkward." As we, both look towards Jessica and Dan.

"I have never seen you around before, have we never met?" He takes a handful of popcorn into his mouth.

"I am not sure," I lie. A part of me wants to remind him of him and Morgan's comments last year, but I hold back.

"Thanks for deciding to be my date to the junior prom," he says, sliding his hand back into the bowl of popcorn. "My ex-girlfriend, Morgan, who graduated last year, refused to come to a high school dance. We broke up shortly after she went away to college."

"Sorry to hear that." What I really wanted to say was, *sorry you dated such a bitch.*

For the rest of the movie, Jake and I talk. My opinion of him changes which is not something I would have ever expected. And when Jessica pulls back into my driveway to drop me off home after the movie, he actually gets out of the car and walks me to my door.

"I had a great time," he says. "You're a cool girl, Emma."

Under the gleam of the porch light, I watch the way his smile releases into a pucker.

"I had a good time too," I say. And before I know it, his face moves in closer to mine as he presses his lips against my own. My lips, timid and scared, don't return the same pucker onto his.

"See you around," he says, making his way down the steps with a smile upon his face.

Paralyzed by what just happened my eyes follow him as he walks back to the car. I see Jessica's face through the windshield, grinning from ear to ear. Her reaction is rather annoying, so I turn my attention towards the direction of Logan's front lawn instead. My eyes take a few minutes to focus through the darkness and when they do, I see Logan standing there, holding onto his telescope just before I watch it slowly fall to the ground.

"What was that about?" Logan reveals himself into the light, just as Jessica pulls out and drives away.

It takes a second or two for me to respond, for I am still coming down from an unexpected high, a confusing unexpected high at that. "What was what about?" I blush red. Thankfully, the darkness is concealing my face quite nicely.

"You just let him kiss you?" he sounds repulsed.

"Yeah, isn't that what people do after dates? They kiss, right?" I am having a hard time sounding okay with Jake's kiss, because deep down inside, I am repulsed by it too. *Or am I?*

He shakes his head in utter disbelief. The dirt beneath his shoes kicks up into the air, creating a small short-lived fog that barricades him from coming any closer.

"I don't know you anymore," he says to me.

"It's not like it meant anything," I exclaim, heading towards him until we are face to face. "So what is your problem, huh?" My blushful red coloring dissipates only to be replaced by an angered red instead. "I thought we weren't fighting anymore? What is going on with you?"

"Nothing is going on with me," he retorts, "you have changed Emma Rae. You have become so unrecognizable. I don't even know who you are anymore."

"You are making no sense!"

"You don't have time for me anymore. You pay more attention to people that don't know you like I know you or even care for you," he pauses, "like I care for you."

Feeling a mixture of emotions that I am unable to identify I pull his arm towards me as he begins to walk away. "What are you not telling me? If you need to tell me something, then tell me. But don't go acting mad when I am doing something you don't like when you don't tell me anything! How am I supposed to know what is going on in that crazy little head of yours? So, if you have something to say—then say it!"

He pulls his arm back and my hand retracts to my side.

We look at each other through the darkness. Our eyes penetrate deep holes that we cannot see but only feel. "Say it," I yell.

"I have nothing to say to you," he turns, walking away from me.

"Don't be a coward Logan Solway! Tell me, do you like me?" The question blurts from behind my lips, which are still moist from my date's kiss. The words taste as unfamiliar as a curse word. "Do you like me?" I whisper in repetition.

"I think we both know the answer to that," he says, before walking away for good.

I charge into the house where mom is standing on the front porch pretending to be cleaning, when I know perfectly

Chapter Sixteen

The booming music, reminisces the initial feeling I had at the homecoming dance. Girls carry small bottles of liquor in their garters and everyone dances around in small-congregated groups with no particular rhythm in mind. The only plus side, is that instead of being jam-packed into the school's gymnasium, we are at one of the local hotels, jam-packed into a room normally used for wedding receptions and other special events.

Balloons cascade down from the drop ceiling; tables are layered with white tablecloths and pretend jewels around tea light candles; and the dim lighting throughout the room suggests that the event coordinator is trying to create some sort of intimate setting. There are also pretend ice sculptures scattered around the room. And decorated upon the buffet and drink tables, are blankets of fluffy white cotton to suggest the idea of snow, hence the theme of "Winter Wonderland."

Rather than spending time with Jake, however, I feel more content with sitting at one of the tables, flicking away at the jewels. When that gets boring, I run my finger through the small candle flame, which feels more exciting than having to get up and dance. I guess I forgot to mention to him that I have the same amount of rhythm as a cow and that it's best if he dances with someone else. Apparently, my disconnect doesn't dissuade him though, because just as I am about to flick another jewel off the table, he comes over and sits down beside me.

"Why are you not dancing?" he asks, taking a sip of punch.

"I am not much of a dancer," I say, "Sorry, should have told you that."

"What, you are not good at it or you just don't want to?"

"Both, I guess."

"Come on," he holds his hand out for me to take, "if you start to dance horribly, I will dance horribly along with you," he smiles.

Ignoring the glower on my face and the fact that I didn't reach for his hand, he still manages to get me up from the table, and lead me out onto the dance floor. I feel completely out of place. I stand there swaying from side to side unsure of what to do. I look at some of the girls around me in order to replicate their movements, but it's so hard to focus on them and on Jake at the same time. Not to mention, I can barely walk in these in high-heeled shoes, but he doesn't seem to care. He smiles and dances awkwardly along with me. We are like two cows on the dance floor.

The evening finally ends a few hours later with the DJ announcing the final song and when it's over, we all head out of the hotel and locate our limo. After we all pile in, Jessica gives the driver the address to bring us to. I guess, I should have seen it coming—why wouldn't she want to go to a party.

"I really don't think I should go," I whisper over to her. I can almost see my parents' disappointed faces staring back at me.

"Oh, come on, so you had a lot to drink the last time, who cares."

"Who cares? My parents will care. They grounded me for a week because of it. And the only reason why they allow me to hang out with you now is because I promised I would never get into the same situation again." My voice gets loud.

"Listen, this party will not be like it was the last time, okay? It is just a chilled get-together with a small group of people, nothing to worry about," she smiles. *Gosh, how I don't trust her smiles.*

The door of the limo slams shut and so does the chance for me to escape. I sit down into my seat beside Jake who puts his arm around me, not noticing my angered disposition. I want to remove his hand, but I just end up leaving it there. I am all too focused on where the limo driver is taking us to care about anything else. I stare out of the window, but I all I see is my frustrated reflection staring back at me. Only when the limo slows and approaches an unfamiliar house, does my frustrated face turn infuriated. This is no small get-together. The house is filled to the rim with people.

Dragged along inside, it takes Jessica and Dan no time at all to disappear, leaving me alone in a crowded place, feeling quite alone. Well, there is Jake, but it's not like I know him too well.

"You want a beer?" He asks.

"No, thank you."

"Don't you drink?"

"Kicked the habit," I half-smile.

Looking at me as though I am joking, he pours me a cup from the keg, "here."

"No, I don't want any," I refuse to take the cup. "I should probably call for a ride," I say, but the music turns up louder, preventing Jake from being able to hear me.

He puts his hand to his ear, "What did you say?"

I repeat myself.

"Why don't we go somewhere quieter," he says.

Not entirely certain on what he said, he takes my hand and leads me up the stairs, and down the hallway into one of the empty bedrooms. The bedroom darkened and fairly large, illuminates slightly by the glow from Jakes' cell phone. Other than that, I can barely make out where anything is inside.

"Much better," I hear him say as he shuts the door behind us.

"I should probably call for a ride."

"Already? Don't you want to stay and have fun for awhile?"

I sit down at the edge of the bed; I feel around the nightstand and turn on a small lamp, revealing a phone directly beside it. "No, I should probably head home, I am kind of tired."

Jake takes a large sip of his beer and sits down beside me. His body inches closer to mine, until I feel his shoulder rub up against my own, "I had a good time with you tonight," his alcohol-laced breath advises.

I nod while removing my nose from the situation. He takes another sip of his beer before setting it down on the bedside table. I stare down at the phone, feeling my body inch towards it, but as I move, so does Jake. I turn to see his face looking at me. He smiles awkwardly as his eyes squint towards me.

"I should probably call home," I reach for the phone.

"How about you hang out with me for a little bit and then after, you can call for a ride. I promise you will not have to drink if you don't want to."

I contemplate the offer and ask him what he has in mind. He reaches over me and grabs a remote control from the bedside table, turning the TV in front of us on. *Watching TV?* My mind shrugs off the idea to call home, if all we are going to do is watch television then I can stay for a little while longer, no big deal.

"How about we get comfortable? He slides his shoes off and climbs onto the bed where he rests his back against the pillows. He taps his hand down beside him, signaling for me to come do the same. Sliding of my shoes, feeling the relief in my toes for having been squished together all night, I climb over and sit down beside him. A cloudy scent of alcohol hits my nose quite aggressively.

The TV is playing the infomercial channel, not my idea of a good time. "Is this what we are watching?" I ask.

"You don't want to watch television do you?" His breath releases tiny daggers, turning my nose away again. *Was this how I smelled after the homecoming dance?*

"Well, you turned it on; I thought we were."

Realizing that Jake request for me to stay doesn't seem as entertaining as I thought, I turn back towards the phone, wondering if I should just make the call now. "How about you turn the channel?" I ask, just before he reaches over and pulls me closer to him.

Startled and unsure of what he is doing, my body paralyzes itself under the confusion of the situation. I reach up to try and move away from his embrace, but he ends up climbing over me, forcing his tongue into my mouth.

My hands push against his chest, trying to get him to stop. His hand runs along the length of my dress, where it eventually stops as it slides underneath the opening. I feel his clammy hands against my chest and I yell again for him to stop.

"Come on, everyone gets laid at prom," he breaths onto me. *I want to barf.*

I push his hand away with my elbow and turn the opposite way. Thinking that he finally gets the hint, I find that his other hand, the one I wasn't watching, is now finding its way up the opposite end of my dress. I try to push that hand away too, but my strength is no match to his. And just as I feel that he is about to reach his destination, something within me snaps and I throw him off of me.

"Knock it off!" I yell.

"What is your problem?" He yells back.

"If I tell you to stop, you stop!"

"What are you a tease?" He approaches me, trying to shove his tongue down my throat again.

I push him away and reach for the phone, which he instantaneously hits out of my hand. "You're a bitch," he says.

I sit down on the bed mortified. I want to go home, but my only chance to call for help is sitting on the floor beside his feet. Angered, he kicks the phone a few feet into the air and leaves the room. When he is gone, I grab the phone and call the only person I need right now—Logan.

I dial the number for Logan's house, praying that Mr. Solway doesn't answer. The last thing I need right now is for my parents to find out about this.

"Hello?" Logan answers. I breathe out a sigh of relief.

"Logan, it's me. I need your help," the tears start streaming down my face.

"What's wrong?" He yells panic-stricken through the phone.

As best as I can, I try to explain to him what happened, but I am still trying to make sense of it myself. "Please come get me," I beg.

"Shit, Emma, I don't have my license."

"Then go get my parents," I respond reluctantly, giving him the address that Jessica announced to the limo driver a little while ago. Trying not to hyperventilate from my intense crying, I watch the door with fearful eyes, hoping that Jake doesn't find his way back inside.

"I will figure something out," Logan explains. "Go outside and wait."

Setting the phone back down on the receiver, I slowly put back on my shoes, keeping my eyes glued to the door the entire time. Why would someone try to do what he did? I feel violated, scared and alone. I just hope someone gets here soon. At this point, I don't care who.

I walk out of the bedroom, unaware that the upstairs hallway is now flooding with people. I weave in and out of it as best as I can, keeping my eyes peeled for Jake in the process. But just as my high heeled shoes descend the first step, a hand appears on my shoulder, turning me around. It's Jessica, looking like she did the morning after the first party she took me too.

"Where are you going?" She asks with the same untrusting smile.

"Home," I remove my shoulder from her grasp.

"Did you and Jake not hit it off?"

My eyes narrow, and the fury within me boils right out of my tightened lips. I ascend the one stair until we are face to face. "Did we hit it off?" I yell, feeling the tears swell up within my eyes again.

Jessica backs up noticing my reaction as the smile wipes clean off her face. "What happened? Emma, are you okay?" The tears seem to temporary sober her up, because it takes no explanation on my part for her to put two and two together. "I am going to kill him!" She storms off, but I don't wait. I simply pull myself together and head outside.

The cold night cradles me gently as I sit on the front curb. I stare up at the stars, trying to find Logan's mom amongst all the others, but the tears are making it quite impossible. "Logan, I need you," I continue to cry.

Just then, a loud roar hits my ears, blocking out the sound of the music emanating from the house behind me. I look up and see Mr. Solway's tractor rounding the street corner, with none other than Logan behind the wheel.

I stand up just as he parks it in front of me. He climbs down and wraps his arm around me. I see in the back, he brought his outdoor blanket. "Where is this guy?" He asks. I feel the heat from the engine penetrate my skin.

"Somewhere inside," I wipe at my tears.

"Get on the tractor and keep yourself warm; I will be right back." Logan storms off and heads into the house. I try calling him back, but he doesn't listen. He is stubborn no matter the situation.

Staring at the tractor and back at the house, I realize, that I can't leave Logan in there all by himself. I tear off my shoes; throw them into the back where the blanket is, and take off into the house after him. He can get mad at me all he wants. I refuse to sit back not knowing what he is about to get himself into.

I pull open the door and see a crowd of people in the living room. I squeeze through several people, until I come to find Logan and Jake standing directly in the middle. *Are they about to fight?*

"Listen to me, if you ever touch Emma or even look at her again, I will kill you," Logan yells. The look on his face scares me. I have never seen him so mad.

"Dude, you need to relax, okay? Don't worry I won't touch her, she's nothing but a prude anyways."

Logan raises his fists and Jake cocks his head towards him. "What are you going to do?" Jake taunts him, pointing at his own cheek. "You want to punch me? I dare you."

Thinking that Logan is not stupid enough to fall for it, his fist glides towards Jake's face, smashing into his cheek. Startled by his own strength, Logan looks at his fist, unaware that Jake is about ready to return the gesture, which immediately causes Logan to go crashing to the ground.

"Logan!" I scream, falling to my knees beside him. Blood is pouring out of his nose. "Someone go get me a towel!"

From outside of the crowd, Jessica storms through the circle. I bunch up my dress and hold it carefully to Logan's nose until someone eventually hands me the towel I requested. From the corner of my eye, however, I see Jessica, marching over to Jake. In one quick movement, she slaps him across the face.

"That's for being a jerk to Emma. And this is for punching her friend in the face," she slaps him again.

I hold the towel to Logan's nose, while helping him get to his feet. "Let's go," I whisper to him.

When we finally leave that night, all I remember seeing is a familiar star shining a little brighter than all the other ones…I think it's safe to say that someone's mom was awfully proud of her son tonight.

* * * *

The summer sun shines through my window, caressing my face with a welcoming hello. It is the last day of school and I couldn't be happier. So much has happened in such a short period of time that I am finding it hard to locate the parts of myself, which somehow got lost along the way. The friendship I had with Jessica, only recently mended when she apologized for everything. She even called me Emma, which made me think she was trying to be sincere. But there seems to be a lot of damage there, so I choose to keep my distance.

As for Henry, Kevin, and the rest of my lunchtime group, I found my loyalty resting with them much more, especially after I explained what happened to them. A part of me felt embarrassed, but the other part felt that if they were my true friends, they would be there for me. And they were. I even went to Kevin's *Harry Potter* marathon, which was spread out over three weekends. I think all is forgiven between us now.

Jake on the other hand, avoids me altogether. Rumors spread throughout the school regarding what happened at prom. Some say I let him go all the way. Others have said that I didn't. But I learned the greatest lesson here, people are going to say and do whatever they want and you have to know that you have no control over them. The only person you have control over is yourself. As long as you know the truth, that is all that matters. And the people that truly love you will be there for you regardless. Just like Logan was.

And from that day forward, I tossed all my makeup in the trash. I boxed up all of Jessica's donated clothes and donated them to the church. In the matter of a day, I returned back to my normal self. *Gosh, I missed her.* There was nothing wrong with her. And as Logan said, *the original is so much better.* I couldn't agree with him more.

Besides Logan, however, no one else back home knows about what happened. It became a secret between us, bringing us even closer. I finally have my friend back and once again, all is right with the world.

Chapter Seventeen

Turning sixteen is a true celebration. Dad finally gives me permission to drive the tractor today and I immediately run out of the house to grab Logan to begin teaching me. Turning the engine on, I slam on the gas and accidentally chase down a few cows halfway through the pasture.

"Slow down!" Logan yells, holding on for dear life.

"Where the hell is the break?" I scream.

I turn the steering wheel and we go charging back to where we came from. But I am not slowing down. *Why aren't we slowing down!*

"Slow down!" Logan wails. His hat flies off as we go heading straight towards the barn. Suddenly he climbs over me and practically sits on my lap to prevent a collision. When the tractor comes to a screeching stop, he turns his head and breathes a sigh of relief. "Do you have a death wish on your birthday or something?

"I guess it's safe to say I need more practice."

"You think?" He smirks.

After lunch with my parents, I run across the front lawn and then into Logan's house, just as Mr. Solway is making his way outside. "Happy Birthday, young lady," he says, tipping his hat to me.

I laugh, "Why are you doing that?"

"It's a sign of respect. Logan told me you like things like that," he smiles, walking out the door.

I make my way inside looking around for Logan, hearing his voice; I climb up the stairs to see that he is on the phone again. I hate when this happens. I never know if whether I should turn around or stay put.

"Yea, they are seeing a lot of each other lately. I was against it at first, but he seems really happy." Logan refers to his dad's relationship with Cassie. The two have been spending a lot of time together and from what I overheard from mom and dad, things between them might be getting serious.

"Yeah, well that's not the only reason why I called you," Logan breathes through the phone. I decide to make my way into his bedroom. He sees me and motions for me to sit down. I guess he doesn't care that I am here.

"Grandpa Charlie is not doing well at all. Grandma Jane had to put him a home or something. I guess, she is unable to take care of him all by herself," he pauses for a moment. "Can you just come and visit?"

I sit upon Logan's bed feeling worried at the response he is about to be given.

"I don't understand?" Logan sighs. "You never visit— you never come home—I never get to see you—forget about dad, he is too preoccupied with Cassie now."

Logan looks behind him and meets my gaze. My eyes hold his for a moment as though trying to hug him. I watch as the phone slides off his ear, while George's voice faintly comes through from the other end. Logan shakes his head before turning away, just as he carries the phone out into the hallway.

I wait apprehensively upon his bed, sitting upon my hands. I hear the phone click back onto the receiver followed by the footsteps from Logan reentering his bedroom. He tries not to make eye contact with me, but I already see what he is trying to hide. He wants to cry. I nod as if to say, *go ahead,* but instead, he does something that completely surprises me.

He walks across his bedroom and stands before me, his eyes fall to my sneakers shuffling across his carpeted floor. My shuffling slows until It stops altogether as I am trying to focus on what he is about to do. A smile sweeps across his face and I catch his eyes once more, leaving me vulnerable to the fact that his foot has risen in the air and is now beginning it's journey to my shoe.

"Chase me Emma Rae!" He calls out, booking it out of his room.

"Wait, you're supposed to chase me!" I yell back.

As we race down the stairs, with Logan only a few paces ahead of me, I am about to reach for his shirt, when all of a sudden, he tumbles and falls down the remaining stairs, hitting the landing with a thump.

"Logan!" I yell, "Are you okay?" I rush to his side as he holds onto his leg. "Are you bleeding?" I remove his hands from his leg and turn him gently over. As his luck would have it, he fell again on the same leg. "You're so clumsy," I tease. "Come on, stand up."

I reach for his hand to pull him onto his feet, but just as I let him go so that he can find his balance, his leg gives out and his body goes crashing upon the landing.

"Go get my dad," he says. "I think something's broken."

* * * *

I hate hospitals. I hate them because they smell horrible and the idea of sick people, scare me. I don't like it. I don't like being the patient and I don't like sitting in the lobby waiting on someone else to be the patient either. And there is no amount of visits to the vending machine to make me feel better about the situation. I just sit next to Mr. Solway asking for the time every few minutes to keep my mind off things—things about Logan and things about sick people. I don't like the idea of sick people.

About an hour or so ago, Logan was finally taken back into a room, where a doctor suggested they run some tests. The good news is, is that nothing is broken, which means that Logan will be back to normal in no time at all. But I still don't understand what else they are looking for. I am no doctor, so I try not to think about it too much.

The constant smell of disinfectant nauseates me. It hits my nose every few seconds until it becomes a permanent resident. And not even the occasional bout of fresh air from the outside can diminish it. I turn to face Mr. Solway, wondering if he too is sharing similar effects, but just as soon as I am about to ask, the nurse comes out and tells us that we can go into Logan's room to see him.

I practically run down the corridor until Mr. Solway orders me to slow down. And when I finally make it to Logan's room and open the door, I see him propped up on the bed, ready to go home.

"The doctor will be in, in a few minutes," the nurse advises, before shutting the door behind her.

I round the hospital bed and sit down beside Logan. "How are you feeling," I brush a piece of his hair away from his face.

"Much better, they gave me some pain medicine and I am able to walk much better."

"That's good. See, nothing to worry about," I smile reassuringly.

Mr. Solway sits in the corner chair peeking out of the room's window every few seconds. The nervous bouncing of his leg is setting my nerves on fire again and I am unsure if whether I should be nervous too, but what for? Logan seems perfectly fine.

"Hi, I am Dr. Parker," a tall grey haired man walks into the room. "You must be Logan," he reaches out to shake his hand. "Well, like the nurse advised earlier, there are no broken bones, but a few things came up during your examination that we want to have tested—"

"Like what?" Mr. Solway cuts him off.

"We are going to run a pathology report on the area around his knee. Logan said that the bump has been there for quite some time now and we just want to test the area to make sure that everything is fine."

"You mean like cancer?" Mr. Solway runs his hand along his beard.

Dr. Parker sighs, apparently trying not to utilize the term, because immediately Logan sits up in bed further. "You think I might have cancer?" he looks at me, and then back at the doctor. "My mom died of cancer." He whimpers.

Mr. Solway stands up and walks beside Logan. "Everything will be alright son, I am sure this is normal procedure, right?" He looks at the doctor for not only reassurance for Logan, but reassurance for himself.

"Yes," Dr. Parker responds, "I will have my office call you as soon as the results are in."

When the doctor leaves the room, Mr. Solway looks down at Logan. "Just a routine procedure," he says.

But something tells me that Logan doesn't believe him, because instinctively, he reaches for my hand and doesn't let go.

Part Three

"I walked over to the hill where we used to go and sled. There were a lot of little kids there. I watched them flying. Doing jumps and having races. And I thought that all those little kids are going to grow up someday. And all of those little kids are going to do the things that we do. And they will all kiss someone someday. But for now, sledding is enough. I think it would be great if sledding were always enough, but it isn't."

-Stephen Chbosky, *The Perks of Being a Wallflower*

Chapter Eighteen

The cloudy skies roll in, as does the rain. It arrives with a gentle pitter-patter against the window glass. I press my face up against it watching and waiting as the fog from my breath floods the surface, which my finger quickly wipes away. A few times, I catch myself drawing pictures to pass the time, but there are only so many renditions of smiley faces, hearts, and stars, that one can draw, before getting bored. And I am already bored. Then with the roaring of thunder, the rain begins to pour violently into waterfall-like streams, making everything beyond the glass blurry. And the only thing that I can see, is my anxious reflection staring back at me—still watching, still waiting.

Since waking up this morning, I knew things were about to change… again. This time, it has nothing to do with school or friends. In fact, it directly affects the farm and everyone around it. But there is nothing that I can do to stop it. Not even Logan. He doesn't want her here as much as I don't; therefore, we will have to try and make the best of the situation.

You see, it all started, just a few days ago, when Logan and I were out in the pasture. He was helping me get the hang of driving the tractor again.

"You almost got it," He said to me. "You gotta press the clutch pedal down to the floor."

"With what foot?" I shrieked. My feet began to sway back and forth nervously. Everything my dad taught me instantaneously escaped my mind.

"Your left," he pointed.

I did as he said, but other than that, I had no idea what to do.

"Engage the brake pedal with your right and then push the throttle forward," I watched him turn the key to preheat the cylinders, before turning the key again to start the engine.

The engine roared and I took off. I only got a few feet, before I noticed Mr. Solway coming out of the back door of his house, waving for Logan to come inside. Something seemed off in the way that he ushered Logan towards him. He didn't offer a wave or smile; but then again, I was too busy paying attention to the tractor than anything else.

"I wonder what he wants," Logan looked at me, before shutting the engine off and climbing down. "You're definitely making progress though," he smiled.

"Well, I need to be able to drive this thing before my dad will let me drive the car. He finally came to his senses on me needing the practice." I tightened the band around my ponytail.

"The rate you are going, I will have my license before you do—and I am a year younger!" He ran his fingers through his hair like a comb.

I, however, remained seated upon the tractor, watching Logan as he ran off into the distance. In a few weeks, the doctors want to remove the bump on his leg, saying that the results came back 'inconclusive', whatever that means. Therefore, they believe that it's best to just remove it instead of retesting the area. Again, I am no doctor. Logan, however, hasn't said too much about it. I think it's because he is a little scared. And I don't talk about it either, because, you see, I am a little scared too.

But just as I was about to climb down, I noticed the back door to Logan's house open again. It swung like a pendulum until it caught on the hinge. Logan came out, but he just stood there, looking down at his feet. My pace slowed, waiting for him to meet my gaze; but it took him a good couple of minutes before he even looked up at me.

When he did, I noticed that his eyes were red and pooling with tears, which eventually cascaded down onto his cheeks. He didn't stop it nor did he care that I was witnessing him cry.

"Grandpa Charlie died," he cried out to me. And all I could do was cry with him.

As for the funeral, it was horrible; we all drove about two hours away to where Mr. Solway's parents lived for the ceremony. Logan was a mess. He cried the entire way there. Several times, I reached for his hand, but it only ended up hanging loosely in my own. I didn't mind, because I knew he was hurting. I decided just to 'be there' for him. I knew that he would tell me if he needed me for anything, so I remained at the ready.

Ms. Griffin, or Cassie, came too. She sat beside me the entire time throughout the services, trying to talk about anything else but Grandpa Charlie. She talked mostly to me about graduating early this year, thanks to her finally convincing my parents. She even discussed some other random things about school and extracurricular activities she felt like I would benefit from. Other than that, I remained silent. It wasn't until twenty minutes into the ceremony that my lips parted with a breath of shock. There walking down the aisle was George. George, the elusive older brother who ran away, finally had returned home.

The gasp heard from pretty much everyone in attendance became much louder than the previous sobs. His entrance although warranted, was not expected. He walked in with his military uniform crisp and pressed. His stride, although confident, displayed a heavy sense of uncertainty whenever his boots hit the ground. My eyes lingered in his direction, admiring some of the similarities between him and Logan. It was weird for me to see him outside of a photograph, because on some level, he never seemed real to me. George was no longer the selfish little boy I had pictured in my mind for so many years. He grew up.

When he made it down the center aisle, he approached no one but Mr. Solway. Initially, they both shook hands, but then I watched their handshake turn into a hug. I really thought I was dreaming. Logan probably thought the same thing too, until he felt his brother's arms around him as well. And even though I knew he was sad at that very moment, his heart couldn't deny how happy he suddenly became as well.

George's visit didn't last long, considering he was scheduled to ship out in a few weeks and needed to be back for training. I decided to give Logan some space while his brother visited and I was surprised to see Mr. Solway's excited reaction to see his son. What I didn't expect was walking in on Grandma Jane discussing the story behind George's absence to Cassie.

"How old is George?" Cassie asked, while Grandma Jane was busying herself around the kitchen. I slunk by the stairwell extending my ear as far as I could to eavesdrop.

"There is about a seven year age difference between the two boys," Grandma Jane replied. I hear the teakettle scrape across the stove. I am familiar with the sound because of Mr. Solway.

"So what happened, if you don't mind me asking?"

"Well, when their mother, Abigail, initially got sick, they didn't think they could have anymore children after George. Logan was a surprise you see, a miracle as she called him. She found out she was pregnant during remission and everyone was so excited, but shortly after he was born, she got sick again and passed away a few years later." Grandma Jane said over her tea.

"How awful, that must have been so tough on those kids and of course—"

"Of course it was hard. But George started exhibited major behavioral problems and fought with his father a lot. He became defiant and one day decided to go move out to Denver and live with Abigail's parents."

At that point, I inched my way closer to the threshold and peered into the room. Thankfully, my position didn't give me away and I was able to watch them more closely. Grandma Jane appeared calm and rested, especially considering that she had just lost her husband.

"And George never came back?" Cassie's eyes widened. I was sure she thought the situation was just as bizarre as everyone else I know does.

"His father tried to get him to come back, but it wasn't until George was about fifteen that he was actually ready to come back, I believe. Those two have been bumping heads ever since and neither one of those stubborn boys wanted to apologize."

It was strange to hear Grandma Jane talking about George in such a causal manner, maybe because Logan and I always tiptoed around the subject. Either way, I didn't tell Logan what I overheard. It didn't matter, his brother was home and the past didn't seem to matter much anymore.

As of right now, however, I am still waiting for Logan to come home. He and his dad are driving back home with Grandma Jane. From what Logan told me on the phone last night, Grandma Jane is now going to come live with them. He didn't seem too happy about it and frankly, neither did I. I just hope that she doesn't get on me about hanging around the farm like she used to; otherwise, she and I will be bumping heads. I was lucky enough to have escaped her attention throughout most of the funeral services; but here on the farm, I don't think I will be that lucky.

An hour later, I hear a car door shut and I know that they are back. The rain is starting to die down, so I run down the stairs, throw on some shoes, and head outside to meet Logan in the yard. The damp and soggy grass mashes against the threads in my shoes, causing me almost to slip a few times, but I keep running towards him regardless.

Mr. Solway is leading Grandma Jane inside, while Logan grabs her suitcases from the trunk as soon as I approach. It scrapes across the opening of the trunk until he sets it down upon the puddle-filled driveway.

"Welcome back," I say, catching my balance on the side of the car.

"Thanks," he smiles, as his cheek crater fills with a few droplets of rain.

I help him grab the last suitcase and follow him inside. Grandma Jane is sitting at the kitchen table, while Mr. Solway is making a pot of tea.

"Why don't you two bring Grandma's suitcases up the stairs and put them in the spare bedroom," Mr. Solway says, reaching in the cupboard for his box of tea.

"Well, hello there Ms. Jensen," Grandma Jane peers over at me, "And how are we this evening?"

"Fine," I say. My feet rock back and forth unsure of where her introduction is heading, knowing her, nowhere good. I hate the way she peers at me. Those judgmental beady little eyes of hers feel like tiny bullets firing away at me.

"Logan here says that you are attending a nearby high school. It's nice to see that you are not still running around the farm like a hooligan anymore."

"A hooligan?" I snap; although, I have a feeling that my glare is not as powerful as hers is on me.

"I think what she means to say is 'buffoon,'" Logan smiles, before yanking me out of the room.

* * * *

The room is decorated with football memorabilia and all Dad can do is float around the office pointing and smiling. Trophies, pictures, ribbons and even a large banner drapes across a wooden bookshelf. It is aged and stained, yet celebrated as the key component of what looks to be an evocative shrine.

"This is me!" Dad yells over to me, "I was about your age when this was taken. Gosh, there are so many memories on this shelf." A brightening effect takes over his complexion as he smiles from one object to another. He is like a kid in a candy store or better yet, like mom in any store.

I smile back at him, because he is having a hard time controlling his excitement and when the Principal, Mr. Harper, enters the room, they both charge at each other as though they are back out on the field. "Ted Jensen! It's so good to see you!" Mr. Harper exclaims, rounding his desk. "Emma here tells me that you work on a farm now, is that true?" He plops down into his desk chair, scratching at his balding head.

The other day, I was called into his office, to discuss not me or my education, but to discuss my father. Apparently, I needed to debrief Mr. Harper on my father's life before this meeting. A little, "catch up" before the "catch up".

"Guilty as charged. I used to work for Holmes Insurance out of New York City, but I gave that all up and moved back home," dad smiles down at me.

"Well, I am glad everything is going well."

Why I am here right now, I do not know. This meeting seems to be nothing more than a chance for dad to share his football memories with someone who was actually there. The entire course of the conversation is an uncomfortable stroll down memory lane, but I am the only one being dragged down it. And after about thirty minutes of listening to nothing pertaining to my education, I excuse myself and go back to class. I doubt either one of them noticed. *Why the heck was I even asked to come?*

"Hey Emma," Henry speeds up alongside me in the hallway. I wonder where he is headed during the middle of class.

"Hey Henry," I say.

"Good summer?"

"Yeah, how about you?"

"It was good. I went away to camp for most of it. I volunteer as a camp counselor up in the Adirondacks during the summer; I love it," he pauses. "It's been like a good few weeks into school and I feel like I haven't seen you at all. I hear you are graduating early?"

"Yeah, I am."

"Well, hey, listen, Friday night, Kevin is having people over and we all wanted to know if you would like to come."

I turn to him, "Sure, what's the marathon this time?"

"No marathon, just our annual anti-football game. You missed it last year, but we usually just make fun of the sport and have a good time."

"Sounds like fun; I will be there."

We part ways and I head off towards my Science class. The one class I dread going to, not because I hate the subject, but because Jessica is there and she and I hardly ever speak anymore, which makes me rethink leaving Mr. Harper's office a hasty decision on my part. In class, I have been keeping to myself mostly. I am perfectly aware that she had nothing to do with what Jake did to me last year; but on the other hand, she wasn't exactly a good friend to me either.

When class ends, I stay back and talk to Mr. Harris about tomorrow's test. He gives me a few pointers and tells me what key terms to memorize. Thanking him, I leave the classroom and head to the bathroom before lunch. But once the door swings shut behind me, I am greeted by the sounds of someone crying in one of the stalls.

Lingering apprehensively, I can't make up my mind whether to stay or leave. I shuffle my shoes across the tile floor, wondering if I should interrupt the soft cry of a girl who apparently came in here to cry alone or simply leave. I decide to leave, but before I do, I accidentally bump into the trashcan by the door. The metal cylinder wobbles until it bangs level with the floor.

"Who's there?" The girl cries out.

"Are you all right?" I decide to ask in return. Identities shouldn't matter. If I don't know who is crying, then why would she need to know who accidentally overheard her?

The crying stops for a moment, but I hear nothing in response. "Are you all right?" I repeat again.

"Emma—is—that—you?" I hear words scattered amongst the continuation of sobs.

Reluctantly, I dig my hands into the pockets of my jeans, "yeah?" I reply. *Who could it be?* But it doesn't take me long to figure it out.

The door to one of the bathroom stalls opens with a fierce creak and behind it comes Jessica, red faced and tear stained. I have never known her to show any emotion besides excitement towards makeup, clothes, boys, and parties. We make eye contact for a few short moments, before she walks over to one of the sinks to splash some water onto her face. Instinctively, I grab a few paper towels and hand them over to her.

"Thanks," she says in reply. I watch, as she rubs not only the tears off her face, but her makeup off as well. To me, she actually looks better.

"You all right?" I ask.

"Dan broke up with me," she cries into the paper towel. It shreds underneath the pressure of her tears. "And you will never guess why."

"Why?" I ask, hoping that she actually wanted me to ask.

"He hooked up with Megan over the summer. Apparently, she was cheating on Pete, with *my* boyfriend. Can you believe it?"

My eyes widen at the information. The star of the football and lacrosse team who once called Jessica's bedside table, home, is probably decorating her bedroom floor in a million pieces right about now. I feel terrible. She really liked him. I just feel bad that there isn't anything that I can do to make her feel better.

"Or maybe it's because I am a horrible person. I mean, look what I did to you?" She nods over her tissue into my direction.

"I told you, forget about it."

"Please, you told me to forget about it last year, but that didn't mean that you wanted to be my friend anymore. You didn't call me over the summer nor did you return any of my calls. I mean, we are in the same science class and you have barely said two words to me since the start of school."

"I know, listen, let's just forget everything and try to go back to normal. Okay?" I place my hand on her shoulder as a welcoming gesture.

She nods as her eyes fill up with tears again. Unsure of what to do, I reach over and give her a hug, feeling a few tears fall down my shoulder. A vulnerable, sad Jessica is not the Jessica I am accustomed to seeing. And when she pulls away from our hug, I look at her. Her outfit is something that I would wear a simple pair of jeans and a plain t-shirt. Her makeup is mostly on the paper towel in her hand, and for the first time, I feel like she and I are finally...Equals... As strange as that sounds. Either way, welcome to my world, Jessica.

Chapter Nineteen

Mr. Solway is wheeling Logan down the hospital corridor, because apparently, me trying to zoom down the hallways and pretend to knock into the things to scare him, is not "proper hospital etiquette". *Whatever, it is not like I am trying to knock over people.* As for Grandma Jane, she trails behind clutching onto her purse, announcing aloud that her suspicions about me being a bad apple are becoming truer by the day. *She really needs to learn how to mind her own business or I will show her what a bad apple I can be.*

The discovery of Logan's bump, according to the doctor, went all the way into the joint of his knee, *ouch,* so he is going to be sore for a while. They gave him a pair of crutches that I decide to try out before he does. "Just breaking them in," I say, as I pass Logan in his wheelchair.

"The doctor will have the results back in a few weeks," the receptionist advises Mr. Solway. "We will call you once they are in."

"I thought they were not retesting the area?" He signs the remaining paperwork and hands it back to her.

"Normal procedure to test it after removal," she smiles.

Coming home, Logan hops up the stairs and into bed. I help make him feel comfortable by fluffing out his pillows and bringing him an extra blanket in case he needs it. I also bring him meals, keep him company, and whenever he needs to leave the room, I help him up. Thankfully, mom and dad let me stay home from school to do all of this. Originally, they were against the idea, but after arguing with them, they finally caved.

"I have to go back to school tomorrow," I hand Logan a glass of water. He guzzles it down before chewing on a few of the partially melted ice cubes. It crunches loudly against his teeth.

"I know. It's too bad you can't keep me company for a few days longer," he says.

"Well, I still have those quarters," I smile, "I can call you throughout the day to check on you if you want me to."

"That's what I bought them for," he smirks.

Later that evening, I am heading back home, trudging across our two front lawns, gazing upward at the stars and for some reason, I find myself continuously looking back towards Logan's house. I stare up at his glowing bedroom window with no particular reason in mind. I picture him lying in his bed envisioning the stars as I see them so clearly above me now. I make up a fake story in my mind and pretend to send it telepathically to him. I imagine him smiling, laughing even. In this one clear and concise moment, I am without question, grateful to have him in my life. Out of everything that has happened to me these last few years, Logan has always been a constant. He is a constant reminder of what a true friend is, not to mention, a constant reminder of who I am and where I belong. I couldn't imagine a life without him.

When the night of Kevin's anti-football party arrives, I am sitting beside Logan's bedside asking him about a hundred times if he is okay with me going. My hand runs along the seams in his comforter, knocking into some magazines he has been reading to keep himself busy. It only took a few days for Logan to recover, although he is trying to milk a few more days out of being waited on hand and foot.

Even with knowing this, I still feel guilty about asking him to go. A part of me feels like I should remain here with him, regardless if he is more mobile than he was almost week ago. Prior to coming over, however, I was so sure that he would beg me to stay; but to my surprise, he doesn't. He responds with an apparent nonchalance and a causal shrug. I am taken back by this, *who are you and what have you done with Logan?*

"That Jake kid won't be there, right?" He sits up a few seconds later.

"No, he doesn't hang out with this group."

"Okay, you can go," he smiles.

"Are you sure?" I ask, hoping that he would change his mind, but he just nods. "Well, how about when I get back, you and I go stargazing."

"Sounds great."

When I leave Logan's house about a half an hour later, I walk into the kitchen where I find my mom cleaning up the counters. Dad is still outside working and dinner is in the oven. She is cooking a rather fancy meal for just a simple Saturday night.

"Did you want something to eat before you take off?" She asks. "I can hurry up and fix you a plate."

"No, Henry should be here any minute and they are ordering pizza over at Kevin's, so I should be fine."

"Well, just make sure you leave a few slices for everyone else," she smiles.

I climb the stairs slowly as though it somehow has an effect on the time. My feet drag underneath me as I ascend each step, but I have the sneaking suspicion that they would rather move in the opposite direction. I pull myself along with one hand on the railing, rounding the corner until I reach my room. Why I came up here, I do not know, because I do not intend to get myself ready. That would mean that I want to go, whereas I don't. Inhaling a few sections of my shirt, I notice the smell of the farm, but I don't care. I refuse to change for anyone anymore.

Henry pulls up a little while later, in a blue Ford Focus with several bumper stickers festooned across the back. Most of them have to do with the camp he volunteers at, besides the one talking about animal rights. I climb into his car and buckle myself in. Unlike Jessica's car, Henry's doesn't have much of a smell. I quite like that about it. It is simple and inviting.

"I am really happy you are coming," He says, backing out of the driveway. Logan's bedroom peels away from my view.

"Me too, it should be fun." I crane my neck to make out a small bit of radiating light.

"I am also really happy you don't hang out with Jessica and her friends anymore."

"Well, Jessica and I made amends, but no, I don't foresee me hanging out with that group anymore."

The darkness looms in the car with a sense of awkwardness. Henry tries his best to continue the conversation with anything that comes to his mind, but I am not that talkative to reciprocate the gesture. I lie and tell him that I am just tired, which he seems to buy, but the truth of that matter is, is that I feel bad for leaving Logan; regardless if he said it was okay for me to go or not.

When we pull into Kevin's large colonial style home, I notice that there are already three other cars parked in the driveway. His front porch wraps around the front of his house to the back like a hug, with several hanging plants swaying back and forth against the gentle breeze. It kind of reminds me of my own home. When I open the car door, I am greeted by nothing more than silence. No loud, obnoxious music emits from the house nor do I see the house bulging at the seams with people. Suddenly, I feel okay about being here. I might actually have fun for a change.

"The party is around the back," Henry points, leading me through the driveway and into the backyard. He opens up a screen door, which leads down into a basement where I hear everyone's voices billow up from below.

Kevin, Maggie, and the entire gang is downstairs hanging out. They are playing board games, eating food, and the only drinks I see are soda. I breathe out a silent sigh of relief. This has to be the first social gathering that I haven't felt nervous about attending. It's good to know I won't be waking up tomorrow morning on someone's bedroom floor.

The anti-football party did not contain much football bashing as I imagined it would. Although, I did feel compelled to share my dad's reenactments of his childhood plays for everyone to see. A guy named Mike, who sat at the lunch table with all of us last year, gets up and reenacts what his dad does with him too. "He is living in the past," Mike laughs, sitting back down.

"Well, so is my dad, maybe they should meet sometime," I smile.

I also can't believe how much fun this group is. Kevin is hilarious and cracks jokes throughout the night, all of which make my ribs hurt. Maggie constantly comes and sits between Henry and me to talk, although, usually she directs her conversations to him, probably because they have been friends longer. But I find her personality refreshing in comparison to Jessica's. Her dry sense of humor and engaging dialogue of future predications fascinates me. She has quite the interesting take on what she believes will happen with all of us after we graduate, especially with Henry. She predicts that he will become a doctor someday.

Around ten, I have Henry drive me home. I am smiling from ear to ear, because I am so happy to have had such a nice time. "That was a lot of fun," I look out the car window and up at the sky. "It's a beautiful, clear night," I say, primarily to myself.

The excitement towards ending my night under the stars, feels like the perfect ending to an almost perfect night.

The car is silent besides the white noise coming from Henry's radio playing faintly in the background. And the only time that there is a break in that silence, is when his car turns a corner, making his keys jingle together, which my feet tap along in an unconventional chorus with.

"Hey Emma," His voice emerges with a gulp.

"Yeah?"

"I like you," he says, keeping his eyes on the road. His face, expressionless soon bears a weighty look of stone.

"Thanks, I like you too," I say, turning my attention back onto the night sky. I can hardly wait to go stargazing with Logan soon. It's the only thing that I can really think about right now.

"No, I *really* like you," He pulls the conversation back into his control.

Confused, I turn towards him. I ask him what he means, but I can tell that he is having a hard time finding the words to express himself any further than that. And by the time he ends up finding them, he pulls into my driveway and starts his speech all over again.

"I really like you. I have liked you for a while now," he pauses. "I know this may sound crazy and I am sorry to put you on the spot like this, but I can't foresee a better time to tell you."

"Put me on the spot for what?" My eyes narrow. "What do you need to tell me?

"I want to tell you that I want you to be my girlfriend."

His words take me aback as my body inches towards the door. It reminds me of the night in the tree house when Logan and I expressed our feelings towards one another. Mouth gaped and palms full of sweat, I stare back at him, unsure of what to say. Even though I am close to a door, I see no exit in sight.

His anxious expression lingers as all confidence within him wanes. I know this because; his eyes pull towards the floor in response to my silence. My lips don't move, but only tighten with each passing second, before they curl inward towards my mouth. I bite at what enters and feel a small amount of blood ooze nervously onto my tongue— *I have to say something—but what?*

"You don't have to," he finally says, but his eyes never leave the floor of his car. "I am sorry I asked. Just forget about it, okay?"

But can I? I can't hurt him, I would feel terrible and right now, my inability to answer is making him look like I already have. "Sure," I say. The response even surprises me, because I actually jump at the sound of my own voice. *What the hell did I just agree to?*

"Really?" He perks up.

"Yeah," I unbuckle my seatbelt and stare longingly out the car window, feeling his eyes on me. "Well," I turn back towards him, "have a great night."

I climb out of Henry's car, shutting the door behind me. I don't have the courage to turn back around and face him, so I keep walking, praying that I find an exit strategy from this situation fast.

I head over to Logan's house with the decision not to talk about what just happened. I climb the back steps of his house and walk straight into the kitchen. I don't knock, because I never do, But when I take a few steps forward, I realize that someone is staring at me. It's Grandma Jane. She is sitting at the kitchen table drinking a cup of tea. I freeze at the very sight of her.

"What, you just walk into people's homes without knocking?" She sets her cup down hard against the surface of the table. Her eyes throw piercing daggers into my direction. My body instinctively ducks.

"I never knock."

"Well, you should adopt better manners, young lady. I don't think your parents would want to hear that you are just walking into other people's homes without extending the courtesy of a knock." Her lip curls in disgust.

"Mr. Solway doesn't care," I say affirmatively.

"Well, I care. And since this is now *my* home too, I would appreciate it if you knock." The words roll off her tongue as though they taste repulsive, even to her.

I say nothing, as I slowly make my way out of the kitchen. And just as I step foot on the staircase, I hear her call me a bad apple again. This woman really needs to lay off me.

After our slow escape from the house, Logan and I make our way across the street. We were able to exit out of the front door of the house without Grandma Jane none the wiser. This time, I am carrying the telescope and blanket, while he tries to balance himself on his crutches. I am really surprised on how quietly he was able to make his way down the stairs and out the door without a sound. I would have probably knocked into everything in sight.

"Your grandma hates me," I say, spreading out the blanket a few feet from the dark grey house.

"I think she hates everyone."

"I don't ever hear her talk to anyone like she talks to me. It's like she is out to make my life miserable or something. What did I ever do to her?"

"Yeah, well, ignore her. Dad says old age makes some people grumpy," he hops over to the telescope.

As usual, we do our best to amuse each other with stories from the shapes we see in the stars. But my mind suddenly wants to focus on Henry's request for me to be his girlfriend. I don't know what it means and how I should act, but I know that my impulsive reasoning to not hurt his feelings, may actually hurt him more in the end. I don't like him anymore than a friend. Yet, I have somehow allowed myself to agree to become more.

I lay beside Logan watching his breath release silently into the air. So many confusing thoughts enter my brain, which end up silencing me as a result. He turns over to make sure that I am okay. But am I okay? Here I am someone's supposed girlfriend, a role that I have no idea on how to fill. Better yet, do I even want to fill it? I am pretty sure the answer is no.

"What do you know about love?" I ask, staring up at the sky.

"Love?"

"Yeah, love; what do you know about it?"

"Not much. Why?" He yawns. He stretches his arms out, as he gets more comfortable. I notice out of the corner of my eye that he is getting into his sleeping position. *Is he that tired already?* "Well, I guess, how do you know if you love someone?" I continue to ask.

"I guess you would just know." He yawns again. "Why do you think you love someone?"

"I don't think so, but I think someone may love me." I respond, just as I watch him drift off to sleep.

Chapter Twenty

The course of my proverbial relationship with Henry spreads throughout the school like wildfire, thanks to Jessica and her big mouth. When I confront her about it, however, I only end up finding out that it wasn't her doing at all; that it was in fact, Henry's. Apparently, he has been gloating about it to everyone and the only reason Jessica found out, was because she overheard him talking about it in the hallway. The whole situation angers me, because I was not under the impression that such news had to be shared with the world. Why couldn't this "relationship" be just between him and me? I am beyond annoyed right now.

As for me telling Logan about Henry my lips have remained tightly sealed on the topic. I did try several times, but I always cowered, because I didn't know how he would react. The only person I managed to say something to, was unfortunately mom, who of course, freaked out in excitement, completely blocking out the parts where I discussed not liking Henry and wanting to end things with him. I think she loves any excuse where she can shop and buy me new clothes.

Thankfully today is Friday, the end of the school week. I have had enough of the constant visits from Henry at my locker. I hate the way he has somehow figured out my schedule so that he can plan to bump into me by "accident" throughout the day. Before this whole relationship ordeal, I barely saw him in school, now I see him more than I did during my entire high school career. Something has got to give.

Heading down the hallway to leave school for the day, I hear footsteps coming up from behind me. I turn and see that it's Henry, *shocker.*

"Hey Emma, what are your plans this weekend?" He asks with a big grin on his face.

"I don't know, probably just working around the farm," I say. I don't return a smile, in fact, I actually pick up my pace a little.

"Oh, nothing else?"

"I don't think so, why?"

"How would you like to go do something?" He grins with anticipation.

I reach the top of the stairs and teeter back and forth at his offer. "Call me, I guess." But knowing him, he'd probably call me even if I told him not to. And the lack of enthusiasm in my tone doesn't seem to dissuade his excitement in the least. He barrels down the hallway parading his happiness for all to see. *Ugh, what have I gotten myself into?*

Arriving home, Logan greets me and for some reason, his face doesn't display a warm welcoming. He kicks at the ground as I approach. When he finally looks up at me, I can see the red in his eyes. "Is there something you want to tell me? He snaps.

Mom briskly walks on by me and makes her way up the porch steps. Logan's eyes follow her briefly and it doesn't take me long to realize that she let it slip out about Henry to Logan.

"What do I need to tell you?" I play dumb, hoping that I am wrong.

"About Henry."

"What about him?"

"Really, Emma, we are playing this game?"

"It's not what you think. Listen, he practically cornered me in the car last weekend, asking me to be his girlfriend. He looked like he was on the brink of devastation if I didn't say yes—what was I supposed to do?"

"You could have told him no, that would have been smarter."

"And then what? I didn't exactly want to hurt his feelings." *I want to yell at my mom right about now.*

"So you spared his feelings by dating him?" he scoffs. "So, what are you going to do, stay with him forever, because you are too chicken shit to break it off and hurt his feelings?"

I never thought of that. "I will figure something out, okay? It's not like I like him like that."

He shakes his head at me, "Then how do you like him?"

"Like a friend," I reply.

"Oh, like me?"

"What's that supposed to mean?"

"It means that the lines between your friends and boyfriends are quite blurred. Perhaps, I should include *that* in your list."

"Well, maybe I should include how ridiculous you act sometimes!" I yell.

"Oh yea?" He approaches me.

"Yea," I step in closer to him.

We are face to face and the only sounds we hear are of each other breathing. His warm breath grazes my cheek. I never lose eye contact with him, staring into those never-ending blue skies of his. They swallow me up hole. I almost lose my balance. Catching myself, I return my gaze. His lips move in and out of his mouth until they stretch outward and upward. His Solway trademark peeks out of the shadows of his face and before I realize it, he is smiling. Unconsciously, I smile too.

"I don't know what to do about you sometimes," he says, trying hard to conceal his smile.

"I could say the same thing about you," I fight against my emerging smile as well.

"Yea, whatever, you are just a handful."

"And you will be the death of me someday."

The conversation with Logan only confirms that my situation with Henry is a ticking time bomb. I need to put a stop to this before things get too out of hand, but when I make my way up the porch steps, I decide to confront my mom first. The thought of upsetting my best friend and losing him over a relationship that I don't want, is pointless. Not to mention, she had no right to tell Logan what she did. It would have been better coming from me and it wouldn't have seemed like I was trying to keep something from him. I can actually feel the smoke coming out of my ears.

"Why would you tell Logan about Henry?" I yell at her. "How is that any of your business to share?" The front door slams in my wake.

"I am sorry, I thought he knew. You tell each other everything."

"Yeah, well, in the future, don't share things with him unless you ask me first." My tone hardens.

"I am sorry sweetie."

"Listen, I am going to break things off with Henry. I do not intend to keep this charade up any longer. And if you were listening to me the other day, you would have heard me saying that I don't —like—him."

Her face goes grave.

"What?" I feel my own burning up.

"Oh, nothing," she tousles the leaves of one of her indoor plants.

"What did you do?" *Why does it feel like there is a volcano inside of me ready to erupt?*

Without facing me, she tells me that while I was outside talking with Logan, Henry called and she agreed on my behalf to go out on a date with him tonight.

"What!" I scream, just as dad, comes barreling down the hallway to see if everything is okay.

"I thought you would want to go," she says, just as he enters the room.

"What is going on in here?" Dad looks to both mom and me, while drying his hands off with a rag.

"*Mom* is sticking her nose into *my* business. She set up a date with Henry when I didn't want one."

"How was I supposed to know? He is your boyfriend after all" Her hands fly up into the air.

"Boyfriend?" Dad peers down at me. "Since when do you have a boyfriend?"

"Since I was forced into having one," I groan.

"Who forced you?" He asks concerned, looking over at mom.

"Henry," I reply. "Well, he looked at me so sad. I was afraid to hurt his feelings." My posture weakens.

"Well, why don't you just give him a chance? You may end up liking him," mom advises. "You never know." She uses the same tone of voice she used when she tried to get me to wear makeup.

"I doubt that." I grit through my teeth.

Unable to muster the courage to turn down Henry's request for a date, I am now getting ready against my will. Mom is in my bedroom, trying to take control of the situation, while she picks out outfits for me to try on. She is making a big deal over the situation that I couldn't care less about. I don't know how many times I have asked her to leave me alone, yet, she still won't listen. She is relentless.

An hour later, Henry pulls up and I timidly make my way down the porch steps. He gets out of his car, just as I spot Logan making his way out from the barn. I wave over to him, wishing that he would come save me, but instead, he stays put. His expression is unreadable providing me with no insight to what he is thinking. *I wish I knew what he was thinking.*

"Hey, Emma, you ready to go?" Henry approaches me.

I turn my attention back towards Logan seeing him walking away. I know he is angry and this time, I know it is all my fault.

The car ride becomes an enclosed space where my remaining fury is contained. The steam fogs up the windows, making Henry click the defrost button. He smiles the entire time, unknowingly adding more fuel to the fire. He gets under my skin like that itch you just can't seem to scratch.

For the first part of the night, he takes me to a small diner for dinner. At first, I hardly make eye contact with him, even at the times he is looking at me. When the waitress brings us over our menus, I hide behind mine, even after I decide on what I want to order. I was kind of upset when she took them back, because she ends up taking my only means of hiding away from him.

After an awkward dinner of useless small talk and stories about camp, he drives over to a bowling alley so that we could play a few games. Within an hour, however, I feel myself begin to loosen up. The tension releases like a heavy sigh and I against all prior notions, find myself having a great time. The annoying Henry that I began dating, ends up becoming this funny, outgoing, and all around good guy. Perhaps, I prejudged him. *Well, of course I did.* Maybe he isn't such a bad guy after all, And by the time he drops me off for the night, my idea of breaking things off with him doesn't sound like much of a good idea anymore. Therefore, I decide to remain his girlfriend until I am sure if I actually want to be it or not.

The next morning, I wake up early with full intentions of getting most of my chores done before Logan makes his way into the barn. I slide into my work clothes, throw my hair into a ponytail and make my way downstairs.

"I don't think we should start to worry now. Too soon, don't you think?" My dad's voice hits my ears.

"Yes, but, then again, looking at the history—"

"Sometimes you can't do that," dad cuts my mom off. "Sometimes, these things have a mind of their own. But promises are promises and we just have to respect their privacy."

"Respect whose privacy?" I ask, rounding the corner into the kitchen.

Dad and mom turn towards me surprised. "Oh," mom begins, "A friend of ours."

I grab a box of cereal from the panty, "Everything alright?"

"Everything is fine." Dad says with a smile.

* * * *

Okay, I admit, I like Henry. I don't mind holding his hand down the hallways or when he kisses me when he drops me off home from school. I even find myself willing to devote most of my free time to him. When I confronted Logan about my change of heart a few days after my date, he told me that once again he doesn't know me anymore. I asked him if he needs to alter his list again, but he just walked away from me without another word.

Months drag on and Logan and I are still at odds with each other. I want to make things right between us, but it is obvious with Henry in the picture that nothing I say or do will make any bit of difference. My walkie-talkie collects dust and no matter how many times I turn it on, I can't seem to bring myself to call him. 'Lima Mike' rolls off my tongue in a faint whisper that not even I can hear. I miss him so much. *Have I really lost him for good?*

When Christmas arrives, there is no amount of holiday music or decorations to put me into the Christmas spirit. As usual, dad is wearing his traditional holiday sweater. Mom wears the dress she bought a few years ago and I somehow found the time to crawl back into my pajamas after church. My intent was to pretend as though I caught the flu or something, but mom and dad are not paying enough attention to notice my fake attempts at coughing and sneezing. Therefore, I have no choice but to put back on my original outfit and join the family.

Even with the two new additions to our holiday table, it feels somewhat lonelier than it has in the past. I sit next to Logan, right across from his Grandma, who stares at me the entire time griping about my lack of table manners. I am really not behaving in any particular fashion that would warrant such a response, but the woman continues glowering at me and making snarky comments under her breath. Turning to Logan, he is of no help, because all he seems to be paying attention to is his buttered roll, which he spends most of his time at the dinner table, tearing bits and pieces off, and throwing them into a pile upon his plate.

Reaching for my glass, the light from the chandelier above reflects gently off the hanging pendant from the bracelet Henry bought for me for Christmas. It is white gold with a pendant of a star, because he said that he always catches me admiring them, which is true. Earlier today, when Logan saw it at church, he wailed on about how stars were "our thing" and that I am allowing some other guy to come in and take it away. I told him that I wasn't allowing such a thing and that Henry was only trying to be nice, but something told me, Logan didn't believe in what I was saying. He made my words seem as though they were laced with a sense of betrayal.

"I am so looking forward to your apple pie," Cassie turns to Mr. Solway, interrupting my thoughts. "I rave on about it to everyone." She sips at her wine.

"Well, he is very protective of his secret ingredient. I have been asking him for almost ten years now and he won't cave," my mom smiles.

"Well," Mr. Solway begins as he leans into Cassie's ear. Logan immediately perks up and watches how his dad begins to whisper something to her.

"What did you tell her?" Logan asks aloud.

"Really?" Cassie responds, unintentionally ignoring Logan. "*That's* the secret ingredient? You know, a lot of people use that."

My face turns to Logan, watching his every move. Below the table, I catch him gripping his hands tightly to the seat of his chair. His skin is a mixture of red and white.

"Yes, perhaps, but not as much as I do," Mr. Solway chuckles. "Really calms the body down after a long meal."

I watch as Mr. Solway and Cassie flirt obnoxiously across the dinner table. Mom and dad just smile, while Grandma Jane slowly chews at her food.

Then, out of nowhere, Logan jumps up from the table and pushes back his chair. "Did you tell her?" The chair fumbles backward at the release of his tight grip.

I stand up too, because Logan is my best friend and it feels unnatural for me to continue sitting, although, I am just as confused about we are standing as everyone else is.

"Did you tell her?" He shrieks again.

"It's no big deal Logan," Mr. Solway tries to calm Logan down. "It's just an ingredient."

"Then why haven't you told anyone else at the dinner table, huh? That wasn't your secret to share. It was moms!" He storms out of the room. His chair knocks to the floor at the whip of his hand.

Everyone looks to me as if I have the answer to his sudden behavioral change, but I don't. I simply pick up his chair and slide it back underneath the table. "I am going to go after him," I say. But no one seems to worry too much about Logan, because just as I leave the room all I hear is someone rattling on about Brandy in my wake.

The front door is still swinging on his hinge, which I catch just as I am putting on my gloves. The cotton fabric smears the condensation upon the glass; leaving Logan's previous hand marks a faded memory.

"Slow down," I call after him, while I struggle to get my coat on. The frosty air immediately tightens my lungs. I cough to release some of the sensation.

He continues plowing through the snow towards his house, leaving behind me the dissipated sounds of the snow crunching beneath his shoes. I have no choice but to run after him and yank him by the sleeve of his coat to slow him down. And with the icicles forming in my once warm lungs, I am finding it hard to match his speed.

"Stop for a second!" I yell at him, spinning him towards me.

He whips his head around and looks at me, "What do *you* want?"

"I want to know if you are okay." My tone softens.

"What does it matter to you? He shrugs my arm off his shoulder. "At this point, what does anything matter?"

"It matters to me because you are my best friend, that's why."

"Listen, I don't have time for this. Dad doesn't give two shits about how he makes me feel or even mom; does he not love her anymore? What about me?"

I take a step back almost losing my balance. "Of course he does, Logan. But maybe he needs to move on. Your mom would want to see him happy. I mean, don't you want your dad to be happy as well?"

He stands there staring at me, waving the falling snowflakes away from his face. "I don't know. Sometimes I am okay with it, but other times, I am not." The fury in his eyes dims.

"How about we go back inside and get warm?"

"I am kind of over the holidays," I catch him looking down at the star pendant dangling from the sleeve of my coat, "among other things."

* * * *

I carry with me three balloons, one red, one blue, and one yellow. And in my other hand is a perfectly wrapped present in shiny metallic paper. It's Logan's birthday, which I usually celebrate just on Christmas, but something tells me that this year, he needs a little bit of a pick me upper. I walk into the kitchen, without knocking, bypassing Grandma Jane and Mr. Solway. They don't say anything to me and thankfully, the balloons block my view from Grandma Jane's face, which I presume possesses her normal scowl.

With the balloons bobbing behind me, I run up the stairs and burst into Logan's room, finding him sitting on the floor looking through a car magazine.

"Happy Birthday!" I cheer, throwing the balloons into the air. They float up to the ceiling, before drifting over to the corner in a small cluster. Logan is still in his hunting clothes from earlier this morning.

He looks up with a smile, "What's all this?"

"It's your birthday and since we never really celebrate it properly, I thought I would change that this year." I hand him over his present. He and I haven't talked much since the

Christmas Eve dinner the other day. "So how do you feel about Cassie's gift to everyone?" I continue. After Logan left that night, Cassie announced that she bought a weekend getaway for everyone at some nearby casino in a few weeks. Grandma Jane of course, denied her gift and said something about gambling being a sin.

"I don't care," he finally responds, fumbling the present in his hand. He opens it up revealing a framed picture of him and me. My mom took the picture of us before the first day of my sophomore year; I thought it would be nice to give him a copy. "Thank you," he looks up at me. I watch as he sets it on his bedside table, facing it towards his bed.

"I am glad you like it."

"Listen, I need to talk to you," he says, tossing his magazine off to the side.

"About what?"

"Well, about why I have been so angry with you lately." His hand runs along the back of his neck.

"I know," I cut him off. "It's about Henry."

"Well, kind of, but not entirely." He now stares down at the floor, fumbling his hands in his lap. "I just don't want time to run out on me before I am able to say something."

I lean in towards him about ready to put my arm around him, because I know he wants to apologize, and he really doesn't need to. He has the right to feel the way he wants to and I am not exactly innocent enough to deserve an apology from him either. But as soon as my arm is about to extend over the length of his shoulders, his moves in closer and kisses me gently on the lips.

A weird sensation flows throughout my veins. I am petrified. I pull back, eyes wide, heart palpitating, looking at my best friend in a way that I wasn't prepared to. *What just happened?* My mind screams.

Shocked, I breathe heavy, tongue-tied and in despair. I see that he awaits my reaction, which I am too distraught to provide. There is only one thing that I know to do and that is to run the hell out of the room, so I do. I don't think I have ever ran this fast in my laugh, even when Logan chases me.

I run straight home without looking back. I have no idea why I am running, but what I do know, is that I could not stay there in his room and face what just happened. *Logan my best friend kissed me!* He kissed me without warning or regard to how I may react in return. He kissed me as though I expected it. But the only thing that his kiss brought to me was clarity. It all makes sense. Logan is mad, because he *likes* me. But something tells me that I already knew that. I guess I was too afraid to face the truth.

I make my way inside and throw myself onto the living room couch with a sigh. My brain tries it's best to coordinate with my heart on how to respond. Thoughts circulate in no coherent pattern, making me dizzy. Thousands of pieces from a confusing puzzle cloud up my mind's eye. But unfortunately, none of the pieces seem to fit.

A few minutes later, I can hear dad walk in from the front porch. He stomps across the foyer, before he turns and notices me burying my face into one of the throw pillows. I let out a yell into the room, which sounds like nothing more than a cross between a groan and a shriek.

"Is everything alright?" He asks, making his way into the room, dusting the snowflakes off his shirt.

"I don't know," I mutter into the polyester fibers of the throw pillow.

"Is this about us going away next weekend? I know you don't like Grandma Jane, but try to make the best of it, okay?" He taps upon the pillow softly.

"No, no, no—it's not about that," I groan. "Even though that woman has had it out for me since the day she met me."

"Then what's the problem?" He sits beside me on the couch. Even through the pillow, I can smell the farm on him. My mind flies right back onto Logan.

"It's about Logan," I respond, immediately regretting it.

"You two get into another fight?"

"No, not exactly," I uncover my face.

"Then what happened?"

"He kissed me."

"Wow," he leans back into the couch. "I am surprised."

"I know; can you believe it?" I gasp.

"I mean, I can't believe that the boy finally mustered up the courage to kiss you. Took him long enough, don't ya think?" he chuckles.

But all I can do is watch my jaw slowly hit the floor.

Chapter Twenty-One

The only way that I can describe it, is feeling like there is a heavy fog or mist circulating around my heart. Each beat is as indecipherable as the next and no matter how I try to analyze and reanalyze my situation; I am no closer to an answer than I was at the very beginning. I avoid Henry during school, which is easy, because he is in none of my classes. Not to mention, I have changed my routine, so that he doesn't get to "accidentally" bump into me throughout the day. My like towards Henry has quickly turned into a confusing mess of dislike and annoyingness. I don't know why or how my feelings have changed course so drastically in such a short period of time, but I do nothing to stop it. I just let it crumble before me.

Jessica however, is the only person who seems adamant about figuring the reason behind my sudden muteness and attitude. I waver on how much I can really trust her and if telling her would even be beneficial to me. Regardless, I am desperate for some kind of help and I know that she has had several relationships and is more familiar with the complexity that is, boys.

"Well, do you like him?" She asks during our science lab work. We are sitting far enough away from any eavesdroppers. She hands me over the small box of slides that we need to analyze under a microscope.

"I do," I hesitate, "or at least I think I do. I don't know, he is my first boyfriend and I don't really have much to compare him to."

"Well, how about Logan? Did you feel anything when he kissed you?" She peers over at me, watching the way my face flushes. I can't believe I told her about that.

"Yea, shock," I respond. "I never thought—I mean, okay, I had an idea, but I never thought his feelings were anything this serious. I just don't want to ruin my friendship with him, because I know that if I decide to break things off with Henry, he and I will probably never be the same again. I wouldn't want that for Logan and me."

"Yeah, that's the tough part," she sighs. "Listen, I think; if you value your friendship with Logan, don't risk it. Love complicates things and people sometimes never get over heartbreak no matter how close they were as friends before."

"You think so?" I move one of the slides under the microscope. It scrapes gently across the metal holder.

"I know so. If I were you, I would just let your relationship with Henry run its course until you figure out what it is that you want. Who says you need to make a decision right now?"

"True; at least with my parents being gone this coming weekend, it will give me time to think this over. My mom has a tendency of being kind of pushy in these matters," I scoff.

"Wait, did you just say your parents are going away?" She moves the microscope away from me.

"Yeah, why?"

"Are you having a party?" Her eyes widen at the thought.

"I thought you and I talked about this? I am not much of a partier and I don't think that I want people drinking and having fights in my house. You want me grounded for life?" I yank the microscope back from her.

"Listen, I said I was sorry for dragging you to all those parties last year and whatnot, but I am not saying throw a blow out or anything. You are technically a senior and you should at least throw some kind of get-together before you graduate. You can even choose the people you would want to invite. I just think it would fun to have people over and have a good time," she exclaims through a single breath.

"No alcohol?

She looks off to the side as I ask her again.

"None; scouts honor," she smiles. "Well, maybe a little. But you don't have to drink any and I won't ask you to."

"I still don't know Jessica, Logan's Grandma who hates me, is going to be watching over me and the house—"

"What, is she staying there with you?"

"No, but she is right next door and the last thing I need is for her to look out of the window and see a party. She will have me killed."

"Well, you figure out what to do with Grandma and I will be your party planner. I promise to not do anything that you will not like."

I hesitate on her words. "How about I think about it first?"

The next morning, I wake up and head out into the barn. Logan is out there feeding the animals and I decide to grab a shovel and start picking up some of their mess. His behavior is as ordinary as it always is. Not to mention, he doesn't bring up anything that happened between us, which makes me wonder if he regrets it or is just trying to pretend as though it never happened. Maybe I have nothing to worry about after all. He hands me a clean handkerchief to tie around my face. Everything seems back to normal.

"So, Jessica wants me to throw a party when everyone leaves next weekend," I say causally over the horse's stall.

"Did you forget that your archenemy is going to be watching over you like a hawk?" He snickers.

"No, I didn't forget. Do you think that there is anything that we could do about it?"

"Well, her doctor prescribed her sleeping pills, which he never takes, maybe she will actually take them the night of your party," he smirks.

"Too bad her doctor didn't prescribe her happy pills too," I laugh, "but wouldn't a party be fun?"

"I guess. Is Henry coming?" He asks, kicking at a bucket near his feet.

"Yeah, I mean, he is technically still my—"

"I don't care," Logan cuts me off. "I am over it." I watch as the bucket kicks over.

"Then, what about—"

"The other day?" He laughs, "It was just a joke Emma."

"It didn't seem like one to me."

"Well, it was. Take it easy," he puts his hands up defensively. "You used to be able to take jokes a lot better. Love has changed you," he turns away, but I can detect the shadow of his dimple appear, which lets me know he is smiling. Perhaps it was a joke after all.

* * * *

Mom and Dad's luggage are waiting by the door, two expensive looking suitcases, which mom had to dust off, prior to packing. Since the announcement of the weekend getaway, the twinkle hasn't left my mom's eyes. I recall the conversation Dad had with me awhile back on the way to school, which makes me think that deep down inside, mom wants out of this life. And any escape that she can find, she clings to… desperately.

But leaving also causes some anxiety within her as well. I don't know how many times she has checked the stove, fire detectors, and windows, to make sure everything is as it should be before they leave. It's almost as if she keeps forgetting that I will be here while they're gone.

From the front window, I can see Cassie and Mr. Solway waiting outside in the car, when dad pulls me off to the side and gives me a great big hug.

"You behave while we are away, alright?" His embrace around me tightens.

"Yes, dad," I struggle to breathe.

"And if you have a party, clean up after," he smiles.

"I am not throwing a party," I try to lie.

"Just don't let your mom know; otherwise, she will want to stay and participate," he winks, giving me another hug just before mom comes over.

"The emergency numbers are on the fridge as well as where you can reach us if you need to. Remember that Grandma Jane is next door," She pulls me away from my dad for a hug.

"How could I forget?"

"Oh and Mr. Solway hired extra farmhands this weekend. Make sure you and Logan look after things." Dad butts in.

"We will."

She gives me another hug and when she releases me, she pulls me in for yet another. She stalls long enough for dad to carry out their luggage and for her to see Jessica pull into the driveway.

"So good to see you sweetheart," she hugs Jessica. "You girls are going to have a sleepover tonight, huh?" Her eyes sparkle against the porch light.

"Yeah," Jessica smiles.

"Try to get this one to revisit makeup. She threw everything she had away in the trash," she frowns at me.

"Come on Charlotte, we have to get on the road!" Dad yells from the driver's side of the car.

"Okay you girls have fun and behave. We will we see you Sunday when we get back,"

The party however, is not until tomorrow night, because Logan is still trying to work out how he is going to get Grandma Jane distracted. He won't tell me his plans and I don't ask. Tonight, however, Jessica and I decide to get the house ready. She says it's best to put everything expensive away.

"It's just a precaution," she assures me when my expression worries. "You don't want anything breaking by accident."

She slides some of mom's glassware into cupboards just when I hear the phone ring. I answer it. It's Henry. I give him some quick excuse to get off the phone, but for some reason, he doesn't hear me and calls right back. In fact, he calls well into the evening. All he wants to do is talk and mostly it's about nothing important or it's about things that we have already talked about. There is only so much I can take of listening to him breathe on the other end of the phone. Finally, I just hand the phone over to Jessica who disguises her voice as mine.

"That bad, huh?" she asks after hanging up the phone. She throws herself onto the living room couch.

"I don't know. I like him, I do, but I just don't know if I like him enough to want to be his girlfriend, you know?"

"Yeah, I dated this one guy named Jimmy for like a few months or so, but it felt like a lifetime—and not in a good way," she laughs. "I liked him, but he and I were just better off being friends."

"Did you stay friends after?"

"Ugh, well, we tried, but he said it was "too weird" so we just stopped talking."

"That's what I am afraid of," I say, just before I hear the front door open.

"Hey Emma, I figured out what to do about Grandma Jane," Logan voices sounds off. He rounds the corner and sees

Jessica and me sitting on the couch. "Oh, hi," he says, primarily to Jessica, I think.

"Hey Logan," she smiles. It's good to see you again."

Immediately his face flushes. "Hi," he eventually says back. "Well, I've got to go." He turns to leave.

"Wait, aren't you going to tell me what you figured out about Grandma Jane?" I stop him.

"It's no big deal," he says, heading out the door. I don't bother getting up and going after him. It seems apparent that he doesn't want to be followed.

"Is he shy?" Jessica asks as soon as Logan leaves.

"He can be," I come back into the room.

"He seriously has the brightest blue eyes I have ever seen," she turns to me with a smile.

"I know, I always tell him that he has skies for eyes."

Chapter Twenty-Two

Okay, I am wearing makeup, but only a little. Jessica put a little blush and lip gloss on me for fun, but I ended up liking it, so I left it on. It's nothing dramatic. Not to mention, she even lets me wear what I want to wear without any fuss on her part. I just make her promise that she will not breathe any word of this to my mother.

In exactly one hour, the party will begin. Logan still hasn't told me what he is planning on doing with Grandma Jane, which worries me with each passing moment. I decide to walk over to my nightstand and grab my walkie-talkie. Seeing this, Jessica starts laughing when I call for Lima Mike through the mouthpiece. And when Logan's voice appears on the other end—she calls me a nerd.

"Is operation 'Insane Jane' underway?" I blurt through the mouthpiece. Jessica continues to chuckle in the background.

"Normal people have cell phones," she snorts under her breath.

"Don't judge me when I tell you what I have to do," his voice comes through.

"I can only imagine."

After I disconnect with Logan, and Jessica and I get ready, we busy ourselves putting up decorations and putting out chips, dip, and plastic cups that she had concealed in her overnight bag.

"Pretty clever, huh?" She zips back up her bag.

"Your parents never suspected a thing?"

"Oh, gosh, no, they don't care. I did this all for your parents!"

Pleased with the result of our decorating, Jessica and I pour ourselves a couple of sodas and sit down in the living room to wait for everyone to arrive. The clock on the fireplace mantel ticks away, reminding me that very soon my house will be full of people ready to have a good time. But will they? I also think about how Henry and Logan will be under the same roof with one another. Henry probably couldn't care less, but something tells me that Logan might. I also think about how Logan tried to play off the kiss between us as being nothing more than a joke. It didn't feel like a joke, but only confronting him about it would make things even more uncomfortable between us. My head is starting to hurt again…

"What are you thinking about" Jessica turns to me.

"Ugh, nothing," I reply. The puzzle pieces reappear in my mind without any hopes of connecting seamlessly.

"Come on, you better talk with me now before everyone gets here. It may be too hard then."

"Okay, I am just thinking about the whole Henry and Logan situation again."

"Are you any closer to an answer?"

I know that something within me is telling me not to ever cross that line with Logan. Risking our friendship for something that may or may not work between us is foolish; not to mention, could I even think of Logan in that way? Then again, I don't even think of Henry that way. Henry to me was a friend, no different from Logan…right?

"What is your opinion?" I ask, unwilling to determine my own, just as another puzzle piece adds into the pile.

"Well, I already told you. Don't a mess up friendship if you don't have to. Plus, it doesn't sound like you are sure of how you feel about Logan anyways. And with Henry, I said to just ride it out. Let the relationship fade on its own. You will know what to do when the time comes. No sense in trying to rush things."

The front door opens and Logan walks in. He is wearing one of the nicer outfits he wears for holidays or when we go to church. Overdressed, yes, but he looks really nice. I can't help but to smile.

"How did it go with your Grandma?" I ask when he makes his way into the room and sits down.

"Out like a light. She probably won't be up for at least six to seven hours."

"What did you do?" Jessica gasps. "Did you knock that old lady out?"

"Technically, yes."

"Logan! What did you do, hit her over the head with a shovel?"

"Oh, gosh, no, Emma, who do you think I am?" He sits back into his seat. "I ran her over with the tractor," he smirks.

Jessica's jaw hits the floor, but I just laugh. "So you used her sleeping pills on her, huh?"

"Doctor's orders," Logan smirks.

"I didn't see that coming," I smirk back.

Soon, the music blares and light floods throughout my entire house. I may not know half the people here, but it doesn't seem to bother me. Jessica assures me that generally parties consist of people you hardly know, which opens up the doors to meeting someone new. As for Henry, he follows me around the house like a lost puppy. A few times, I purposely pretend to have to go to the bathroom just so I could get a break from him. I mainly just sit inside and clean up a bit. Thankful to have lost him again, even though I am sure only temporally, I spot Kevin in the hallway as soon as I come out of the bathroom for what is my fourth time in the last hour.

"Hey Emma, thanks for the invite," He high fives me.

"I am glad you could come. Doesn't compare to your parties though," I laugh.

"Not much does," he grins.

"Where is Maggie? I thought she would have come."

"Um, well, you see, it's kind of hard for her," His hand wipes across his face as though he is uncomfortable with me asking.

"Why? Does she have to work or something?" I causally survey the perimeter for Henry.

"No, it's not that, it's—"

And there he is. Two cups in hand, one for me and one for him. He dances his way down the hallway towards my direction with a huge grin on his face. Suddenly, I don't feel so good.

"What's the reason?" I quickly ask before Henry approaches.

"It's—" Kevin looks to Henry.

"Hey you two," Henry butts in. He hands me my cup of soda.

"We will talk later, all right?" I speak to Kevin who only nods his head in reply.

Since an hour into the party, Jessica has been bouncing from person to person, playing hostess. Logan is lost among the herd and a few times, I have spotted him talking with a few guys from my school, while he was demonstrating what looks to be the punch he delivered to Jake's face last year. I have never seem him interact with other kids our age, which I find rather rewarding and interesting to behold. He would have done well with me at high school and to think, it will be all over very soon.

Clambering down the stairs with my shadow at tow, I round the corner and enter the kitchen to locate a phone book. I decide to call up Maggie and see if she wants to come. Maybe she thinks I don't like her or something and I would hate for her to think that.

I open up the bottom cupboard and try to maneuver around some of the items that Jessica put in here so that they wouldn't break. I spot the phone book, but just as I am about to slide it out, one of mom's crystal bowls slides out along with it and hits the ground, shattering.

"Damn it!" I yell. I hate breaking glass; it's such a pain to clean up.

Trying to collect some of the large pieces in my hand, I watch as Henry bursts into the kitchen. Seeing the mess, he offers to help me clean, which I appreciate. He grabs the broom and dustpan from the corner of the room and starts sweeping up the visible shards. Several times, I look up at him, as we bend down to scoop up the glass. His determined and serious face does not excite nor inspire any feelings of happiness or giddiness I would presume that love would provide. This guy, my boyfriend, means nothing more to me than some of the strangers at this party. Yet, he holds me up on this pedestal, which I strangely yearn to be knocked down from.

He catches me looking at him and smiles. I smile back out of politeness, but for no other reason. The glass slides across the dustpan and from what I can see, we have gathered all of it up. But glass is so tricky that I may end up finding pieces of it weeks later. From the corner of my eye, however, I see the vacuum cleaner floating towards the kitchen, but when I return my attention back to Henry to let him know that I will pick up the rest, he leans in and kisses me. The vacuum falls gently to the floor beside me.

"Here," Logan says, looking down at me stone-faced.

"Thanks," I say, wanting so badly to wipe Henry's kiss off onto the sleeve of my shirt.

Henry is still looking at me, while I am staring back at Logan. My concentration on him doesn't wane, even when he walks away, leaving me nothing but the back of his head to look at.

I quickly vacuum, wash my hands, and grab the phonebook from the floor beside my feet. I leave Henry in the kitchen and tell him that I will be back in a few minutes. I make my way up the stairs and into my parents' room. I don't usually come in here, but strangely, I find the ambience quite comforting. So many thoughts are darting through my mind and I have no idea what they are about or even how to slow them down. I open up the phonebook looking for a Maggie's information, but it takes several tries before I get the number right.

"Hello?" Maggie answers.

"Maggie, hey, it's me Emma," I say. "I was wondering why you didn't come tonight?"

"Oh, well, I am busy," She explains quietly.

The door to my parents' bedroom creaks open and Henry walks in. The darkened room doesn't deter his brisk walk over to me. His body anchors beside me on the bed, reminiscent of the night Jake tried to take advantage of me. I move slightly over in response. *Didn't I tell him that I would be back in a few minutes?*

"Can you hold on a second?" I put my hand over the mouthpiece and turn to Henry.

"Who are you talking to?" He leans into me with smile. I pull back the phone towards my ear.

"It's Maggie."

"Hello?" I hear Maggie's voice emit from the phone.

"Hi, sorry," I answer.

"Who are you talking to?"

"Henry."

"Oh," she goes silent again.

Henry looks at me and for some strange reason, I hand him the phone. "Talk with her; I need to get some fresh air."

I quickly get up from the bed and leave the room.

My instincts feel strangely aroused and aware. But what they are conscious of, I do not know. I head down the hallway and stairs as though somehow everything feels right with the world. A peculiar sense of clarity has struck me, but I have no idea what it is that I am to see. The party is alive as ever. People are laughing and carrying on in small congregated groups and I move through them like a ghostly silhouette of myself. If someone were to ask me if I could have pictured myself in this moment five years ago, I probably would have laughed.

I look for Jessica, but she is nowhere to be found. The streamers that once cascaded down from the ceilings, are now being carried throughout the room underneath people shoes, resembling bits of unsuspecting toilet paper when someone exits a public restroom. Balloons are used as makeshift volleyballs, making me glad for the precautions Jessica had suggested. I can't imagine what would have happened if we left everything out. It's funny how I am the only one who ends up breaking something.

I can smell the faint scent of alcohol throughout the rooms and I am proud not to have sampled even the tiniest sip, besides the stale residue I tasted after Henry's uninvited kiss. I reach the staircase landing and round the corner towards the living room. Jessica is not there nor is she in the dining room. I weave in and out of the groups, trying to spot her. Logan by now is probably home. I know there is no way that he stayed after what he saw. I am sure that I will hear about it tomorrow.

Heading back towards the kitchen, I spot a side view of Jessica. A few people lingering by the walkway block the other half of her out. When I squeeze on by them, I finally see her. But I don't just see her. I also see Logan. They are standing next to each other. Well, they are not just standing next to each other they are face to face. And it takes several eye rubs to believe what it is that I am seeing. They are kissing. Logan and Jessica are kissing.

I stop dead. My heart stops and sinks into the pit of my stomach. All sounds, smells, and sight has been viciously yanked from me, leaving me paralyzed with nothing more than the feeling of wanting to crumble to the ground into tiny pieces. *Logan, my best friend, is kissing Jessica!* Even thinking that sentence in my head doesn't make sense. Not to mention, seeing that image unfold doesn't make sense. In fact, the world I was so sure of a moment ago, and the clarity I thought I had no longer makes sense. That too, has been taken out from under me, leaving me bare and vulnerable to face the things I had no idea I was bound to face. The wetness swells from behind my disbelieving eyes. *What do I do?*

Logan's blue eyes are closed and I am surprised to see the entanglement of their lips still taking place. Did they not feel the world stop or see me shatter like broken glass onto the floor? Have they no idea that my lungs have stopped requesting air and that I am seconds away from either fainting or dying? I am in disbelief. I feel betrayed. My throat clears and against the music, it falls silent into the background of the noise.

Feeling movement in my limbs again, I march over to both of them and pull them apart, I can smell the alcohol radiate from Jessica's breath and taking one good look at her, I know she is drunk. How is it that Logan is kissing her with that breath? His blue eyes sparkle without any trace of alcohol present. He is fully aware of what he is doing, which only angers me even more.

"How could you?" I say to no one in particular. I can't face either one of them. I storm out of the kitchen and charge through the guests. Several of which I knock into without rendering an apology.

Henry hangs nearby with Kevin in living room. Spotting me, he calls out my name.

"What?" I yell back at him. My head whips with an unfamiliar ferocity, forcing the wetness to seep out from my eyes and stream down my face.

He takes a few steps back, looking over at Kevin for help. "I am sorry," he begins. "Are you okay?"

"Listen, I am sorry. This isn't working." I can't even look at him to see how my abrupt breakup in front of pretty much the entire party has affected him. I just continue charging my way out of the house and into the pasture, leaving everything and everyone behind.

The icy chill in the air is no match to my fury. I pound through the snow and don't ever once look back. That is until I hear Logan's voice call out to me. I am halfway through the pasture when my body unexpectedly turns around. He stands there with his hands in his pockets. His eyes staring back at me with worry.

"What!" I yell back at him.

"I am not going to chase after you Emma," his voice carries over to me. "Not anymore."

"Chase after me? Who asked you to chase after me?"

"I am tired of it."

"Tired of what Logan, you are not making sense! Then again, you never do."

"No, I always make sense, it's just you never listen to what it is that I am saying. So I am done."

"Done with what?" I sob. *With our friendship?*

"Done chasing after you; I chase after you whenever you ask me or tease me to. I chase after you for fun, I chase after you out of boredom, and I chase after you because to me," he pauses, "there was no one else worthy of chasing after." He looks away as quickly as the words sneak out of from his mouth.

My posture softens, "Sure there is, what about Jessica?"

"That was a mistake," he walks towards me.

"Yea, a very *long* mistake," I reply sarcastically. I dig my shoes into the snow.

"What does it matter? You have Henry don't you? Go be with him." He points back towards my house.

My eyes narrow and glower into his direction. "Just leave me alone."

"Now you know how I feel," I hear him call to me as I continue to plow through the pasture away from him. A quick turn of my head I see him beginning to walk back towards my house. Is this how Logan feels? All those times I have brought other guys into the picture, he had to stand back and watch it happen. I discredited his feelings and accused him of just being his stubborn self. But he wasn't being stubborn, he was being hurt—by me. And *I* was the one too stubborn to realize it.

All of sudden, everything makes sense. What he said was right. For the entire length of our relationship, I lived off of Logan chasing me. But never once did I chase after him. No wonder he played his kiss off as being nothing more than a rouse. And what did I do, I ran out of there, leaving him alone to face the courage of his decision. Did I expect him to chase after me then too?

The frigid air melts against my warmed flesh, as all the voices in my head disintegrate at the sound of my beating heart. My feet inch back towards the direction of my house, no longer do they desire for the pasture or beyond. I run back towards him, right foot, left foot, pound into the snow until I am directly behind him. I grab him by the shoulder and against all fear and prior reservations; I pull him in and kiss him. I kiss him full of happy summers full of explorations and adventures; I kiss him full of inside jokes and conversations through walkie-talkies. I kiss him and for the first time, and I understand why our friendship hasn't been the same for awhile. We were just too stubborn to admit it to each other and to ourselves.

I definitely feel like the horse's ass now.

Chapter Twenty-Three

The sleeping pills lasted well after the party ended. And the only reason that they did, was because the party ended quicker than what I had anticipated that it would. Jessica is passed out on the couch, while I am sitting with Logan in the dining room. Below the table, our hands are intertwined as we sit here in complete silence. I never imagined this moment, so my expectations of it are unclear. But something about holding Logan's hand feels right, that much I do know. It feels different from when I held Henry's. With Henry's I felt like I was holding the hand of a stranger, even during the times that I liked him. With Logan, I feel like I am holding my own hand—he is a part of me after all.

A few moments later, Logan pulls our hands up to the table and we face the evidence of what we have become. It's amazing how something so commonplace can turn into something amazing. *I mean what have we become?* Can I still call him my best friend or does him being my boyfriend change all of that?

"There is so many things that I want to say to you right now," he says, staring down at the table.

"Like what?"

"I don't know, a lot; but, I don't want to ruin the moment by talking about any of them."

"Why is that?"

"I think this moment is better suited for silence."

When the next morning arrives, the sun rises as it normally would. I detect no change in my morning routine and when Jessica awakens, unsure of last night's events, I don't get angry with her. Her lack of judgment opened my eyes, which I may have not been able to face otherwise. So as strange as it may seem, I hug her, thanking her for doing what she did.

"I did that?" She gasps. "Gosh, I must have been drunk."

"You did," I smile.

"Well, I am glad to have at least been of help."

"For the first time since we have become friends, you actually were."

When everyone returns, mom and dad enter the house to find everything the way that they left it. Minus the crystal vase, that is.

"What happened to it?" Mom asks visibly upset.

"We were dancing," Jessica butts in, "I accidentally hit it and it fell on the floor."

Mom looks to Jessica and appears to accept her apology without any question, before making her way up the stairs to unpack. Dad, however, lingers beside us. As soon as we hear their bedroom door shut, he turns to us.

"Is that all that broke?" He looks to me and then at Jessica.

"Yes," we nod in unison.

"So, how was it?"

Jessica looks to me for help, but I can't tear my eyes away from my dad. "How was what?" I ask.

"The party, did you girls have fun?" He smiles.

Unsure if honesty is the best policy, I decide to tell him that we did.

"I am glad" he says, "Threw a few parties in my day as well." His eyes glaze over with nostalgia. I push Jessica out of the room just in time.

Jessica leaves shortly after and I return up to my bedroom. I fall face first into my bed, recalling all the puzzle pieces back into my mind. Only this time, a picture begins to form, leaving only a few scattered pieces beside it. It's a picture of Logan and me. And even though I am no longer confused, I find myself scared beyond words. Nothing in my life has scared me more than the thought of losing Logan. But at the same time, I don't regret my decision. Too much about Logan and I being together makes sense even with all the chaos and confusion that surrounds it.

* * * *

My locker door slams against its metal frame. It's the first day back to school after my party and the idea of coming face to face with Henry, sickens me. I can't imagine how he must be feeling and to know that I am the cause, sickens me even more. I turn to head towards homeroom when I spot Maggie walking towards me. Her glasses inch their way to the tip of her nose. She slides them back irritatingly.

"Hey Maggie," I say as she shuffles towards me.

"Why did you call me the other night?" She asks.

"I wanted to see why you didn't come," I smile, however, she doesn't smile back.

"That was kind of lame of you, don't you think?" She scoffs.

My brows furrow. I shift the weight of my books into my other arm. "I don't understand."

"You—calling me—and with Henry there and all…"

"Henry? What does Henry have to do with this?"

She looks away for a moment and when she looks back at me, she frowns slightly. "You don't know?"

"Know what?" I ask confused "Are you mad that I broke up with Henry?" Of course, she is; she is his friend. If I hurt him, she without a doubt would come to his defense.

"You broke up with Henry?" She leans against the lockers. "He didn't tell me that."

"Yea, I did. I feel bad for the way I did it. I figured that was what you are mad about; you know, me hurting your friend?"

She shrugs, "I had no idea." A sense of relief takes over her, leaving me just as confused as ever.

"You don't know, do you?" She looks down. Her back slides its way down the locker until she is sitting on the floor. I decide to sit down alongside her.

"Know what?" I ask.

"Ugh, I can't believe I am about to tell you this. The only other person who knows is Kevin." The sound of his name reminds me of my party and how he was about to tell me something; but unfortunately due to Henry, the subject was changed. "I like Henry," she turns away. "When you guys starting dating, well, it bothered me." She says, just as the homeroom bell rings loudly above us, but I don't move and neither does she.

"You like Henry?" I am stunned at her confession.

Maggie pulls her knees to her chest and buries her head. "Yea, since middle school," she groans.

To my side, I just stare at her. Her short black hair and black framed glasses conceal her face, making me unsure of how she is feeling.

"Does Henry know?" I finally ask.

"Please, isn't it obvious?"

"Well, actually, no." I try to recall incidences when I may have thought that, but only come up empty handed.

She pulls herself off the floor and dusts off her clothes. "Hey, since we missed homeroom, how about you and I play hooky today?" She beams at me.

Not wanting to disappoint anyone else in my life, I open my locker, toss my books inside and follow her out to the parking lot, willingly.

We spend the morning at a small diner for breakfast. Ironically, it's the same diner that Henry took me to on our first date. I tell her this, but I also share how I hid behind my menu the entire time with her.

"You did that?" She laughs.

"I did. I felt so bad, because he was desperately trying to impress me and all I wanted to do was run and hide."

She twirls her straw in her milkshake and tells me about her initial crush on Henry in middle school. They were at the eighth grade dance and all she could think about was how she was going to muster up the courage to ask him to dance. But when she finally did, he was dancing with Melanie Hansen. From there, Maggie was devastated, deeming her love with Henry unrequited. Pretty dramatic of her not to at least try again; but who am to judge?

"Why don't you just tell him about you feel?"

"Rejection, I suppose," she says, before taking a sip of her milkshake. "I am not ready to experience *that* kind of heartbreak, yet."

* * * *

The spring sun emerges with a friendly greeting through my bedroom window blinds. My eyes awaken to the sounds of mom in the kitchen downstairs. The clinking of pans and dishes and the smell of cinnamon, signals to me that she is busying herself making French toast for breakfast. But even with all these happy ways of waking up, I am plagued by a bitter sadness, erupting within my gut. I had a horrible dream last night and the emotions that my dream-self experienced have yet to wear off.

My dream was about Logan. My dream was about Henry. My dream was about both of them, hurt at the hands of me. The way I hurt Henry, I ended up hurting Logan. In a crowded room, I left him. I deserted him and embarrassed him, while I ran off into a direction that even now, is still unclear to me. And all that Logan yelled out to me was that he refused to chase me any longer. Heart pounding, tears forming, my eyes burst open in a panic. *Have I made a horrible mistake? And is it too late to do anything about it now?*

I pull the covers off me, exposing my emotions to the world. And even though I am alone in my bedroom, I feel as though the whole world knows how I am feeling. It violates the very core of my heart and I weaken at the thought of where all these feelings would lead me. *What if it takes me to a place that*

Logan would not follow? What if I end up destroying the one relationship I cherish more than any others in the world? This is way too much to think about this early in the morning. I need to get out of bed and figure this all out later. I mean, who says that I have to figure this out now?

As I suspected, Mom is in the kitchen making French toast. She isn't wearing her apron, but I notice a few cracked eggs on the floor and I offer to help her clean up the mess.

"Sorry, I have been up since the crack of dawn. Your father woke me up getting ready for work this morning," she hands me a dishtowel.

"He is already working?"

"Yes, he has been out there all morning."

I bend down to pick up the egg mess and immediately remember the crystal vase I broke here. "Mom, can I talk to you?" The words, unpremeditated, slip through my lips faster than I can stop them.

She twirls around, beaming at me. "Of course you can, sweetie."

After I am done cleaning up the mess, I sit down at the kitchen table. "It's about Logan," I say.

Handing me my breakfast, she sits down beside me with coffee in hand. Her stoned face sips at her coffee, waiting for me to continue, but I begin to second-guess on whether it's such a good idea anymore. Confiding in my mother, although possibly helpful, always turns into some kind of spectacle. And what I don't need right now is a spectacle.

"I like him," I say, refusing to make eye contact with her. The only thing I can see is her coffee cup slowly inching its way back to the surface of the table. I can't even hear her breathe.

"Well of course you like him," she chuckles nervously, her previous tensed posture loosens at my words, "he is your best friend." She picks up her coffee cup and takes another sip.

"No, mom," I already feel the conversation becoming useless; "I *really* like him." *I feel like Henry right now.*

"Oh," the look of denial she held on her face, deflates like a balloon. "So are you two dating?"

"I guess, but I am kind of scared about it."

"What are you scared about?"

"You see, Henry liked me and I liked him, or at least I thought I did. Recently, however, I find out that Logan likes me as well and I like him, but Logan is my best friend and I feel like having anything more with him would ruin that. Not to mention, I don't want to hurt his feelings like I did Henry's. What if I break things off with Logan like I did Henry or what if I end up regretting what I did to Henry, what if—" The words rattle out of my mouth in a panic.

"Well, I was kind of hoping you were still with Henry, he was such a nice boy."

"Yea, well, what about Logan?"

"What do you mean?"

"What's wrong with Logan?"

"Nothing, sweetie, he is perfect." She looks away.

"What if I mess it up and ruin my friendship with him?"

"Listen, we all have "what ifs" in life honey, it's best just to choose the ones you are willing to live with," before she gets up from the table without another word.

Chapter Twenty-Four

No one knew. And what I mean by "no one", I mean, Logan and me. We had no idea. The weekend getaway that seemingly changed everything changed not only the relationship we had with each other, but Mr. Solway's and Cassie's as well. Here she sits at the dining room table, displaying the ring upon her finger. Logan sits beside me, gripping the bottom of his seat again, which I end up loosening his grip, in order to hold his hand within my own. I don't even mind that my hands are now filling with his nervous sweat.

The engagement sparks an excitement within my mother who has been asked to be the maid of honor. "So, you're looking at getting married this August?" She asks, opening up one of the bridal magazines scattered upon the table.

"We thought a small ceremony here would be perfect," Cassie smiles.

Grandma Jane rocks back into her chair and looks into Logan and my direction. *Does she know we are holding hands?*

The news of Mr. Solway's request to marry Cassie was confessed to Logan a few days after they got back. He was furious. He stomped around his room for two whole hours before he let anyone inside. The only person he allowed in was me.

"It's not a bad thing," I said to him. "This happens a lot. People need to move on."

"My mother died still married to him. Shouldn't he still be faithful to his vows?"

"Well, I am sure he is, but he needs to live his life. He needs to share his life with someone. And although, Cassie can never compare to your mother, she helps fill a little of that void. She is second best."

"Who would want to spend the rest of their life with a second-best option?" he barked at me.

"Think of it this way, if you had to pick, would you mind Cassie taking care of your father for the rest of his life or someone you may *actually* hate? She may not have done it as perfectly as your mom, but she can still do a good job," I smiled.

He nodded his head before taking a seat upon his bed.

"If I died, I would want to make sure that you spent the rest of your life with someone who would love and take care of you as much as I would have."

"You are not going anywhere, don't even say those things," he said.

"But it's true. I want you to write that down in my list."

"What what down?" He peered over at me.

"I want you to remember that if anything were to ever happen to me, I would want the next best person in my life to take care of you."

"Oh, yea, and who would that be?"

"Honestly, I don't know, which means, I can't die until I find her."

He smiled at me as I took a seat beside him. He faces the ground, "I guess I would want the same for you."

"Good," I wrapped my arms around his shoulder. "At least we have our whole lives to keep searching."

"Yea, our whole lives."

* * * *

I can't believe that I am doing this. The stack of applications and pamphlets overwhelm the surface of the table and I see no end in sight. College wasn't ever a possibility to me nor was it ever a desire of mine. But with Logan's sudden interest in running away from the farm and seeing the world, we decided to begin applying for colleges together.

Logan talks about getting a degree in agriculture and I find that I have an interest in either communications or journalism. Thankfully, Cassie has been a tremendous help to us. She guides us through our essays and takes the liberty of mailing off our finished applications.

"Logan being homeschooled won't hurt his chances, right?" I ask her as she seals the final envelope.

"No, he has taken the required tests. He will be fine," she smiles.

I nudge at Logan's shoulder as if to tell him that everything will be okay. To think that we are finally going to be in school together again makes me unbelievably happy.

With summer vastly approaching and the end of school around the corner, I am somewhat saddened by the transition. Jessica is going away to SUNY Brockport and begged me for weeks to apply to join her. I told her that I would, but I really have no intention of doing so. I think a good separation for us is what we need. As for Henry, I finally approach him in school and apologize for everything that happened the night of my party. I explained to him how I felt from the beginning all the way through to our bitter end.

"No worries," he laughs. "I knew things between us weren't going to last."

"You did?" I match my pace alongside him in the hall.

"Yea, I mean, I knew you didn't like me as much as I liked you. There were times, however, that I thought you may have, but those moments were short lived."

"I am not much of a girlfriend, wasn't much of friend either, I guess."

"No, you were a good friend, I just went ahead and ruined it," he smiles. "I hear you are with Logan now." He stops suddenly.

"You did?"

"Yea, Jessica told me. I mean, I kind of pushed it out of her, so don't get mad at her for telling me."

I shrug it off, because it's really no big deal.

"It makes sense though, you know. For both of us, I mean."

"How so?"

"I mean, both of us had people in our lives that truly cared about us, but we were too blind to notice. It took something to happen for us to, for lack of better words, see the light."

I lean into him, "Are you saying…"

"Yea, she told me. She even said you gave her the courage to say something. I am glad you did, I think we will really hit it off."

"I am so happy for you Henry. And I am glad that you and I can be friends again. I was really worried that I messed things up."

"Never, I will always be your friend."

He walks away and leaves me standing, smiling, at our recovery. It's funny, as I stand here in the middle of the hallway, lost amidst the chaos and swallowed up by the stampede, I don't really feel any of those things I did on my very first day here. I am part of an ever-changing herd, walking through these doors as no one, but somehow leaving as though I am finally someone. A circle of high school life that I think everyone goes through. We all go down paths, because we are each supposed to learn and take something away from the whole high school experience. No two journeys are the same, and that's okay. I was supposed to be here for a reason, without Logan, no matter how much I wanted him to be here. I may have not come to this point in my life if things were different. I guess everything *does* happen for a reason.

* * * *

"Everyone must stay in line, exactly where I put you," Mrs. Reddins addresses us. I am sandwiched between two kids I have never seen before. The guy in front of me is gigantic. I feel like a hobbit in comparison to him. Thanking the visual reference given to me by one of *The Lord of the Rings* movies that I caught on television the other day. I called up Kevin to let him know that I finally watched it. He seemed more excited about that then my parents seem for my graduation. Apparently, dad feels like I should have stayed back another year. I might be missing out in something, according to him.

My gown is white and I hate it. I hate it because it makes me look pasty and the cap that falls midway down my forehead is already stained with foundation, because mom forced me into wearing makeup so that I can look my absolute best in my photos. I didn't fight her on it too much, because she at least let me do my hair, which is now unfortunately matted underneath this stupid cap.

Underneath my gown, however, I am wearing my work outfit. I laugh, thinking about how all the other girls are probably wearing dresses and skirts, but I am wearing something smelly from the bottom of my hamper. My take on graduation is that if I entered these doors not being who I am, the least that I can do for myself, is leave the way I should have entered in the first place. And that's exactly what I plan to do. Even if that means dressing differently or even smelling odd, I really don't care. This is who I am and no one will ever take that away from me again.

The slow walk down the bleachers and into the stands where the graduating class is supposed to sit makes me rather uneasy. I see mom, dad, Mr. Solway, and Logan sitting off towards the middle of the attending audience. I wave nonchalantly towards them as they smile. Logan however, mouths, *I am so proud of you*, to me.

Once the ceremony commences, I am lost in nonsensical thought. It is only until the valedictorian makes his speech that I actually come to. It drags on longer than the time I believe that he was allotted, instantly reminding me of the cliché high school speeches, I see in movies.

I swear, the way high school is described at this moment makes it seem like the last four years (or for some, three) were the best years of our lives. But were they? I mean, I would hate to think that. The agony of the whole high school experience cannot be summed up into clever words and phrases. It is much more than that. And the only wisest thing that I hear him say is, "is that high school is beginning of your creation. It is the foundation of who you are and who you will become. Your definition and status, will mean nothing in the eyes of your peers, this is only a change that you will see and feel. Welcome to the beginning of the rest of your lives."

Later that evening, mom brings out a cake and we all gather around the dining room table to enjoy a slice or two. Grandma Jane is here and I am surprised to find that she is not paying much attention to me, especially considering this day is in celebration of my academic achievements. Dad slaps me on the back every time he walks by, congratulating me for sticking it out and getting such good grades. Mom is not speaking to me. When she finally saw what I was wearing underneath my gown, her lips pursed in disgust and she has barely said two words to me since the conclusion of the ceremony.

"I am going to go grab the telescope and blanket," Logan says, getting up from the table.

"Oh, are we stargazing tonight?" I look up at him surprised.

"Absolutely; I mean, didn't you see how clear the night sky is?"

I return my attention back to my cake, watching dad trying to sneak another slice when mom leaves the room. Grandma Jane shakes her head, before pointing at Logan's half-eaten slice.

"Someone pick up his mess," she orders anyone who is listening.

"I will pick it up once I am done eating," I say, noticing how Logan left his cake. He loves cake, but I am sure it's because he is more excited about going stargazing.

"Boy shouldn't just leave his plate everywhere," she huffs, "probably best he doesn't eat all that sugar, anyways."

"A little sugar never hurt anyone," Mr. Solway interjects.

"Yea, but I don't think it's wise to—"

"He is fine, mother. All kids eat sugar, right Emma?"

I smile, "Sure do."

When I am done eating, I pick up my plate as well as Logan's and head towards the kitchen. Mom is in there cleaning up the counters and putting away a few dishes into the cupboards. I know that she is still upset with what I chose to wear, but she needs to understand why I chose to wear it.

"You still mad?" I walk up behind her, sliding the dishes into the dishwater. The water rolls from side to side until the plates sink to the bottom.

"Today was a special day for you Emma. Why would you wear something like *that* to your ceremony?"

"Mom, listen, they are just clothes. This is who I am. I am not a dress and makeup wearing little girl that you so desperately want me to be."

"I know," she turns to me.

"I am the girl who would much rather work around the farm and get dirty. I don't care about all that other stuff."

"I know," she says suddenly pulling me in for a hug. "You are so much like your father and I was too busy trying to make you more like me, and I apologize."

"It's okay mom, no need to apologize. You know, being more like dad isn't such a bad thing. You love him for the way he is. Besides, there is only room for one glamorous gal in this house," I laugh.

"Well, can't say that I didn't try."

She releases me from our embrace and I head over to the foyer to throw on my shoes. I walk outside expecting to see Logan out there waiting for me, but he is nowhere in sight. I walk down a few steps from the front porch and wait for him there. I wait for about ten minutes, then fifteen, and twenty, before deciding to walk over and see what is taking him so long.

I enter through the side door of his house without a single knock. Since Grandma Jane is not inside, I feel no need to announce my entrance. I walk around the main floor, looking around for him, but he isn't to be found. Therefore, I begin climbing the stairs, sliding my hand along the banister until I reach the landing into the hallway. Immediately, I see the phone cord stretched from the hallway into Logan's room again. He must be talking with George.

"Is everything going alright for you, at least?" Logan's voice breaks through the opening of his cracked doorway. "Forget about me George," he snaps, "I want to talk about you."

The air goes silent and I hear nothing. Not even breathing or movement from inside of his bedroom. He is as still as a piece of furniture.

"It will be fine," Logan speaks up again. "Everything will be alright. I mean, everything is gone, but I mean, it's not like they aren't going to keep an eye—"

I have no idea what he is talking about, but I surely can feel the frustration in his voice seep into the hallway. Perhaps it's best that I turn back around and wait for him outside. There is no point in staying to eavesdrop for what feels like the hundredth time I have done it. I hate walking in on him when he talks to his brother. Their conversations never feel uplifting to me and I always add a bit of animosity add towards what I already feel for his brother.

I head back down the stairs as slowly as I came. The glow from his bedroom provides barely any light to guide my way down, but thankfully, my memory is sharp, remembering the number of stairs it takes until I reach the one.

The nightly air is warm and feels rather welcoming, as though the summer sun still hangs above in the sky and daylight is still all around. I look around me at the farm. The tractor sits a few feet away. The animals are all in their stalls. The patched roof and newly painted doors on the barns come into view. I admire it all, knowing that I am making a choice to leave this all behind soon to go away to school. But what makes it so easy to leave behind, is that I am taking the one person who makes me appreciate all these things along with me. You see, our adventures do not just exist just in the pasture, the fields, or beyond the brush by the river. They can exist no matter where we are, as long as we are together and I truly believe that with all of my heart.

A few minutes later, I hear the front door to Logan's house shut. He is walking outside with his telescope and blanket under his arms. I catch a small smile appear upon his face even without seeing him clearly. I think it's because I know him so well.

Under the stars, side by side, we soon lie upon the blanket. What makes tonight so much different from all the others is that we are holding hands. His warm hand intertwines with mine and for the first time in my life, this all makes sense. I love Logan. I have loved this stubborn, horse's ass of a boy since the first day I stomped down hard on his shoe and told him to chase me. He wraps his arms tighter around me without any fear or hesitation, which is weird because I am trembling. And the tighter we hold each other's hands the more certain it seems that we feel about each other. And I know no matter how many times my hand reaches out for his, he will always reach back. I have no doubts. The chase is over now, he caught me, and I refuse to let him go, ever.

He caresses my hand again, gently moving his fingers up and down. My head rests upon his shoulder, noticing the rise and fall of his chest. I match my own breathing with his. It doesn't take long, because so much of ourselves seems to be in tuned.

"I love you, Emma, I always have," Logan says amidst his bated breaths. The words reach my ears in a triumphant sweetness that only confirms what I have been only able to admit to myself.

"I love you too," I breathe into his shoulder.

My head immediately pulls off his chest. The movement even startles me, considering it wasn't premeditated. I move the hair that falls over my eyes, turning my head to face Logan as the hair then falls back into the same spot. This time, he moves the few strands away for me. He tucks it softly being my ear and holds his hand to my cheek. Our eyes remain fixated upon each other. Neither one of us seems to blink. Then, his eyes look downward as he stares at my lips. I watch as his lips control the movement of his head, as they begin their journey up to meet mine. When they meet, I can taste the sweetness of his mouth. I cannot pull my lips away. Magnetized to one another, neither one of us can seem to get enough, as our mouths continue to connect without any desire to come up for air. The inside of my mouth feels the gently caress of his tongue. My heart palpitates until it feels like it is about to rip through the walls of my chest. *So, this is what it feels like to really kiss someone…*

I pull him closer, grabbing onto his shirt, until he is on top of me. Our breaths are already labored; yet, we still do not come up for air. I lift his t-shirt up and over his head. I peek down below. Every muscle is heaving with every breath that he takes; *I have never seen Logan like this before.* I never realized just how beautiful he was.

His hand travels up the inside of my body, until it reaches the lining of my bra. It is there that he hesitates and lets his fingers linger. Even through the increased concentration on my part to kiss him, I can sense the fear emit from his tensed lips. I remove my hand from the tie of his pants and pull myself up onto a sitting position. His body bends with my movement, before our lips finally break their seal away from each other, leaving us eye to eye in the pale moonlight.

Through the semi-darkness, I stare at him. I can't get over how beautiful he is. We don't speak and I find comfort in that. I need no words to describe this moment, so I waste no time in finding any. All we can hear is the faint noise from the crickets and the sounds of our breaths. I bite my lip and raise both of my arms in the air. He looks surprisingly at me, as though timid and unsure. I nod to let him know that it is okay.

He moves in closer. His nervous body shakes and his movements seem awkward and unsure, which only makes the anticipation of what we both know is coming, that much more exciting.

I lean in and press my lips against his ear, as his eyes close to the touch, "It's okay," I assure him, pulling him even closer to myself.

I raise my arms a little higher. I catch the dark grey house in my view, but I quickly look away, seeing that his eyes haven't lost their focus on me. The bright blue skies that they are make me forget the darkness all around. I can feel his hands slowly running underneath the sides of my shirt, before he lifts it off my head for good.

My body fills with goose bumps and not because I am cold; but because each touch from him makes my body feel like it's on fire, as if my soul begins to rejoice for the first time in my entire life.

He reaches into his pocket and pulls out a small packet. Where he got one, I do not know. He looks at me as though asking for permission without actually having to. I kiss him softly and let him know that it's okay. For the first time, I feel like a woman and when I look at Logan, I don't see the same boy, I see a man. He positions himself above me and when he is ready, he slowly moves inward and I feel him inside. I can't describe how I am feeling, emotionally or physically, but we never lose eye contact off each other.

He gently kisses me and I do the same. And when the night carries through and our bodies weaken, I am left without any fear. Logan is mine and I am his.

Chapter Twenty-Five

I am wearing a dress with an ugly pale pink color, which in turn makes my hair look fire engine red. I told Cassie when we all went shopping for bridesmaid dresses that color wasn't flattering on me, but she didn't seem to listen. Majority voted that day and I lost miserably. Putting it on today makes me feel just as ridiculous, but mom has been kind enough to remind me that this isn't *my* day, so what I think or feel doesn't really matter…

The only communication I had with Logan all day was through our walkie-talkies. I agree that it is childish of me to still use, but something about seeing mine on my bedside table, like the rooster alarm clock, feels right. Why would I part with something that holds so many memories? If you love something, hold onto it. No matter if it pitifully crows, makes people make fun of you or is even perforated at the seams. *I get it now dad, thanks.*

The ceremony outside is put together all by the hands of my mother, which consists of a small gazebo that was rented for the bride and groom to exchange their vows. From there, there are about thirty white chairs facing towards it with a small aisle adorned in various flower petals down the middle. It is simple, yet, pretty. She didn't do such a bad job and I am actually getting excited to see how everything unfolds.

When everyone arrives, I peek out from the side window to see Mr. Solway standing beside the priest under the gazebo. Logan is beside him and of course, George is nowhere to be found. A few of Mr. Solway's farmhands are in the wedding, men that he has worked alongside with for many years, stand off to the side, smiling. I wonder how much it tears Logan and his father up that George isn't here. To be quite honest, it tears me up a little.

"Okay ladies, it is time to begin our way down the aisle," mom sings aloud.

Two of Cassie's friends are the first to head down. I watch their slow stride and awkward smiles, wondering if I am going to look like that when it's my turn.

"Now you, sweetie," mom says, gently pushing me through the side door. I try not making eye contact with anyone. My feet slide uneasily across the freshly mowed lawn until they grace the beginning of the aisle adorned in flower petals. I casually kick a few up with my feet, realizing that I am probably exhibiting a sense of boredom to all those watching me. I forgot to smile, which forces an awkward one to appear on my face. I know everyone is looking at my hair. I look up and see Mr. Solway, smiling. Then, I look over to Logan, who is smiling too, he mouths, *you look beautiful,* which makes me forget all about my hair and how I almost trip over the hem of my dress when I make my way over to where I am supposed to stand.

The ceremony was nice. The vows exchanged, even though I zoned out for most of it, were nice. When Mr. Solway kissed his bride, I looked over to Logan to gage his reaction. He didn't appear sad. His posture seemed relaxed and I saw his dimple from where I was standing. I am glad to know that he is finally accepting of the situation. I bet it will feel nice to have a completed family now. I am sure his mom would have wanted this.

The reception begins when the DJ starts roaring country music through the speakers. I am not a fan of country music or dancing, which everyone begins to do once the music commences. I am over getting myself something to drink when Grandma Jane bumps into me. Apparently, she has had some of the adult beverages, because her words are a little slurred, even though she tries telling me that all she has been drinking is punch.

"Oh, it's you," She sneers at me.

"Yea, who did you think it was?" I retort.

"You and Logan have been spending an awful lot of time together lately."

"Yea, so?"

"So?" She mocks me, "Don't think I am not watching you. He is my grandson after all. He doesn't need your stinkin' pity, you know?"

"He is doing just fine," I say, "He doesn't need my pity. He is perfectly fine with everything."

"You think so, eh? Would *you* be? Then again, I don't think your little head could even fathom the thoughts that circulate around his."

"What is that supposed to mean?" I turn towards her. I don't even care that she is trying to get a rise out of me. Yet, for some reason, I continue to engage her.

"Just don't think that you need to be all lovey-dovey with him." *Oh, goodness she knows.* "He doesn't need someone to pretend just to make him feel better. Love is no medicine you know, especially fake love."

"Listen old lady," my tone strengthens, "I have no idea what it is that you are talking about. And you need to get one thing straight, okay? I don't pretend with Logan about anything important. I am not that kind of person no matter what you have convinced yourself. Just because Logan's dad married someone, didn't mean that I had to cushion Logan with pretend feelings, alright?"

"What does Logan's dad marrying Cassie have anything to do with what I am saying?" She looks at me.

Just then my mom calls over to me. "Emma, I want you to come meet someone." My eyes don't leave Grandma Jane. I watch her slowly sip at her "punch" and when I hear my mom call out of my name for the second time, I walk a couple inches towards her.

"I have had enough of your judgment and ridicule. I am just as much a part of this family as you and I have never once done anything to deserve such treatment. If you so much as say or look at me in any negative way, I will and I promise you, show you what a bad apple really is."

I walk away leaving her mouth gaped and eyes blinking. I don't turn back or even pay her any more mind throughout the remainder of the night. And when Logan drags me onto the dance floor, I don't even find her eyes to see how she is looking at me. I have had enough of that woman.

* * * *

Mom walks into the kitchen and places the stack of mail upon the kitchen table. Normally, I am not interested in what comes, but ever since mailing out my applications for college, I can't get enough of sifting through the envelopes in search of something for me. Today, I reach over, look through the stack, and find an envelope addressed to me at the very bottom. Excited, I bust out of the back door and into the pasture, and find Logan riding up towards the barn in the tractor.

I wave at him to put his foot on the break. "Did you check the mail?" I exclaim.

"No, not yet, why?"

"I got a letter from one of the colleges we applied to. Go check to see if something came in for you."

"Okay, climb on," he gestures towards me.

I reach up and grab a hold of his hand, squeezing into the seat beside him. Hitting the gas on the tractor, we ride up towards the front of the farm. Once he turns the engine off, he makes his way towards the mailbox and pulls out the stack of mail. He sifts through the pile and finds nothing.

"Nothing," he says, looking over at me.

"Well, maybe they don't respond to everyone's' applications at the same time," I say.

"Maybe," he says, but I hear a sense of doubt in his voice.

"Well, I will wait to open up mine until you get yours."

Days carry on and it's not until a week later that Logan finally gets his letter. He calls me over his walkie-talkie and tells me to come over in an hour so that we can open them together. But I am too excited to wait. And after about forty five minutes of fanning myself with the envelope and skipping about my room, I head over to his house and make my way upstairs regardless.

"There is something I want to ask you," Logan's voice comes through his bedroom. Again, I have walked in on another conversation. I swear my timing is always bad. "I am going to send you something soon, but when you get it, I need for you to call me, so I can explain," He pauses, "I am not done with it yet, it's not that simple."

I decide that eavesdropping is no longer something I want to be a part of; I am either going to make my presence known or I am going to leave. I choose to go with the latter. I inch my way towards his door, quietly. My breaths become heavy, much louder than my steps.

"She doesn't know, no. I can't bring myself to say anything. I don't want her to worry you know, if she doesn't have to at least. It's not going to be for another six months before I know anything anyways."

My hand slides down the wooden door and I push. There Logan is on his bed, staring up at me. His face reddens as mine comes into view. "I have to go," he says," clicking the button on his phone. He gets up slowly from the bed and walks by me into the hallway.

"What was that about?" I ask when he reenters.

"Oh, nothing, just catching up with George," he replies nonchalantly.

"Who is *she* and what doesn't *she* know?"

"It's nothing Emma, don't worry about it. Let's open up our letters."

I walk uneasily into his room and sit down beside him on the bed. At the count of three, we tear through our envelopes revealing the college's decision. I received a yes. Logan received a no.

He turns to me with a frown. "Well, looks like I am still not going to attend school with you," he says.

"No, that's not true. We still haven't heard back from the other colleges we have applied. There is still time."

"Is there?" he says.

"Yea, why wouldn't there be?"

"I don't know," he looks away.

"Logan, what is it that you are not telling me. What is wrong with you?"

He doesn't say anything. He runs his fingers through his hair and then rubs at his face. When his hand reaches back down to the surface of his lap, I take it and hold it in mine. His palms are clammy and I know that he is nervous. His body is telling me that he is keeping something inside. I no longer believe in his words.

"You can tell me," I say, "You can tell me anything and I will never get mad at you or judge you. You know that right?"

"I know," he says.

My initially gut reaction is telling me that maybe this thing between Logan and me is about to come to an abrupt end. Could his feelings already have vanished for me? The thought sickens me and I feel the insecurities squirm around my stomach making me want to puke. My mind immediately shoots back to the night we had under the stars. *Was that it? Was that all this worth?* I can barely allow myself to think that.

"You don't love me anymore?" the tears swell from behind my eyes. I hate to admit that I am crying no matter if it is premature or warranted. I need to know the truth even if the truth will kill me.

In one quick movement, he wraps his arm around my shoulder and pulls me closer. "No, no, it's not that. Of course, I love you; I will always love you. That will never change."

"Do I write that on your list?" I say, trying to stifle a smile.

"Yes, absolutely."

"Then you do the same, because I want you to know that I will always love you too."

"No matter what?" He asks.

"No matter what," I affirm.

"No matter what comes between us?"

I look into his eyes and nod, "yes."

"Even if I tell you that I have been keeping something from you?"

I move out from underneath his arm and stand up from the bed. Looking down at him, he looks frightened and frail. I have never seen Logan like this before, not even when Grandpa Charlie died. I can't imagine what he could be keeping from me. *I thought we tell each other everything?*

"What is it?"

Like a bandage, I want him to rip it off and tell me fast. His eyes burn into mine; "What is it?" I yell at me.

He looks away and fumbles with his hands in lap again, before he reaches down and begins to roll up his pant leg.

Part Four:

"When it is dark enough, you can see the stars."

—Ralph Waldo Emerson

Chapter Twenty-Six

My hand brushes the strap on my luggage as the zipper moves tightly along the seam. I can actually hear the polyester fibers screaming at me that they have had enough, but I do my best to pack pretty much everything I have in my room. I want to leave nothing behind. The idea of leaving for college at the end of high school felt adventurous and exciting; but now, it feels like nothing more than abandonment and betrayal. I want to make the transition as easy as I can and if I had it my way, I would pack up the entire farm and take it with me. Thankfully, I still have the box that Logan made me. It's safely secured in the center of my suitcase.

Mom knocks on my door just before she carries in a large box. She walks over and sets it down between us on the bed. "There's no makeup inside, right?" I peer over at her.

She laughs, "No, it's something much better." She opens up the folded cardboard sections, revealing a box of various items. "In here," she begins, "are things from my past. You know, you and dad are not the only nostalgic ones in the family."

Looking inside I see a few purses, miniature sculptures, pictures, and scrapbooks. I can't help but to wonder why she is bringing this to me.

"I want you to have this," she says, "especially the scrapbook. I started it when I graduated high school and never finished it, but I want you to.

I take the book out and open it to the first page. I can't believe how young my mom looks in all the pictures I skim through. It's funny, because she looks just like me.

"I don't know if I can go," I say, immediately shutting the scrapbook in my hands. "I can't leave, not now, not ever. Not until I know that everything is okay."

"Well, sweetie, you can't live your life in fear of the unknown. You have to trust that everything will happen for a reason and as it should happen. You being here or not will not affect anything. You can't forget to live for you."

"But that feels selfish of me. I can't live for me, knowing that the person who defines me in every way, isn't beside me. I can't do that."

"He defines you in every way?" Her expression is as solemn as mine.

"Yeah, I know, dad already told me that having another person define you is wrong…"

"It's not wrong," she says, which instantaneously perks my head up. "Our soul mates define who we are in every way and there is nothing wrong about that. They balance us and make us better. They complement our souls in a way that no other person in this world could ever do," she pauses, "After all, a mate is part of pair of things, which belong together, so why wouldn't we allow such a beautiful definition in our lives?"

I reach over and hug her. That was probably the best thing she has ever said to me.

Soon, nightfall arrives and darkens my room. I lay underneath the streaks of moonlight through my blinds. Even though college is only an hour or so away, it feels like I will be across the country. A mile is too long between Logan and me. I just wish that he could come, but I have to understand why he can't.

The night of his confession tore a hole in my heart. The uncertainty ripped through my soul like a poignant dagger. I literally fell helplessly to the floor, burying my head within the tiny carpet threads of his area rug. I cried for what felt like hours. I cried for what felt like days. And what surprised me the most was that Logan got up from the bed and knelt down beside me, trying his best to comfort me. *He tried comforting me!* When the reason I was crying was because I was scared for him.

For an entire month, he begged me to go to college, even though I was so quick to throw my acceptance letters down the toilet. He didn't want me to miss out on any opportunity no matter what has happening with him or around the farm. The only thing he made me promise was that I wouldn't change. *Your original is far better than any remake the world would want to do to you,* he reminded me.

The sun reaches through the window with its elongated arms, grabbing hold of everything in sight, before reaching down and opening my eyes. I slept on the floor last night. My head propped up against my luggage, aches when I relieve it from its awkward position. The muscles tremble upon their stiffened release.

I pull myself off the floor and walk over to my window, opening the blinds, I see Logan outside. He causally walks over to the barn, no different from what he does every morning. The reassurance of his routine sits very well with me. It lets me know that all is well, even when there are no words to express it. And something within me is telling me that everything will be alright. There is no way that a routine like his could be broken. The world would never be the same.

I walk down the stairs and make my way out the door. I am not hungry and feel no need to hang around the kitchen with my parents. I head out to the barn instead. When I reach the threshold, I sneak inside and quietly make my way up behind him, putting my hands gently over his eyes, I ask, "Guess who?

"Grandma Jane?" he laughs.

"No," I say.

"*Hmm*...Jessica?"

I twirl him around and reveal myself to him, "not funny," I say.

"I was only kidding," he pulls me in for a kiss. "I am going to miss you."

"I know, because I am going to miss you too. You promise to come visit me?"

"Well, considering I have my license before you got yours, I don't see why that will be a problem," he smirks.

The morning passes gently like a breeze and before we realize how much time has elapsed, I can hear my dad calling my name out to leave. Logan and I had somehow made it down by the river, where we spent the last few hours, lying side by side, listening to the sounds of the birds chirping and of the rolling river a few feet away. Nothing is better than this, until the reality of me leaving surfaces and destroys every ounce of denial within us by nothing more than the sound of my dad's voice.

We get to our feet, brushing the blades of grass off our clothes. I look down at the ground as he ties up his shoelaces.

"Do you hear that?" I ask, trying hard not to smile.

"Hear what? Your dad calling, you mean?"

"No, not that," I say.

"Then what? I don't hear anything," He sticks one of his ears out to be sure.

"It sounds like running," I say, trying to meet his gaze. It takes only a half-second for him to realize my game.

"Oh, yeah," he smiles, "Now that you mention it, I do hear it."

"You do?" I inch my foot closer to him.

"It does sound like running."

"Good," I yell, just before my foot stomps down upon his and we go running into the fields.

* * * *

My room feels like a concrete prison with sterile furniture and no personality. Mom and Dad carry in my suitcases and several boxes, waiting no time at all to begin my unpacking. My roommate has not arrived yet, which is a good thing. I want the storm of unpacking and sorting to die down before I have to meet her.

In comparison to high school, the ambience of college is nowhere near the same. The hallways are not congested and everyone seems to be determined to try to identify who they are without any predetermined statuses. I like that. It kind of makes the transition that much easier on me, because I refuse to conform.

"How about you come home the first weekend in October?" Mom says to me.

"I have to wait *that* long?" I look over towards dad.

"Well, no, not if you don't want to. We can come get you whenever," he says.

I breathe out a silent breath of relief.

"Get everything you can out of this experience," Dad then leans in towards me. "These years will be some of the best years of your life."

"I know," I smile.

Mom motions for dad to leave the room so that she can have what I presume to be a mother and daughter chat before they go. "I stocked up on your female essentials and put them in the bottom of your closet, okay?" she says.

"Thanks," I groan, looking out of the doorway to make sure that dad didn't hear.

"The picture of Logan and you is right beside your bed. I thought you might like that."

I look over and spot the picture, "I do, thank you."

"Remember, you being here is fine. Everything will be fine. I don't want you worrying, okay?"

I nod, even though it's killing me inside being here.

"It's not healthy and I want you to do your best here. Logan would want you to do your best as well."

"I know, keep an eye on him for me, if you don't mind."

She looks at me perplexed, "I doubt he will go running out on you," she smiles.

"I am not worried about that. I just don't want him running off to where I can't chase him."

Chapter Twenty-Seven

School is hard. And it's too far away for my walkie-talkie to pick up a signal to talk with Logan. Still, I keep it by my bedside in case such a miracle happens. I do my best to call Logan every day; though, which is easy, considering there is never a line to the payphone, because no matter how many times I have hinted to my parents about getting me a cell phone, they still somehow seem oblivious to my request. I am probably the only student in the entire school who doesn't have one.

The remaining few coins I have left from Logan's Christmas gift a few years ago, remain in the side pocket of my school bag. I take one out, slide it through the lot, and begin to dial his house phone. The metal phone presses into the lining of my jaw. And after three rings, he finally picks up.

"Hey there," he says. I can't believe how great he sounds. "How is college life?"

"It's okay. I am still trying to get used to it."

"I am sure you are doing great."

"Yea, so how is the farm?"

"Great!" He exclaims, "Couldn't be better."

"What am I chopped liver? I did a lot around there—it sounds like no one misses my contributions," I laugh into the phone.

"I told you, you were never much of a farm girl."

"Ha, Ha," I say.

"Well, good thing hunting season is almost here. It will keep me busy until you come home."

"You better be careful," I order, "I never liked the idea of you hunting in the first place, no matter if it's a "man thing" or not."

Even through all of our phone conversations, I can never bring myself to ask him about how he is feeling. I hate thinking that Logan is sick or that something is wrong with him. He sounds good, which makes me believe that he is, and there is no amount of asking on my part to that would have any effect on that. I can't fear the unknown anymore; and besides, I made Logan promise to never keep anything from me ever again. If he were doing badly, he would tell me.

After dinner down in the dining hall, I walk back to my room to find my roommate, Monica studying. She reminds me a little of Maggie, but has long blonde hair with streaks of brown throughout. Her glasses ride the edge of her nose until she scrounges up her face to try to move them back up to a more comfortable place. I like that about her. She wastes no time on the frivolous things.

Monica, to me, is a breath of fresh air, an undemanding friend who seems to enjoy everything about me and no matter what I have opened up and told her, she always repays me back by revealing something about herself.

"How's it going?" she asks when I walk into the room. Monica has a habit of leaving the door open. She finds the room too confining; not to mention, she is a self-proclaimed "people watcher".

"It's going good," I say.

"How is your boyfriend?" She asks. She always asks, especially after I told her about what is going on, although, she has been kind enough to not use the word that I try my hardest to avoid using myself. The word is laced with unhappy endings and of pain, but thankfully, soon enough we will know something more. I have to believe in happy news. I have to believe that the universe wouldn't want a good soul prematurely wasted. I can barely fathom the thought in my head right now without feeling an urgency of tears.

"He is doing well; he sounds good, at least."

"Are you going to go home this weekend?" She scrounges up her face just as her glasses start to slip.

"In a couple of weeks," I say.

I decided to stay until the beginning of October like my mom suggested. Even though I miss Logan terribly, I never anticipated how much work college would be. If I am not at class, I am studying, and if I am not studying, I am doing endless amounts of homework. But Logan has been rather understanding, which makes the separation a little easier to deal with.

I climb into my bed and close my eyes. The sounds of Monica turning pages within her textbook and the people walking by in the hallways do not dissuade my eyes from succumbing to some much-needed sleep. I haven't truly had a good night's sleep since Logan's confession. I toss and turn for hours on end in fear of the truth that the darkness will reveal. Not to mention, I have somehow convinced myself that sleep is nothing more than a waste of time. And I feel entirely ungrateful wasting any time, especially when I don't know how much of it I actually have to waste.

Several weeks later, I am finally going home to visit. I pack my overnight bag and wait outside of my dorm for my dad to show up. Seeing his car round the front of the building excites me to the point that I bust out of the front doors and practically throw myself onto the car. When he gets out to help me with my bags, I immediately smell the farm on him. The smell of home makes me realize just how much I missed it. It saddens me to know that I am not even finished with my first semester yet.

The drive home is full of updates. He lets me know that the farm is turning around a much larger profit than last year, which means that things are going great for everyone. Logan hasn't missed a day of work since I have been away. Dad does accidentally make mention, however, that Logan is scheduled to meet back with the doctor for his six month checkup in a few weeks. Now with the realization of that day lingering in my horizon, I am unable to think of anything else. So much weighs on the outcome. And we won't even know anything on that day either.

When we finally pull into the driveway back home, Logan runs out of the barn and runs towards me. I can barely open up the car door to get to him; because he is too busy trying to open it up for me. Once I climb out, I immediately hug him. Our embrace tightens in commemoration of all the moments we have spent apart. It feels so good to be home.

Down by the river, we lie side by side. I stare up at the tree house with a sense of longing.

"Have you gone up there at all since I have been gone?" I lean over towards him.

"No, why?"

"You want to go up there now?"

He peers over at me hesitantly, but I remind him that it is not as though I am asking him to sleepover up there again, which I thought he did very well the last time. And with knowing that he will not get up willingly, I pull him off the grass and practically push his way up the tree.

Once inside, he says, "Okay, yep, just the way we left it, time to climb back down."

"Oh, come on you big baby, let's hang out for a little bit."

He sits down upon the wooden floor and looks around. "We finished now?" he groans.

I smile towards him. "I wish you would enjoy it up here," I say.

"What's there to enjoy? Every time I am up here, something bad always happens."

"Well how about we make a better memory for you up here?"

"What do you have in mind?" He says, seeing me smile.

* * * *

Falling asleep in my own bed is a feeling that I can't put into words. I crawled into bed late last night and felt the familiar comforts of my white blanket and soft cotton sheets. I can tell mom washed all of my linen before I came home, because it is crisp and pulled tightly along the length of the mattress.

Waking up sans alarm or mom's singing, pushes me out of bed a lot faster, because I am instantly reminded that I can help around the farm. I think part of it has to do with me wanting to prove myself. Logan made me think awhile back that my contributions weren't that important to the maintenance and running of the farm. Whether he was joking or not, I want to feel validated. I always thought I worked very hard. This morning, I intend to prove just that.

Throwing on my work clothes is like breathing in a breath of fresh air. I admire the stains in my bedroom mirror and try to recall the incidences when I received them. One in particular was when I tripped out of the barn and landed in mud.

Logan laughed his head off at me, because I was pretty much covered from head to toe. Most of the stains came out in the wash, but there is still a small streak right above my right elbow. Apparently, my sweatshirt doesn't want me to forget that day.

The cool press of the morning air seeps into my skin. I reach up and tie my hair back into a ponytail as soon as I approach the barn. My work boots are the cleanest I have seen them in awhile, which makes me wonder if mom cleaned them too.

"Good morning," I say to Logan and a few of the new farmhands. They are inside picking up the animal mess, while laying down new hay. A few feet away, I spot a couple of the guys fixing some of the stalls where the wood is weakening.

Logan smiles to me, "Good Morning," he pauses, "Hey guys, this is Emma. Emma, these are the new guys around here."

"Hi," I try waving towards them all. "What do you need me to do?"

Logan looks up from what he is doing, "We pretty much have everything under control. You could go back to bed if you want."

Puzzled, I stare at him, *bed?* I think to myself, *why would I want to go back to bed?* "No, I can help," I say reaching into my pocket to uncover a clean handkerchief. "I can finish picking up," I reach over for a bucket and a shovel. "I am not helpless."

I begin working, scraping, digging, and carrying the ruined hay out of the barn. I can feel Logan's eyes penetrate through the opening of the stalls at me. Why would he think for two seconds that I would okay with turning around and going back home? I am annoyed slightly at this, especially when it makes it seem to the other farmhands that I may be a tad bit useless around here; but instead of dwelling, I let it roll off my shoulders. Logan wouldn't deliberately hurt me.

Well in the afternoon, Logan finally allows himself a break. Before that, I spent the better part of my morning, following him around like I am his dad's cat. I watched him get involved with things around the farm I never knew he helped with. It's like watching Mr. Solway or my dad work. I am quite impressed, but I don't tell him that.

"I say we run past the river," He says, after we eat our lunch. We are sitting down by the river upon Logan's outdoor blanket.

"I am not chasing you over there!" I point, remembering my fear of the river.

"Come on, I will hold your hand across. The water has gone down a bit and there are a lot of rocks that you can step on across," he says, just as I hear a gunshot off in the distance.

"Isn't it hunting season?" I ask, trying to determine the direction of the gunshot.

"Yea, but no one hunts back here, they go across the street. Too many houses," he says.

"I don't know Logan; I think I heard the sound coming from beyond the river."

"You are just saying that, because you don't want to go with me," he teases.

Then, I hear another shot and this time I almost certain of where it is coming from.

"No Logan, we are not going in the woods."

"Catch me if you can!" He gets up in a flash and darts away from me.

"Stop being a horse's ass!" I yell towards him. "Come back!" I see him make his way across the river.

"Quit being a buffoon!" He yells back to me.

* * * *

I have never heard such loud sirens. Then again, I don't think I have ever heard sirens this close to the farm before. It sends an eerie chill down my spine. The red lights circulate the front lawns as though trying to create a spotlight on the event.

"I didn't know! I thought he was—"A strange man panics in camouflage gear, I watch Logan's bloody body being carried upon the stretcher.

"You know you are not supposed to hunt back there, there are a development of houses on the other side; are you crazy?" My dad screams into the strange man's face.

"I told him not to go in there. I told him that I heard gunshots!" I panic. I keep repeating myself as though no one hears me. I keep repeating myself in hopes that we could go back in time where Logan actually listened. "Is he going to be alright?" I cry into my dad's shoulder.

"Yes, sweetie, he will be fine." But there is too much blood for me to believe in what he is saying.

I climb into the back of the ambulance and grab onto Logan's hand. Mr. Solway looks down at his son with tears streaming down his face. "He was shot in the shoulder, Emma. He will be fine." He takes Logan's other hand into his own.

But Logan is in shock and so am I. I continue to squeeze his hand all the way to the hospital and when they wheel him out of the back of the ambulance, I force myself to stay strong. He looks so helpless and scared and there isn't anything that I could do about it. But when I am finally forced to let go as they wheel him away down the corridor, it makes me feel like I am really letting him go. I want to chase after him, but Mr. Solway pulls me back.

"Let's go sit in the waiting room," he orders softly. I know he is trying to calm me down, while still possessing a sense of control over the situation.

"I want to go with him," I cry.

"I know, so do I, but we can't."

"I want to make sure that he will be okay."

"Me too, Emma, me too."

I fall asleep in the cold plastic cushioned chairs. I position my body into pretzel-like positions in order to find a comfortable way to relax. Mr. Solway spends most of his time drinking coffee. I think I saw him get up to refill his cup about six times, which doesn't include the trips he probably made while I was sleeping.

Hours go on by until we finally hear something. A nurse is kind of enough to approach us to let us know that they retrieved the bullet and are now doing a scan or something to make sure everything is okay. The thoroughness is quite appreciated and hearing that the bullet is out of his body, makes the tense and anxious filled breaths of mine, release more gently into the air.

Not long after, my parents, Cassie, and Grandma Jane, all make their way into the waiting room. Mom sits beside me and holds my hand. "How are you holding up?" she asks. She starts to play with my hair, which instantaneously relaxes me.

"Fine, they retrieved the bullet," I say.

"Well, just think, maybe all he will walk away with is a funny looking scar and a good story to tell someday," she smiles.

"Yeah, I hope so."

She tries her best to make small talk with me and even point things out in some of the magazines to try to occupy my attention, no matter how briefly. But my mind is not here in this waiting room. It has drifted down the corridor and into whatever room they have placed Logan into; I can't help but to worry. I want my best friend.

Around eleven o'clock at night, however, mom and dad decide to head back home, asking that Mr. Solway keep them posted if anything changes.

"I am staying here," I say, as Mr. Solway nods to let them know it's okay for me to stay. Honestly, he doesn't have much of a choice.

"Jane, you want to head back with us?" Mom asks.

She pulls her body off her chair and clutches tightly to her purse, "Yes, please." She turns to her son, "I will make a pot of tea for when you get home," she pats him on the shoulder.

"I am going to stay here too," Cassie announces. I look from the corner of my eye and see that she is holding Mr. Solway's hand. I can't imagine Mr. Solway having to face this alone. I know Mrs. Solway would have wanted someone beside him, holding his hand and being there for him during this time of need. I am for the first time in awe of what I told Logan. Mr. Solway deserves a hand to hold and for someone's hand to hold his back. He really picked the best second best.

Soon, my eyes fall heavy against the fierce fluorescent lights. I agree with myself to close my eyes for only a few minutes. The last thing that I want is to be asleep if Logan were to ask for me. Behind my lids, I can still make out the glow from the lightening, but soon it darkens, as picture Logan and me running through the pasture. It was about five or six summers ago, when we pretended to be shipwrecked pirates…

"Ahoy Matey!" Logan exclaims in his pirate drawl.

"Where ye think thee buried treasure is?" I say, although, I am no match to his pirate-talking skills.

"Arrr! Me not sure, best we start digging!"

"Aye, aye, sir!" I salute him.

He hands me a shovel and I proceed to dig. I dig so far into the earth excited at the prospects of unearthing buried treasure. I imagine mountains of gold and jewels, enough for our families to live comfortably for the rest of their lives. But no matter how far we dig or how many holes we make, we find nothing...

My arm slides off the chair and my eyes open wide. I turn to see Cassie and Mr. Solway talking amongst themselves. From the time on the clock, I fell asleep for about twenty minutes. But just as I am about to ask Mr. Solway if I missed anything, out comes Dr. Parker, asking to speak to Mr. Solway.

"Dr. Parker, what are you doing here?" Mr. Solway gets up to greet him. "Were you the doctor who removed the bullet from Logan's shoulder?" They shake hands.

"No, I was not," his hand falls to his side.

"Oh, then what are you doing here?"

"I was wondering if you and I could speak in private?"

Immediately Mr. Solway looks back at Cassie and then at me. "Okay," he responds, and walks alongside the doctor out of the waiting room.

Cassie gets up and moves closer to me.

"What is that all about?" I ask, hoping that she would know.

"Probably protocol to protect Logan's privacy."

But something tells me that this isn't protocol, it is more of an exception.

Ten minutes can seem like an eternity depending on what you are waiting for. Mr. Solway's exit out of the waiting room feels more like hours or days instead of a measly couple of minutes. Cassie is watching the television above us and I am watching out for any signs of his return. I need to know. If I had it my way, I would probably run out of this room and demand an answer now. But I don't have to do that, because Mr. Solway has returned. He looks just like Logan on the day he found out Grandpa Charlie died. Tears stream down his face and gets lost into his beard. I can't move. I am frozen solid to the plastic cushions. Cassie, however, slides out of her chair and approaches him. He whispers something to her, but I know it's not the secret ingredient to his apple pies. Her hand goes to her face in shock.

"What is it?" I cry well before I even know the reason why.

Chapter Twenty-Eight

I am tearing apart my room. I have smashed what could be smashed. I have ripped what could be ripped. I have tipped over, knocked over, and kicked everything that my adrenaline would let me. I even punched my wall, which sent a piercing pain through my knuckles and up my forearm. I pulled it away, examining it, noticing the blood and scratches I gave to myself. The wall has no visibly damage—I only seemed to have caused the damage to myself.

Beyond my destruction within the confines of my bedroom, I have yelled and screamed, wailed and cried, louder than my soundproof walls could contain. I asked questions without receiving answers and the silence that met my ears in return only motivated me to yell even louder. I can't deal with the silence. Better yet, I can't deal with anything at this time.

My door opens slowly until it reveals my dad on the other side. Checking to see that nothing is flying in the air, he walks into my bedroom and sits down upon my bed. I am pacing two feet in front of him. I am wearing a track into the floorboards.

"If someone is sick, shouldn't they know that they are sick?" I yell at him. I continue to pace, but I don't stop and wait for an answer. "I mean, if people know someone well, shouldn't *they* at least know that, that person is sick?"

I look over at my dad who stares blankly in return. His lips are stiffly pressed against each other with no hint of a reply approaching. He is as still as everything else in my room.

"No one knows Logan Like I do' shouldn't I have at least known he was sick?" This time the tears reemerge. They pour out of my eyes like tiny waterfalls. Unable to see my pacing track any longer, I fall to the floor, covering my face with my hands. A few seconds later, I feel my dad make his way over to sit down beside me.

"You can't blame yourself for this. This is not your fault and it is not Logan's."

"Then who do I blame? This isn't fair!"

"I know," he wraps his arms around me, "it's not fair. It's not fair for him to go through this."

"I want to know, how bad is it?" I look up from my hands. "How bad is he?" I demand.

Slowly my dad's arms fall off my shoulders. "Emma, you know I can't—"

"Tell me," I beg. "I want to know."

He looks off the side, before returning his gaze back onto me. He struggles through several breaths and filler words to avoid the silence from taking over again. "It's not good," he finally says.

There is something about hearing that information coming from someone you love, rather than a stranger or a doctor, which solidifies the seriousness of the situation. There is no need to speculate the ending or find ways to pretend we are living in an alternative universe where this could all be easily solved by a good night's sleep or a good game or two in the pasture.

I cry, much louder and longer than I did before. It brings back the memories of last night in the hospital. I will never forget that look on Mr. Solway's face. I will never forget Cassie's reaction when Mr. Solway whispered amongst heavy sobs into her ears. I will never forget how he knelt down beside me, taking my hands into his own, before almost crying into my lap. And I will certainly never forget how he told me that the reason Dr. Parker was called in, was because upon Logan's examination, they discovered that it spread right on through to his lymph nodes. Upon further investigation, they found a few spots on his lungs. Mr. Solway could not bring himself to say the word that I too have spent months avoiding. It shatters my heart just thinking about it. No one, for that matter, uses the word either. It makes the situation feel too real and without hope.

"Logan's cancer spread?" I say without realizing that I have accidentally made the situation real.

* * * *

This secret or truth lingering over my head like a dark cloud, resurfaces over the passing of the salt at the dinner table, Logan is sick. He is scheduled to come home this evening, which scares me because I am afraid of how I will react towards him, knowing what I know. He has been gone for almost a week in which I have visited him every day. Visiting hours in the hospital, however, are never long enough and I spent most of my time rehearsing the things I wanted to say before entering his room. My goal is to remain strong for him. I don't want him to think that I can't take care of him and I certainly don't want him trying to comfort me.

"I am not going back," I say, playing with the food on my plate.

"To where?" Mom asks.

"To school, I am dropping out."

Mom's fork slowly slides out from her hand and falls onto her plate. "You can't do that," she says. The metal clinks loudly.

"Yes I can. I am staying here until Logan is better."

"You need to go back to school sweetie, Logan would want you to."

"Don't tell me what Logan would want. I know Logan better than anyone does and I know that he would want me here, regardless if he admits to it or not. I am not going. You can call the school today and tell him that I dropped out."

After dinner, I walk outside and sit down on the front porch steps, waiting for Mr. Solway's car to pull into his driveway. I must have been outside for a good two hours before I see his headlights coming down the street. Instinctively, I stand up and make my way across the yard.

When Logan gets out of the car, he is not what I imagined him being like. His movements are not weak and he doesn't even possess a sickly complexion. He is as he always was before, besides where they patched up his shoulder. I give him a hug and he does his best to hug me back, but reaching up hurts his wound, so he holds me tightly around my waist. When we let go,

I hold his hand all the way up into his bedroom where I get him to climb into bed.

"Gosh, I am so sick of lying in bed," he says with a groan.

"Yea, I know, but the doctor said you are going to need your rest."

"But I am not tired."

"I know," I smile. "Just think you will be extremely well-rested when he allows you to get out of bed and we will be able to do whatever you want."

"Yeah? Promise?" His eyes beam at me.

"Promise."

I sit at the edge of his bed, holding his hand in my own. He is warm and so very much alive that the idea of him being sick doesn't seem plausible. I guess I have a hard time believing in the things that I can't see. So for now, with what little imagination I have left, I pretend as though nothing is wrong. Logan simply has the flu or something. He will bounce back in no time. The idea of this, calms my nerves considerably, but again, I hate that my imagination has me using it to escape the harsh reality, and not for fun, but in order to function and survive.

"I want to talk to you," Logan says, caressing my palm with his thumb.

"About what?" I ask.

"Remember what you told me about my dad? Well, I want you to know that I put a lot of thought into that conversation this past week. And with knowing that there is a chance I may not be able to take care of you forever, I want you to know that I will stop at nothing to ensure that you will be taken care of even after I—"

"Stop it!" I yell, "Don't you dare talk like that, do you hear me? I don't want to hear it."

"Seriously Emma, if anything were to ever happen to me, I want you to be taken care of just as if I am still here," he continues, "I would want you to trust me to know that I would forever take care of you, even if indirectly."

"Stop it," I beg, "Nothing will ever happen to you, do you got that?"

"We don't know that and honestly, I am going to have to plan as though something will."

The silence returns and frightens my inner core. It makes my heart beat fast and then without warning, I feel an abrupt stop within its beating. I can't help but to fall victim to the silence myself. I have no idea what to say, and I refuse to let him see me cry.

"I would never leave you though," he continues, pulling himself up in bed.

"Don't you dare make promises you can't keep."

He nods weakly, "I know, but this is one I know I can."

Strangely, I know exactly what he means, but I refuse to ponder over the idea a second longer.

Chapter Twenty-Nine

"**I** feel great! I don't know what the hell everyone is talking about?" Logan exclaims in the middle of the pasture. He breathes in and out with a huge smile upon his face. "If my lungs were so messed up, could breathing feel this good?" He looks to me as he pounds upon his chest like Tarzan.

He does look good; I can't deny that. I watch the way that the sun softly glistens down upon his face and makes his golden hair shine. Those vibrant blue eyes are brighter than the sky above and even with winter just around the corner, standing beside him makes me feel like summer is still in the air. I detect not a single moment where I can smell the scent of it passing. It's as though it will stay with us forever.

As he continues to pound upon his chest, all that I can do is smile. I have been not one for words lately, because I never seem to choose the right ones. What I have been successful at, however, is with the continuation of me pretending as though everything is okay. In the make-believe world that I have created in my mind, Logan is not sick. There is nothing for him or I to be afraid of and our greatest struggle in life is deciding on whose turn it is to ride the tractor. In my mind, I always let him win.

For an entire month, my plan works. Logan only missed a few days' worth of work for doctor's appointments. When he was gone, I just pretended as though he was out shopping or something. However, as days went on, Logan developed a very persistent cough, which I would simply blame on allergies or a seasonal cold. I would blame it on the changing weather or the dust, anything that sounded better than the real reason. And because of my dedication to this perfect world, my parents have grown increasingly nervous about my delusional sense of denial. But I have a different way of coping than they do. I need to pretend as though everything is okay for Logan's sake. It is the only way that I can stay strong for him.

Logan is still in bed this morning; I find this out when I head out to the barn and find only a few of the farmhands inside. I tell them that I will pick up Logan's slack and spend my morning working away until everything is accomplished the way Logan himself would have done it.

Taking a break, I decide to head over to Logan's house. I walk through the backdoor and see Mr. Solway sitting at the kitchen table with Cassie. Grandma Jane is taking her morning nap on the couch, and the only sounds I hear is a ticking clock and the occasional sigh.

"Logan asleep?" I ask, walking further into the kitchen.

"He wasn't a little while ago when I went upstairs to check on him," Cassie answers.

"Is he doing alright?" I know the question doesn't seem right for me to ask. Of course, he is not doing all right, why would I ask such a thing?

"He seemed fine; he was talking to George when I was up there. George is heading to Afghanistan in a few weeks. I don't think Logan liked hearing that," she continues.

"Well, of course, he didn't like hearing that. He probably needs his brother right now." I can feel my anger bubble to the surface. "Do you have George's phone number?" I ask.

Mr. Solway reaches for a small notepad and pen in the center of the table. He writes down the number and slides it over to me. "Don't cause any trouble," he says, just as I take it into my hand.

"When have I ever?" I say, walking back out the door where I came.

Mom is in the kitchen and dad is still outside working. I walk up the stairs to my parent's bedroom and take the phone off the receiver. I dial George's number about five times before I let it ring. I am not sure what it is that I want to say, but finally decide just to wing it.

"Hello?" George's voice comes through the phone.

"George?" I ask, knowing exactly who it is.

"Yes, who is this?"

"It's Emma, Emma Jensen."

"Oh, hi, Emma, how are you? Is everything okay?

"Well, I hear that you are going on another deployment. Don't you think that it's kind of bad timing?"

"It's not my choice Emma; there is nothing that I can do about it."

"Your brother is sick, George," I feel the layers of my pretend world start to peel away. "What are you just going to abandon him just like you did after your mom di—?"

"Emma, stop, you are overreacting. I am putting in a request to come home, but I can't do anything until I am approved. I already told Logan about this."

"You have no idea how much he needs you," I exclaim. "You are his brother. Wouldn't you want to spend time with him in case something was to happen? Don't you see the severity of this situation?"

He goes silent. I only know that he didn't hang up by the sounds of his breathing muffled by the background noise seeping into the phone.

I can't help but to yell at him a few more times before I smack the phone back down upon the receiver. I don't leave my parents' room. Instead, I crawl underneath their covers as I used to do as a child whenever I had a nightmare. It seems fitting, because my life feels like a nightmare lately, it's just no amount of hiding underneath covers can alleviate.

Hours pass before I finally resurface. My feet gently glide across the wooden floorboards, producing not a single sound. I float like a ghost down the hallway and steps until I stop at the bottom to the sounds of voices coming from the kitchen.

"He asked for it?" My mom gasps. I hear her cup hit the surface of the table.

"He did," Mr. Solway's voice, replies.

My dad clears his throat, but says nothing. *Why isn't he saying anything?*

"Did you give it to him?" Mom continues.

"Yes, Charlotte, I did. What choice did I have? He may be too young, but I don't want to upset him with anything right now. If he wants it, he can have it."

"Has he—?"

"Not that we are aware of," Cassie interjects. "He hasn't left his bed. Poor boy seems to get worse by the day. I guess we all hoped it wasn't as aggressive as Dr. Parker advised."

"Does he know? Does Emma? I would hate to think that they are aware that there is some ticking clock hanging over their heads. They are still kids; they don't deserve to know that kind of feeling."

"It feels like only yesterday when my wife went through this; and now it's my son. What have I done, where did I go wrong?" Mr. Solway sighs.

"It is not your fault," Mom responds. "We will be here every step of the way."

"I just don't feel like there are many steps left."

I make my way out of the house and over towards Logan's. Grandma Jane is in the living room watching television, as I head up the stairs. When I open the door to Logan's room, I find him looking through a car magazine. His pale face immediately perks up at me. The one thing I do notice is that no matter how sick he may or not be, his eyes haven't lost their luster.

"Hey, Emma, do you want to see the car I am going to buy in a few years?" He coughs.

"Absolutely," I smile as I make my way towards him.

"Isn't she a beauty? Probably will cost me a fortune, but I have saved up almost every penny I earned working on the farm."

He motions for me to sit closer beside him, as he wraps his arm around me. "George and I got into a fight today," he says.

I pretend to be none the wiser. "You did?"

"Yea, I am kind of through with begging him to come home. Not to mention, I feel foolish."

"Why do you feel foolish?"

"I have asked a lot of him and most of what I have asked he has yet to come through on. I guess if I had to choose though, I would much rather he keeps his word on the important things."

I nod as if I understand, but I really don't. Instead, I nestle my face into chest, listening to the sound of his beating heart. I feel sick, so sick that I want to throw up. My mouth is pooling with saliva and I make no hesitation, before I lean over and grab his trashcan and throw up. Barely anything comes out of me, because I have not exactly had much of an appetite, but what I did consume, wanted so badly to come out. The sick feeling almost mimics the hangover I once experienced.

"Are you okay?" Logan asks, rubbing my back.

"I feel awful," I say, wiping my lips upon the back of my hand.

"You coming down with something?"

"Probably, I haven't eaten much, might be a stomach virus."

When I know that I will not throw up anytime soon, I lay back down beside Logan. We stare up at the ceiling pretending that we are underneath the night sky. We make believe that we can see the stars and the funny shapes we think they make. He tells me stories and I do the same, it feels better to escape for just a moment or two, but I feel a tear forming out of the corner of my eye when I see his shiny red telescope collecting dust in the corner of his room. I wonder if we will ever use it again.

"Have you spoken to your mom?" I ask.

He turns to me, "No."

"Do you think she knows about what is going on?" I immediately hate myself for asking.

"I think so. I doubt she isn't looking down on me, whether I can see her or not."

"I can go talk with her if you would like."

"I would like that," he smiles.

Soon, he closes his eyes and falls asleep. When I know that he is safe and sound, I creep softly out of his bedroom and make my way down the stairs.

When I hit the landing, Grandma Jane's eyes pierce through the darkness at me. She looks me up and down, but instead of scowling, her eyes grow wide. She looks at me as though in shock, leaving me perplexed at the sight.

"What?" I ask.

Her mouth is gaped, as I try my best not to allow the sick feelings within my stomach to return. They churn around and around, until I find myself running towards the kitchen and throwing up for a second time there.

I am dry heaving over the trashcan, wanting so badly for it to stop. I can't be sick right now; Logan needs me too much. And just as I am about to wipe my lips again on the back of my hand, I look up and see Grandma Jane handing a few paper towels over to me.

"Bad timing, eh?" she says to me.

Chapter Thirty

Dad pulls into the driveway, unloading boxes of my belongings from school. He went there and packed up my room for me, because I have been sicker than a dog these past few days. Thankfully, mom is great at taking care of me. I have her make Logan and me chicken noodle soup, because it has a tendency to make me feel better, which I hope has the same effect on him.

It takes dad several trips up the stairs to bring all my things into my bedroom. Seeing everything back here provides me a sense of relief knowing that I don't have to leave again. I am where I belong and no amount of pressure from my parents will change that. I refuse to leave.

"We can unpack these boxes later, okay sweetie?" Mom asks, setting down a glass of ginger ale upon my bedside table.

"That's fine," I say, rolling over onto my side.

Later in the afternoon, I awake feeling strangely better. Mom allows me to go next door and see Logan, but forces me to put on a facemask in case I am contagious. I walk into the kitchen where Mr. Solway, Cassie, and Grandma Jane are sitting, enjoying their afternoon tea. Cassie looks exhausted and I know that she has been working very hard taking care of both Logan and Mr. Solway as best as she can.

"Hi Emma," she says, seeing me when I enter. "How are you feeling?"

"Much better," I reply, "Mom wants me to wear this in case I am contagious," I reveal the facemask to everyone.

"Well, it's good to play it safe," she smiles.

"I doubt the child is contagious," Grandma Jane peers over at me. She surveys me up and down as she did several days ago. For the first time, we actually agree on something, because I don't think that I am contagious either.

"I am going to go upstairs, is that okay?" I ask pretty much everyone.

"Yes, that is fine, but if he is sleeping, let him sleep."

I nod, "Okay."

It only takes me to reach the top landing of the stairs to find out that Logan isn't sleeping. I see the hallway phone cord stretched through the opening of his door, which makes me wonder if he is making amends with George or not. If it is George, I hope that he doesn't share with Logan about my phone call.

"Yea, I asked for it. Didn't think you wanted it," Logan says. He pauses for a reply. "Oh about that, I am almost done with it. I will send it out as soon as I can. Thanks for giving me an address though. I wasn't sure how to reach you when that time comes."

I don't know why, but I don't think he is talking with his brother. My experience with eavesdropping doesn't detect the same tone of his voice he would generally use. I am curious to know who is on the other line and what exactly Logan needs to finish.

"I know you don't understand," he continues, "but I am hoping it all makes sense once you receive the final version. This is all I want from you, nothing else. It will be our secret until the time is right."

I teeter back and forth and find myself wanting to bust through his bedroom door to yell at him. I thought he would no longer keep things from me. *Logan a liar?* But I can't react like that. I can't upset him anymore; therefore, I turn around and head back down the stairs.

"Back so soon," Cassie says as I walk back into the kitchen. "Is he sleeping?"

"Yea, he is sound to sleep," I lie.

I head home and plop down at the kitchen table, mom is making dinner, and dad in the living room reading the paper. I watch the quick movements of her knife as she begins slicing and dicing some vegetables.

"Do you want some help? I ask, willing to do anything to keep my mind off Logan.

"Sure, sweetie," she hands me a knife. Can you slice a few of those green peppers for me?

Getting up, I feel fine, but as I make my way over to the counter, I start to feel nauseated again. My clammy hand grips around the knife as best as it can, as it slices into one of the peppers. The smell turns my nose up. My free hand shoots to my mouth as though trying to prevent myself from throwing up again. Mom turns her attention away from the stove and sees the look on my face.

"What is wrong with you?" She walks over.

"Gosh, these smell awful. Are you sure they are not bad?"

She picks up the peppers and examines them. "No, they are fresh. We normally eat them cooked so you are probably not used to the aroma," she smiles.

At dinner, I pick at my food as best as I can. I nibble here and there and do my best to produce some kind of dent in the heaping amount mom served on my plate. I know she wants me to put something into my stomach, but nothing wants to stay in there. I finally just excuse myself from the table and go upstairs to bed. I am not tired, but I crawl into bed anyways. Mom walks in a little while later.

"Still sick?" She walks over to me and presses her hand against my forehead. "You are not warm, so you are not running a fever, which is good."

"Yea," I muffle against my pillow.

"How about I unpack? I think I know where everything goes."

I nod to let her know that it's okay. It saves me from having to unpack all myself. She opens up several boxes and begins placing pictures back in their rightful places. The rooster alarm clock and walkie-talkie have made it back to my bedside table. Seeing the walkie-talkie again makes me want to call Logan. But I don't feel like reaching for it now.

She takes my clothes out of the luggage and puts them away. I watch her attention to detail as she folds and hangs up everything. When it comes to my personal items, she places my toiletries on my dresser, which she advises she will bring into the bathroom when she leaves. Then, I see her grab all of my female essentials and put them down next to my shampoo and soap. Seeing her take such good care of my things makes me smile, but then all of a sudden, my heart slams into the pit of my stomach, *Oh, my god...*

* * * *

With the arrival of Christmas, I am in no need to celebrate. Shopping doesn't happen and I find that there really isn't much to be joyous about. Mom decorated the house as usual. The tree is alive with ornaments, tinsel, and lights, but underneath is barren with nothing more than a dusty tree skirt. This year, however, given the current circumstances, mom has convinced Mr. Solway to throw the Christmas Eve dinner at his place sans the normal gift exchange.

"I will make all of the food," she smiles when Mr. Solway hands her a fresh carton of eggs.

"Would be better, the boy has been having a hard time getting out of bed. Dr. Parker wants us to already consider hospice, but I don't remember them coming this soon with my wife," he looks down at the floor.

"Maybe it would be best. You and Cassie have been running raged over there these last few months. It would be great to get some help; look at it that way."

"I suppose," he sighs.

"What are you guys talking about?" I ask, approaching the door. I heard everything that they were talking about and even if I didn't, I know that it is about Logan, it's always about Logan.

"Nothing dear, just finalizing our plans for Christmas."

Later on, which even surprises me—I call Jessica. I haven't spoken to her since I left school so I thought I should make the effort and call her. I tell her about everything that has happened after she fills me in for a half an hour about college life.

"Oh, jeez, Emma, I am so sorry," she sighs into the phone. "I can't imagine."

"Now they are talking about has-spice or something?"

"You mean hospice?"

"Yeah, have you heard of it?" I ask.

"Yes I have. When my aunt was sick two years ago, my uncle had to call in hospice; generally, that isn't a good sign."

"What do you mean?" my voice quakes.

"It means that it's close."

"What's close?" I ask, but she quickly changes the subject on me.

An hour later, I put on my shoes and head next door. I walk in and make a quick beeline up to Logan's bedroom where I see him lying in bed. He almost blends into his white cotton sheets. I want to hug him, but I am afraid I would break him. He looks so frail and weak, but the one thing that still hasn't faded, is his eyes. Somehow, it makes me feel better seeing him this way. His eyes provide a sense of reassuring comfort.

"Merry Christmas," he coughs when I enter.

"Merry Christmas," I muster a smile, even though I so desperately want to cry. My jaw hits the floor with a bang. Logan is wearing my father's favorite Christmas sweater. "Is that—?" I point.

"I was cold earlier; your dad insisted I wear it. Don't I look festive?" He smiles.

I sit down on the bed beside him, "You do," I say, "Dinner will be ready soon, are you going to want any?"

"I don't have much of an appetite, but you better have some."

"No, I am not hungry." I say just as my stomach growls. I can't help but to smile.

"I have your Christmas present," he says to me pointing over to his bedside table. He motions for me to open the door, which apprehensively, I do.

"I didn't buy anything for anyone this year," I frown, holding the small bag in my hands.

"Just open it."

I open the tie on the small gift bag and reach through the tissue paper. Once my fingers reach the bottom of the bag, I retrieve a small velvet box. "What is it?" I ask before I even attempt to open it.

"It's a gift for you, ya buffoon, open it."

I set the gift bag off to the side and bring the box towards me. Slowly, I crack open the box as though it is one of those trick containers where snakes fly out and surprise the unexpected opener. But when I open it, I don't see snakes. Instead, I see a small ring. I take it out of its holder between two of my fingers. I hold it out in disbelief.

"I can't get down on one knee, but I will try."

"Logan no—" I yell at him, as I watch the covers slide off of him and his tired and weak body pull itself out of bed.

"Sadly, I don't think I can chase you anymore," he laughs.

"Don't worry," I say, holding my hand out in case he falls, "I am not going anywhere for you to have to chase me."

Down on one knee Logan looks at me with those amazing blue eyes of his, "Emma, I love you, will you marry me?" He beams up at me.

Even with everything in my life telling me that the end is near, I take the ring onto my finger and tell him yes. I would rather pretend we have a lifetime together than admit to the fact that we don't. I would rather live a thousand lives within my pretend world within the small window of time reality will give us. I have to learn to ignore the ticking clock. I have to appreciate the time we have left.

Shortly after, Logan climbs back into bed; I leave the room with the ring upon my finger. My stomach growls again, this time I place my hand upon it, feeling how bloated I am. Grandma Jane is just coming out of her bedroom, draping a shawl around her to keep warm. She looks over at me and stops for a moment, but she doesn't give me a dirty look, instead she begins walking towards me.

Her slow pace doesn't feel slow at all, because we are face to face well before my brain registers that she is coming over towards me. I try my best to keep an expressionless look upon my face, but something tells me she is about to yell at me for something. I can't imagine what I have done now.

"I know," she says. Her beady eyes survey me up and down.

I guess that she knows that Logan proposed, but soon everyone will too, so what does it matter. "You do?" I play dumb.

"I have known for awhile," she continues, "probably even before you did."

"Well, I just found out."

She looks at me perplexed, "You *just* found out?"

I nod in reply. "Logan just asked me."

Immediately, her eyes shoot down at my left hand, noticing my ring. By the look on her face, she seems surprised. She shakes her head, "I had no idea, I mean, I knew he was thinking about it," she continues. She takes my hand into hers and looks at the ring, "this was his mother's, you know."

I was not aware of this, but somehow, knowing this, makes me like it even more.

"Well, you and I have never saw eye to eye, I guess its best we start now, what with all these changes," she smiles, taking me by surprise. She pulls me in for strange hug. Her embrace feels awkward and cold.

I realize after she lets go of me that she hasn't explained to me what she knows. Hesitantly I ask her.

She looks at me with a smile and her hand moves from her side and places directly onto my stomach, "I know," she says, "best you go down stairs and eat."

Chapter Thirty-One

The snow melts, but still there is an icy feel to the air. It's crisp and cruel in the way that it rips through your lungs as though it's comprised of tiny knives made of ice. Logan hasn't been allowed outside because of it; but on occasion, I open up his bedroom window just so that he can get some fresh air and smell a little bit of the farm. It's comforting to him.

As for things with me, well, things haven't been quite the same. Grandma Jane knew something, that to be honest, I really didn't know about. I mean, I had my suspicions don't get me wrong, it seemed more like an impossibility than anything else; but then, I remembered that afternoon in the tree house and I knew. I knew then without a doubt.

Telling my parents terrifies beyond comprehension. I asked that they meet me in the living room to talk. I feel it's best to tell them now and get it over with, considering I haven't seen a doctor yet, and I am sure, at least for my baby's sake, that I make an appointment soon.

"You're what?" Dad's face goes pale. He stands up and immediately starts pacing, while mom tries to calm him down. "How did this happen? When did this happen?"

"A few months ago, I think when we were up in the tree house."

"I should have torn that thing down several summers ago when I had the chance!"

"Ted, tree house or not, they are kids, they would have gone elsewhere."

"How can you be so calm about this? Our daughter is still a child and she is about to have a child of her own!"

Mom takes dad's hand into hers and gets him to sit back down. "Does Logan know?" She asks. I shake my head. "It's best he doesn't know. It would make things that much harder on him, agreed?"

"I feel bad keeping a secret from him though."

"I know sweetie, but it's to protect him."

For an entire month, my lips remain remained sealed. I wear the baggiest clothes that I can find to ensure that he doesn't take notice of the rapidly growing bump in my belly. Thankful to have finally seen a doctor, they reassure my mom and me that everything is going well. The baby is healthy and so am I. That is the best news I have heard in awhile. I just wish I could share it with Logan.

Hospice has been really good to Logan and they are kind enough to let me spend hours on end with him. I am there for every meal and activity in between, but it's hard to see him struggle as much as he does. He coughs more than he breathes and watching him waste away is starting to waste away me just as much. I can barely stand it any longer. I am finding it hard to remain strong.

An oxygen tank replaces the spot where his bedside table used to be. The table instead, has been pushed several feet away from his bed full of medicine and cups. Most of Logan's fluids now come via IV and I hate seeing the bag hanging over his bag as it slowly drips down into his veins. He can barely keep his eyes open most of the time, but I still sit by his side for hours just listening to him breathe. Listening to him breathe lets me know that he is still holding on, that he is still fighting.

A week later, I am sitting next to the hospice nurse playing cards. Logan has been asleep for the last hour.

"Go fish," the nurse smiles at me.

"Gosh, I haven't played this game," I say, fishing for a card in the pile, just before I peek over at Logan. "I really wish his brother could be here. He probably would want that more than anything."

"If that is who he has been talking to, I think Logan mentioned a week ago that they were fighting."

"They didn't reconcile?" I ask surprised.

"Didn't sound that way to me," she says, "So how far along are you?" She asks as she surveys her cards.

"What?" I look at her surprised.

"I am sorry, am I wrong?" She sets her hand down.

"How did you know?"

She smiles again, "I *am* a nurse, Emma, plus it's obvious."

I look down and then back up at her. "Is it that obvious?"

When it's time for Logan's next round of medication, the nurse walks over to his bedside to wake him.

He coughs at the sound of her voice. It sounds so painful. After he takes his medicine, I walk over and sit down beside him, holding his hand.

"I love you Logan," I say to him.

He tries his best to keep his eyes open, but he still manages to tell me that he loves me too.

* * * *

A few weeks later, I wake up the world feels strangely silent. I pull myself out of bed and make my way down stairs as I am greeted by voices coming from the kitchen. My parents, Mr. Solway, Cassie, and Grandma Jane, are all gathered around the table, faces red and eyes bloodshot.

"What's going on?" I say, finding myself backing away from the room. My father gets up from the table and I know what he is going to say, but I don't want to hear it. I run down the small hallway to the front door, grab my shoes and begin running.

"Emma, get back here, you can't run in your condition!" He yells at me, but I don't listen. I just keeping running and I don't stop.

I run as though I am being chased, but every time I look back, I don't see him. I don't hear him. I am chasing myself. I keep facing back, as I burst through the brush, leaving the pasture and field behind me. However, I am unaware that my feet have graced the water and by the time I become aware of it, I plummet straight into the river. I immerge from beneath the water's surface, tears blending in with water. I can barely keep myself afloat.

I rub my eyes, as he appears before me. There he stands perfectly dry in the water beside me. I can't swim, but I don't care. If anything, I want to join him. He holds his hand out to me, which I can't help but to reach out for. I give him the hand where his mother's ring now calls home.

"I will hold your hand across" He says. His voice echoes strangely in my ears.

"I don't want to get across. I want to be with you." My arms flap violently against the water. I had no idea just how deep this water is.

"You will always be with me, as I will always be with you."

I scream and cry, feeling my body reach the other side of the river. I climb out and lay upon the surface of the ground. *How did I get here? I want to go back into the river, the one place I never wanted to be.*

"You know where to find me, right Emma?" His vibrant blue eyes sparkle into mine

"Beside your mother?" I cough some of the water out from my lungs.

He shakes his head and points to the blue sky above. "You always said that I had skies for eyes, so that will be me watching down at you."

The tears continue to fall as I feel his hand slipping away from mine.

"I will see you soon ya big buffoon," he smiles at me as I watch his image fade to a ghostly silhouette.

All I can do is watch him, even after he disappears from me. I don't even look away as I hear my dad trudging through the brush to come find me. Instead, my head gently falls to the grassy surface as I whisper, "In a flash you horse's ass."

Present day…

Chapter Thirty-Two

We sit down by the river, staring out through the wooded area. It's not the same spot I have spent many times before, but it will do. George doesn't say much and neither do I, which I strangely find comfort in. The silence doesn't feel as threatening as it has in the past. I am okay with listening to all of the sounds around and feeling the gently kick within my stomach.

"You want to feel?" I ask George, taking his hand and placing it on my stomach. "I have quite the kicker in here," I smile.

"Do you know what you are having?"

"No, I want it to a surprise."

He smiles.

Staring back at the river, I begin to think to myself. I wonder, if I were to have known that this all of this was going to happen, would I have changed things, would I have done things differently? But every time I ask myself those things, I have to remind myself that everything happens for a reason. And even though I gave up precious moments to spend with him, I may not have fallen in love with him the way that I have, if it weren't for those moments. Losing him in small dosages was enough to show me just how much he meant to me. And losing him for good, well, it showed me just how much of myself went along with him.

Logan defined me in every way. He was my soul mate. Our lives were seamlessly intertwined making it almost impossible to know where he ended and I began. I truly loved my best friend.

"Here," George hands over the envelope he showed to me a little while before. "Go ahead, read it."

I take it loosely into my hand, watching the way that he looks at me. I open it up slowly and see the letter inside. I immediately make out Logan's handwriting and already the tears start to fall…

George,

I know with when you start reading this, you will not understand. I don't blame you. It's hard for me to even wrap my own head around it. You see, Emma said something to me awhile ago, she said, if she were to ever die, she would want the next best person to take care of me, and well, I want the same for her. And with thinking of that, I realized that it was you. You are second best for her.

I want you to take care of her, so here are some things that I need for you to know about her, things I promised her I would never forget if we ever grew old together. Unfortunately, I will never live to see that day. But I need for you now to keep that promise for me. Please say that you will.

You see, she needs to look into someone's eyes that remind her of mine. She is convinced that I have skies for eyes, and since your eyes are almost like mine, I feel like the transition wouldn't be that hard.

You are also as stubborn as me; she needs that. Apparently, it pushes her to fight for what she wants and she likes the challenge. She is a handful, you see, a bit of a spitfire.

You must always keep her in check, reminding her never to change who she is. She is the best person I know and any change, whether with her personality or appearance, I feel would be a disservice to her. Remind her that she is beautiful every day.

She needs to be around the farm. If your take her away from it, she tends to go crazy. Let her ride the tractor now and then, just make sure that she doesn't try to kill any cows or destroy the barn.

She doesn't like to hurt people, which means, she will do and say things sometimes hat she doesn't want to do. Remind her that it's okay to be honest with other people, even when it may hurt them.

Most importantly, chase her. Chase after her every chance you get. She is worth it. And the best part of it all is that I always caught her in the end, but from now on, it has to be you.

Please take care of her and love her like I have since the very first day I panicked when I thought she was going to drown in the river. Even at such a young age I knew that if I was to lose her, I would never be the same again.

I know this is hard to understand and I can't imagine you not being confused, but you are the closest person like me in this world. I know you will be there for her and take care of her, just like dad took care of mom and you took care of me. I never shared just how close we were even with you gone for so many years, it was our secret, I know. I apologize for yelling at you the other day, I am sure Emma thinks you and I are still fighting. Please explain to her that we are okay.

Logan

P.S Emma doesn't know that I know. I think she thought telling me would make it harder to let go. But she knows exactly where to find me. And I will look down on both of them until we are together once more.

I can barely hold back the tears. My head falls into George's chest, where I continue to cry more.

"It's okay," he says to me, "I will take care of you," I promise.

Never in a million years could I have seen this coming, never in my wildest dreams. "I want to see him," I say," looking back towards the parlor.

George immediately stands up and offers me his hand. "Let's go."

Epilogue

"Chase me!" I yell at him, as I dart across the pasture and into the open fields. The grass whips across my ankles, but I continue charging right through it. The smell of the farm wafts through the air and hits my nose in a strangely pleasant manner. It used to be that I couldn't stand the smell, but now it just screams home to me. From a short distance away, I can hear the sounds of the grass crunching beneath his shoes. He really is picking up speed now, which only pumps up my adrenaline even more. "You will never catch me!" I continue to yell back at him. I know exactly why I provoke him; because I love the way I let him catch me in the end.

What little hair he has on the top of his head, glistens like gold in the sunlight. I can't help but to turn around and swoop him up into my arms, "Ah ha! I caught you!" I laugh into his belly. He giggles loudly at my touch.

"Do you know who that is?" I point up at the sky.

He giggles again.

"Do you know who that is?" I tickle at his tummy.

"Dada," he sputters out between giggles.

"That's right that is your daddy."

Turning to the side, I see those familiar blue eyes, not as vibrant, but still recognizable, waking towards us. He stops and shakes his head with a smile and I can't help but to smile in return. And even though he doesn't have skies for eyes, they really are second best. Logan always knew what was best for me even when I didn't. He knew that if he couldn't catch me in the end, he would make sure the next best person could.

CPSIA information can be obtained at www.ICGtesting.com
Printed in the USA
BVOW03s2023291113

337729BV00004B/12/P